GREENLAND

GREENLAND

A Novel

DAVID SANTOS DONALDSON

AMISTAD
— 35 —

An Imprint of HarperCollins*Publishers*

Permission to quote a passage from *Maurice* by E. M. Forster © 1971 has been generously granted by W. W. Norton & Company Inc., New York, and by The Society of Authors as the E. M. Forster Estate.

Permission to quote from the poem "The Snow Man" from *The Collected Poems of Wallace Stevens* by Wallace Stevens © 1954 has been granted by Alfred A. Knopf.

An excerpt from *Stolen Life* by Fred Moten is used with the permission of the copyright holder © 2018 Duke University Press. All rights reserved. www.dukeupress.edu.

The epigraph quoted from James Baldwin's essay "The Creative Process" is republished with permission of Beacon Press Inc, from *The Price of the Ticket* by James Baldwin © 1985; permission conveyed through Copyright Clearance Center, Inc.

HarperCollins books may be purchased for educational, business, or sales promotional use. For information, please email the Special Markets Department at SPsales@harpercollins.com.

FIRST EDITION

Designed by Nancy Singer

Library of Congress Cataloging-in-Publication Data has been applied for.

ISBN 978-0-06-315955-6
ISBN 978-0-06-327520-1 (ANZ)

22 23 24 25 26   LSC   10 9 8 7 6 5 4 3 2 1

To my mother, who

read Baldwin to me in the womb,

bought me an orange Olivetti when I was ten,

and unlike some mothers in this story,

has always believed in her two sons

It is a peculiar sensation, this double-consciousness,
this sense of always looking at one's self through the eyes
of others, of measuring one's soul by the tape of a world that
looks on in amused contempt and pity.

—W. E. B. Du Bois, *The Souls of Black Folk*

But the conquest of the physical world is not man's only duty.
He is also enjoined to conquer the great wilderness of himself.
The precise role of the artist, then, is to illuminate that darkness.

—James Baldwin, *The Price of the Ticket*

CONTENTS

PART 1

The Very Last Englishman

One may as well begin with the gun. I'm holding the neat little thing in the palm of my hand. A Glock 22. It weighs like a sinker with the magazine fully loaded. Ten Golden Sabers. Such a glamorous name for bullets. The truth about my current situation is that I am locked up in this basement study, confined here for three weeks, and I have a gun.

I'm sure you've already figured out that since there's a gun, there's sure to be a violent death. But I can assure you I will do my best to avoid it. I despise violence. Honestly. I've actually taken a solemn vow against killing even a tiny insect.

I know you barely know anything about me, aside from the fact that I'm locked up in this basement study. My name is Kip Starling. Kip is short for Kipling. I was named after my father's favorite writer, the staunch British colonialist. A problematic literary destiny set from birth. It may seem like too much information to say what I'm about to say, but we don't have time for niceties. Three weeks is all I have for this entire crazy endeavor. There's no time for the old literary conventions. "Show, don't tell," they say. I know. But I think it's more important that we start off on the right foot. I need to be crystal clear about one thing: the reason why truth is paramount to me.

Eleven years ago, when I was twenty-six, after I was essentially kicked out of my Columbia MFA writing program—feeling lost, with no purpose—a concerned friend dragged me along with him to a meditation center on the Upper West Side. We sat on the floor and chanted beautiful but incomprehensible words in Sanskrit. It initially seemed silly to me, but to my surprise I had a mystical experience—something truly mind-blowing. In my meditation I experienced a self I instantly recognized as the true me. It's hard to put into words exactly. But I became expanded, infinite. And yet infinitesimal too, all at the same moment. The stars and the oceans sang through me. It was pure ecstasy. I wanted that experience to last forever. After that, I was convinced that the spiritual path was my new purpose in life. So I signed up to become a monk—a sann-yasi in the yogic tradition. In less than a month, I found myself in India, living in an ashram, shaved head, saffron robes, vows of celibacy—the whole nine yards. Nothing was stopping me from attaining that ultimate truth.

Well, the monastic pursuit lasted about a year before I fell in love with another novice, Darren Albury, who had an equine bum and the cross-eyed, inward-looking gaze of a saint. We were the only Black guys in the entire ashram—and both of us of Caribbean descent! Narcissus's magnetic pull got too strong to resist, along with my eternal struggle of sacred and profane, the spirit and the flesh. Darren and I were quickly discovered and dismissed from the ashram due to "adharmic behavior." We slinked our separate ways in shame. I had failed again, first at my MFA writing program, now at spirituality. I stopped meditating altogether, out of spite, I sup-pose. What a proud fool I was!

But despite being cast from the Garden of Eden—wayward and, admittedly, ever entangled in the outlying brambles of sen-suality—I am still that same honest truth-seeker who made those vows of nonviolence years ago. You must believe me. I wouldn't be writing this story otherwise.

What else is this mad literary endeavor, if it isn't my attempt at finding my way back to my lost, unadulterated true self? In the ancient Indian Vedas, the pursuit of becoming a sannyasi is summed up with three simple questions: Who am I? Of what do I really consist? And what is this cage of suffering? I'm still searching for the answers to those questions. If I had a motto, it would be "Seek only truth!" *Sola veritate!* That's what all this is for.

On the other hand I am also Black, Caribbean, Brit(ish)—as Afua Hirsh puts it—and now Americanized, living in Brooklyn in 2019, floundering in the wake of a peculiar invention called Whiteness.

"Is there really such a thing as race?" you may ask. Isn't it all a Kantian philosophical invention? Yeah, sure, that's all true, but now we're neck-high in centuries of the Grand Delusion. Fred Moten, the African-American poet-philosopher, says ever since the invention of Whiteness, "Black" has become a stand-in for something fugitive, "a spirit of escape and transgression . . . An outlaw."

From the look of me—slight of stature, with my Harry Potter glasses and preppy oxford button-down shirts—you'd never peg me as an outlaw. I even have a new, persistent bulge about my waist— "skinny fat," they call it. The worst of both worlds. If you had to size me up, you'd probably guess I was a burgeoning history professor, or a hopeless enthusiast of Dungeons & Dragons, or maybe even a struggling youngish writer (and you'd be correct there). But I have to agree with Fred Moten: despite what some might describe as my humble appearance, I am—by the very nature of my nature—an outlaw.

The Outlaw and the Legend

My crazy situation—being locked up in this cramped basement study—starts with the fact that I'm a novelist. At least that's what I call myself. As of yet, no publisher has wanted to grant me that identity. But I have a literary agent, Wilson—a genuine gentleman and a scholar. He's a tall, seemingly liberated WASP. Fashionably youthful enough to wear edgy, thick-framed Italian glasses but old enough to be that rare, nearly outmoded literary professional who believes in nurturing raw talent. He's taken me on and is representing a manuscript I presented to him two years ago. A novel based on the life of the great British writer E. M. Forster.

My historical novel focuses on the three years Forster lived in Alexandria, Egypt, during World War I, when he fell in love with the Black Egyptian tram conductor Mohammed El Adl. At the ripe age of thirty-eight, Edward Morgan Forster (known as Morgan to friends) had never had sex. The affair with Mohammed is well-documented as Morgan's first and most meaningful sexual relationship and unfortunately, it was a doomed one. I had written the novel in a voice close to Morgan's perspective. I myself am in many ways like the shy, self-doubting gay British writer—I was even raised in Weybridge, the suburb of London where Forster lived. Wilson liked my novel, a real-life story of gay star-crossed lovers. Also, *A Passage to India* was one of Wilson's favorite novels. It was one of mine too—along with *Howards End* and *Maurice*. And who doesn't adore the Merchant Ivory films with Helena Bonham Carter and Emma Thompson? *A Room with a View*— gorgeous! Wilson, like me, was a fan of the gentle British soul; he sympathized with the repressed homosexual writer, and he helped me to refine my manuscript.

After a year of gut-wrenching rewrites ("Kipling, cut this part," "I don't think we need this part either," "Can we add flash-backs?" "What about flashing forward too?" "It's great! Just one more thing . . . we need to shave it down about half the length. Make it lean, sharp, snappy!") it was finally polished—no fat, lean. Nearly emaciated, I thought. But better. I secretly thought it even had moments of brilliance. We—mostly Wilson, really—titled it *Morgan and Mohammed: A Love Story.*

But after a year of submissions, no publishers took it up.

Then, two days ago, a major literary editor in the publishing in-dustry contacted Wilson. She was intrigued by the novel, she said, and although she would not be offering on it, she expressed interest in having a meeting with me and Wilson. Wilson confessed to me that this was highly unusual. Normally a publisher either accepts or rejects a project and rarely meets with the author after declin-ing. We were both perplexed but also hopeful. I couldn't sleep that night; my heart and mind were racing like dueling drumrolls. Ex-citement and fear must be one and the same, I was convinced. Was it finally going to happen, the dream of my life? And not with just any editor; this was the biggest literary editor in the business—a publishing legend!

A day later, just yesterday, we found ourselves in the editor's huge Madison Square Park office—a tasteful, sunny room with tall windows, a gray leather Milo Baughman sofa with matching arm-chairs, white metal bookshelves, and a towering fiddle leaf fig tree.

The publisher—a straightforward, handsome woman with short silver hair—sat upright on the sofa with the warm yet detached air of a Buddhist nun. She said she admired my book, that the novel was moving. It was clear I had talent and that I'd done a great deal of research but *that*, in fact, was the problem for her: she disliked my adherence to historical facts, some of which I had interpreted differently from the way she did. (She clearly knew a lot about Forster.) She said she wanted to encourage me as a writer, but as Wilson and I knew, she wouldn't be publishing this novel. Forster's story had already been told by biographers and his voice was already known through Forster's own work. Although my novel was well executed, she said, it offered nothing new in content or style.

When I realized my golden opportunity was slipping like sand through my fingers, my heart leapt to my throat and my palms got sweaty. I cannot let her say no, I said to myself—not when I've gotten this far.

All my life, through all the various ups and downs, I've only had one enduring dream: to be a published writer. I'm useless at anything but writing. In school I was the awkward kid shunned at every turn. The only ones who truly appreciated me were my teachers. "Kip writes wonderful stories," they told my parents. "He has a rare and vivid imagination." And they encouraged me too. "You're a real talent, Kip. Your parents didn't name you after the great Rudyard Kipling for nothing. It's your destiny!"

I knew I had to dedicate my life to becoming a writer. I had no time for friends; my extracurricular hours were consumed with obsessively studying novels. Between the ages of twelve and fifteen, I read *Crime and Punishment* five times because my mother had mentioned that Dostoyevsky was a great writer. I had to drum his narrative techniques into my brain to become a great writer too. That was the only way I was finally going to matter. Me, the skinny, awkward Black boy who, for some reason, imagined he was going to fit in with his school peers. In my first year of secondary school, I discovered *Giovanni's Room* and realized that becoming a writer had successfully exalted the skinny, gay Black American James Baldwin, so I decided I had to go to America to write, to be saved. Then I too would matter. Even my parents, despite their disappointment at having a "batty boy" for a son, would see that I could be a success.

I could not say all this to the publishing legend yesterday, of course, but I also could not take no for an answer. "Please," I said to her, my voice betraying my desperation with a quiver. "Tell me what version of my Forster story would theoretically interest you for publication." I needed to understand where I had failed to appeal to this gatekeeper of the literary market.

She tugged at her brown tweed jacket and then clasped her hands on the knee of her pleated wool trousers. "Mr. Starling," she offered with an earnest frown, "a commercial media conglomerate is acquiring my publishing company in four weeks. Your novel would have been my last acquisition before the merger, and frankly I don't know if literary fiction is something the conglomerate will be interested in publishing—they seem more interested in highly commercial authors."

"But—" I was unable to contain myself. My insides were jumping like popcorn in a popper. "Sorry, but I must ask you this: If—*if* it were possible," I said to the publishing goddess, hearing my own voice come out strained but deep, more aggressively than I'd intended, "*if* I could get you a new version of my novel in *three weeks*, before the merger, a version you'd *really* want to publish, what would need to change for you to say yes?"

The publishing legend tilted her head back and caressed the string of tasteful white pearls around her neck. She gazed up high, above the plant.

"Well," she said, focusing on me again, speaking firmly, "perhaps if you were to tell it from the perspective of *Mohammed. That* would be interesting!"

H ere I go: *Mohammed's Story*. A draft the literary legend cannot refuse. I only have three weeks. Time is of the essence. I'll have to work nonstop. I'm not leaving this basement study until I've finished the entire manuscript.

To secure my success, I've taken some drastic measures: I've boarded up the door from the inside, with seven planks of two-by-four pinewood nailed across the doorframe (that's why I needed weapon number two: the hammer). If I leave this room, it will not be on impulse. I have all the necessary provisions with me—five boxes of Premium Saltine Crackers, three tins of Café Bustelo, and twenty-one one-gallon jugs of Poland Spring water—occupying almost all of the desk's surface. That's all I'll need until I'm done. I can't escape. I can't sabotage my life's dream. Drastic times require drastic measures, don't they?

The logistics of this endeavor are not pretty, I must warn you. I have my essential writing supplies: my MacBook with its power cord and an Oxford English Dictionary (the shorter, two-volume set). My iPhone is stored away in the bottom drawer in case of emergencies—I barely get a signal down here anyway—and I've turned off the internet router. I want no distractions from the external world. Yet there are the internal distractions to consider, the bodily necessities. In the study there's a tiny "half bathroom," as they call it—a little water closet—but we never use it; the toilet doesn't always flush properly. I'll save flushing for when it's abso-

lutely necessary—otherwise I'll piss down the sink; that ought to
help. They say W. H. Auden, while a don at King's College, cus-
tomarily tinkled in his study sink. The expediency of poets! Art is a
savage undertaking.

The only other distraction is, of course, people. In my case, two
specific people: Ben, my husband of the last seven years, who announced last week he's breaking up with me—he wants a divorce
(details to come)—and my ex–best friend, Concepción (Concha). I
haven't spoken to Concha in eight months now, or rather, she hasn't
spoken to me—not since our disastrous lunch at the Broadway
Diner last April. It was either a colossal misunderstanding we had
or else too much truth told all at once. In any case, it ruptured our
perfect "friendom," the private kingdom we'd created for ourselves,
fortified, I thought, with bulwarks as thick as the old city walls
of her Spanish hometown, Seville, where we first met during our
college years. Now our friendom has been pillaged and abandoned.
But Ben has somehow rallied Concha to break her silent treatment,
to help him save me from what he calls "the madness of my extreme
measures." Together they've been outside my study for an hour
now, pleading for me to unbarricade myself.

They claim they are worried about my approach—not against
the work per se, but against the insanity of locking myself away
like this. "Write your book," says Ben, "but just do it in a practical
way! You don't have to *harm* yourself, Kip!" Even in my ire I have
to smile when he says "harm" the way we Brits say "ham." I still
find his Boston-Irish brogue adorable—damn him! Concha warns
me against "starving" myself. She learned English in London and
has an even posher accent than mine. If you close your eyes, you
can't tell it's not Emma Thompson speaking. The only difference is
that Concha's gestures remain very Spanish. She emphasizes her

words like an orchestra conductor bringing a baton to the down-beat. Her every move, no matter how small, seems to carry the flare of flamenco—always a stomp of defiance against the cruelty of life. Now, together, Ben and Concha have come as a unified choir to save me from myself.

I'm ambivalent about them both right now. My heart actually feels like it's melting in my chest at the thought that they care enough to protest. I almost wish they'd break down the door to prove how much they really love me. Then we'd all embrace, beg forgiveness, and sob in each other's arms. But on the other hand, they have both broken my heart terribly, and I can't forgive them. How can I trust in their motives? I'm not sure if either of them ever truly loved me. The real me. But then, my therapist, Margaret, suggests maybe it isn't their fault. "Do you ever show them the real you, Kip?" she asked me.

Do I ever show myself the real me? I thought. *Who is the real me?* Isn't that the existential question? The same question posed in the ancient Vedas?

I can hear the two conspirators whispering now. Do they think I can't hear them? The study door is paper-thin—another reason why I've nailed up the two-by-four planks. I hear every word they're saying: Ben wonders if I'm taking our breakup too badly. Concha says she's been worried about me since last year. I've been getting more and more unstable as my Forster novel's not getting sold, she says. "He's completely self-absorbed, Ben. Obsessed with nothing but that book."

"I know, I know," says Ben. "Do you think we should call his therapist? There's something really off about this stunt of his. Manic. Nailing up boards over the door? Who *does* that?"

"I know, I know," says Concha. "And only eating *crackers* for three weeks?"

"Maybe we should take him to Bellevue," says Ben. I bet he's deepening those vertical furrows between his fifty-six-year-old brows, his "empathy marks." I can practically see his pale, freckly face. "Kip should probably be on medication. Maybe a mood stabilizer. I actually wonder if he's becoming delusional."

"Really?" says Concha. "Is it that bad?"

I shouldn't have told Ben that Margaret recommended medication. But the truth is, Margaret actually set up an appointment for me to meet with a Dr. Brian Welch, a psychiatrist on Eighty-fourth and Riverside Drive. As soon as possible, she said. I was supposed to have the appointment today. But I don't need to see Dr. Welch, and I don't need medication. I just need to be published. There are some of us who know our raison d'être. Publication, that's my cure!

With all their fuss outside the door, I'm realizing that domesticity is the enemy of Art. I should have planned this better. I should have gone away, stayed in a cheap motel somewhere off the New Jersey Turnpike. A Motel 6 in Elizabeth or East Brunswick. Artistic genius has come from New Jersey, after all: William Carlos Williams, Amiri Baraka, Bruce Springsteen. New Jersey would have been the best idea. Far away from home and loved ones. Loved ones are the most dangerous threat to one's self-realization.

"Please, please, *please* bugger off! Both of you!" I finally shout through the door.

I hear the hysteria in my own voice. Are they right? Am I going mad?

There is a precedent for this kind of madness—writers sequestering themselves to create in a flurry of inspiration: Proust locked himself away in his bedroom, refusing all visitors; Virginia Woolf insisted on a room of her own; and Tolstoy raged violently at the slightest disturbance from his needy wife, Sophia Andreyevna. As for speed writing: The Nobel laureate Kazuo Ishiguro wrote *The Remains of the Day* in four weeks. Dostoyevsky wrote *The Gambler* in twenty-six days. Robert Louis Stevenson wrote *Strange Case of Dr. Jekyll and Mr. Hyde* in only three days.

Surely, I can survive three weeks on my saltines, espresso, and water. Gandhi lasted over twenty-one days with absolutely no food at all. Jesus fasted for forty days in the desert—the Spirit led him into the wilderness, where he wrestled with the devil. The final temptation was overcome only in absolute isolation.

This is my own sort of wilderness in here, isn't it? My test: to wrestle and to overcome my demons. I can write Mohammed's tale and come out a free man. But I need my wilderness—at least this metaphoric place of solitude away from civilization. But to be honest, I've always had an ambivalent relationship with the real wilderness. I crave the freedom, the space to be, and yet I fear the loneliness of it. But now it's time to be brave, to finally be alone in this wilderness of mine.

Five hours and not a word of the novel written yet. I couldn't think clearly with the disruptions from Ben and Concha. But now they're gone. Thank God.

I'm staring at my MacBook, waiting for her to speak to me—I've named her Sophia. She has a lustrous, rosy golden hue. Okay, Sophia, I say, how should we begin this great work? Sophia is stubbornly silent today, just when I need her most. It's absurd, I know. I'm personifying a silly inanimate object. Projecting my needs for nurturing and support onto this little slab of aluminum that was shipped here from a factory in China.

Ben says I've created Sophia out of my need for what he calls a "transitional object." In psychology-speak, that means something substituting for the "primary object" (i.e., the parent, the comforting one, the desired one). It's like a pacifier in the absence of the mother's teat, says Ben. I hate it when Ben analyzes me. Come on, who doesn't have mother issues? Anyway, even though I realize what I'm doing with Sophia, I can't help myself. I feel betrayed by her withholding now. A heavy sinking in my chest. Two can play at this game! I get up and sulk towards the window. If Sophia's playing hard to get, I'll get my inspiration from nature.

To reach the high-up window and peer outside, I have to stand on top of the black combination safety box that's on the floor. The study only has this one vista, the size of a small birdcage. Through the black, wrought-iron grates, I have a worm's-eye view of the back garden.

We're in a Brooklyn brownstone on DeKalb Avenue. Ben bought the place with his inheritance after his father died. It's lovely, with way more rooms than we need. I moved in with him eight years ago. That's when I installed this basement study. I could have chosen any one of many rooms upstairs but I wanted my own space, free from Ben's history. Yet it's impossible to escape history in these old houses. We're just opposite Fort Greene Park, the hilltop park that was conceived by the great American bard Walt Whitman. I look outside this birdcage window for inspiration, but I only face the backdrop of the old cedar fence beleaguered with lime-green moss. If I crane my neck, I can see a dishwater-gray sky, and next to the snowcapped red barbecue grill is our snowman.

Last week Ben and I made this snowman. It was after this year's first big snowfall. A bright, crisp, blustery day. It already seems so far away—a happier, more innocent time. The snowman's carrot nose has now drooped considerably; pigeons have shat green-gray on his wobbly head; and the coals for his eyes seem to peer down in judgment at me behind my window's iron grates. I'm free, the snowman seems to say, and you're still in a cage!

A cage or a jail? Yes! The Muses have finally sung! I'll start the new novel with Mohammed writing his story from jail. In real life he was jailed for six months, in 1919. Locked away as I am now. We are not so different, Mohammed and I. All right, Kip, let's get to work!

I turn back to face the hoary redbrick walls again—this stuffy old cell. I probably should have chosen a bigger, airier office, like Colson Whitehead's. I once saw Colson in a magazine photo from *Time*, sitting at his desk, with white floor-to-ceiling bookshelves, tastefully placed African statuettes, abstract paintings on the wall. The study of a real Pulitzer winner. All I have is a nine-foot-high, overcrowded Ikea bookshelf, still rickety despite several brutal hours of assembly. Stacks of cardboard boxes of my old crap. And on the floor is a single-burner hot plate with my rusted espresso pot. Then, of course, there's the black combination safety box I'm now standing on. That's where I've locked up the hammer and the gun. I don't know the combination, on purpose. I'd have to fetch the instructions from upstairs—and I can't do that. Not unless all else fails and the gun is finally necessary.

Why, you ask, would I have a gun? Oh, I can't tell you everything all at once.

I return to my desk and readjust the height of my swivel chair—it was too low. I plant my Adidas-clad soles on the creaking floorboards, shut my eyes, and pray Sophia is kinder to me now. After all, I've got an original idea of my own: Mohammed is writing from his jail cell. And then, like a miracle, Sophia awakens my fingertips. I feel them tingling as she lifts them swiftly across her keyboard, and before I know it, together we are delivering my new opening words.

MOHAMMED'S STORY

A Mind Like Winter

Winter in Alexandria is my favorite season. It's wet and gloomy. But it can also be a strange comfort. It's like when ice is held to your bare skin—it's bracing, vitalizing. Somehow you even miss the burn when it's lifted. You crave it again, as much as you fear it. I look back fondly on my winters in Alexandria, especially a particular winter, two years ago, when I was twenty-one. My life changed then. Morgan. He was the icy sting I craved, that I feared. His wintery touch comforted. But then it scorched me too.

That winter of 1917 was no different from most. Rain bombarded the Mediterranean coastline. You felt as if, somehow, you were drowning in the ancient, brooding metropolis. There was also the peculiar odor of antiquity everywhere, a moldiness seeping up from cobblestones in the labyrinths of Turkish Town; from the porous limestone of the old city wall, and from cracked pavements of grand streets like Rue Fouad, the former Canopic Way, where Cleopatra once rode; where mules now stomp up mud as they carry red Berber carpets for sale; where horse-drawn calèches trot by with their brass bells tinging against the quiet roar of rain; and where culverts overflow with sludge and piss and shit. All these heavenly showers and filthy fluids—the great blessings of Osiris.

I only wish winters in Alexandria were colder. Even when there's a chilly sea-wind rushing in on the Corniche, I am stirred to attention like a soldier. Heat makes one slow and lazy, but the cold prepares one for war. I want a mind like winter. Why else do the northern countries dominate us Egyptians? I would love to see snow just once, to *feel* it. I dream of escaping, not only from this miserable cell but from Egypt entirely, far away from all civilization. What good has it done me? Have all the many books from the Great Library of Alexandria made me immune to heartbreak? Am I any more fit to survive alienation from the beloved? Oh, to be free and roam the artic wilderness! If I were an Eskimo, I could trek through the ice and freezing winds, and I could find safety by making my own igloo. Then I'd know I was truly fit for survival.

Sometimes I wake up in the middle of the night or early in the morning, before the first call of the muezzin, and I'm in a sweat, my white djellaba plastered to my skin, coughing and confused. Then slowly I remember I'm here, locked up in this cell. What is my crime? Defence of the Realm Act, they say. They insist I'm an outlaw, a threat to the British Empire. Guilty of the possession of unregistered firearms. Never mind that it was only a trade I made with an Australian soldier—my rationed bag of beans for his old gun. They accuse me of planning a revolt against the Empire. Me, a poor, consumptive, Black boy! But I know the truth. It is because I have tried to love, that's why I'm really in here. Because I have dared to call Morgan my best friend. They cannot abide that. Imagine if I had said the whole truth: he's my lover! Ha! I would be dead already.

Curled up on this cold floor, I try to console myself, rubbing at my protruding ribs as if I were strumming an old oud. What's happening with Morgan and me? I ask myself. How will our strange love story end? Morgan once told me that in fiction it doesn't matter how a love story begins, but there are only two ways it can possibly end—either the couple lives happily ever after, or one (or both) of them dies. I know I will die young, that seems certain now. But, then again, ours is not the usual love story. It is something far more dangerous.

So far I haven't heard a peep from Ben or Concha today. I can write in peace. I readjust the desk chair height—too high now. I stare at the blinking cursor on the empty Word document. Ready for Sophia and me to tackle Mohammed's tale. I take a deep breath, the kind of yogic *dirga pranayama* breath I learned at the ashram, inhaling air through my nostrils, slowly filling my abdomen, then exhaling through my mouth. Ugh! I feel fat. I should do more sit-ups.

Suddenly I hear a strange fluttering behind me. I stiffen, my breathing stops, my heart is pounding. How did a bird get in here? I spin around, raising my arms, prepared to defend myself against the intruder—wings that loud must belong to a very large bird. I squint up at the ceiling, scan every corner, but there's nothing there. Then I hear a tremendous thump. At first I think it's coming from above. Has Ben fallen down the stairs? Then it comes again—*thump*—and now I think it may be outside the study door. It comes a third, fourth, fifth time—*thump, thump, thump*—increasing in speed. And I cannot tell where it's coming from. And it's a very unusual sound. It's the thwapping thump of dragon-size wings displacing the air.

And then I hear a whisper. At first I can't quite make it out. But it comes again, only louder now—a woman's voice with a deep, smooth, intoned whisper: *"Come!"*

What the fuck?

"Concha? Concha, is that you out there?" I shout through the door. Silence.

I jump up and look around again, ready like a crouching tiger. But there's definitely nothing in here. I must be hallucinating. You're losing it, Kip. It must be the stress, the pressure of this ordeal. If I just concentrate on the writing, I'll be okay. I sit down at the desk and force myself to focus on Mohammed again, to get inside his head. That's all I need to do. Breathe, and focus on the work.

According to my research sources—Forster's letters and diaries, and books by him and others—Mohammed was quite strident, a tough young man. He'd had a difficult childhood, and that gave him an edge. That's where I needed to speak from in order to write from Mohammed's perspective properly. I have to find where I relate to him.

Like me, Mohammed was keenly aware of how being Black affected his life. He told Forster he was much darker than his siblings. He also had more sub-Saharan features—fuller lips, wider nose. He suspected his mother had had an affair with a Sudanese man. His father must have also suspected as much, because Mohammed was never fully accepted by his father. He wasn't allowed to eat with the rest of the family, and his father refused to pay for his education. It was that strange fate that caused his mother to find alternatives for Mohammed and enroll him in the free American Missionary School. He ended up with a far better education than his brothers got; he became "Westernized" and perfectly fluent in English, for which he had an exceptional proclivity. One door closed and another opened. But it didn't compensate for what he'd lost, said Mohammed. Even his mother rejected him, he confessed to Morgan. She always held him at a distance. He was proof of her transgressions. Mohammed felt he had, in a manner, raised himself. He had never been able to rely on his parents for their affirming love.

Before writing Mohammed's next chapter, I must get myself into the head—no, the heart—of Mohammed, the broken heart of someone who never felt accepted. And before I know it, for some reason, I'm thinking more about myself than Mohammed. About little Kip.

Memories seem impossible to control. Like stones in a pile, I cannot pick out just one without causing an avalanche. Isn't this what happened when Proust cooped himself up in his bedroom? He was overtaken by memories, the avalanche. A simple bite of a madeleine released long-forgotten memories, the most vivid sensations, recalling seminal events. They all came tumbling down upon him. In trying to find Mohammed's voice, it seems I have now released my own avalanche.

More British Than the British

At thirteen, I was deep in the closet. Not the proverbial closet—I had no conscious idea of my sexuality at that age. No, I had literally closed myself up in the closet of my bedroom, hiding in a dark corner, huddled under a heap of dirty laundry.

It was a Friday evening in April, just after my parents and I had returned from my school's annual arts festival. The fateful evening had started off well. My parents showed up on time for the school event. It was my first year at the posh independent secondary school in London, and I was eager for my parents to see my artistic efforts. Mum and Dad were in pleasant, collegial moods, it seemed, friendly and chatting with the other parents, mostly white, harried, middle-class professionals who'd rushed there from work or the uber-relaxed aristocrats, disheveled from a long day of lounging, or gardening, perhaps.

Growing up in London's Home Counties, in Weybridge, I lived in a three-story, modernist town house. It's part of a now much-coveted Span Development, the Templemere Estate. My parents still live there to this day. On the estate, the boxlike brick and glass houses are spread among landscaped gardens and set back some distance from the road.

When I was young, there was only one other "Black" family

on the entire estate—the Shardas, a wealthy Indian family from Agra, whose son, pudgy Panav, has recently become a leader with the Tories, is chums with Boris Johnson, and to my horror, has been a major proponent of Brexit. You can never predict who will come out of Weybridge—or where we will go.

To my knowledge, I am the only child of Delores and William Starling.

Delores is a sharp, lean, brown-skinned woman. At six feet, she is always the tallest woman—and often the tallest person—in any room. Dad only has an inch on her. She's a former invest-ment banker with Deutsche Bank. She specialized in global capital markets—a job that nearly killed her, she says. She has a straightened perm that remains in beauty parlor shape. Now in her mid-sixties, she has remade herself after an identity crisis in which she nearly left Dad (because how could she be herself while being his wife?). But she found herself again after an arsenal of self-help books from Waterstones and stayed. She now has a new, more rewarding life as a water aerobics instructor for seniors at the YMCA in Central London. Never mind the feat of being a Caribbean female in the finance world; if you can appreciate the sacrifice a Black woman must make to get her hair wet three times a week, you'll grasp the grit of this woman.

William is quietly commanding, Indian-looking, with silky, gray hair, and he's etched like a tall spear. He has warm, kind eyes behind his horn-rimmed eyeglasses. He never raises his voice, but everything is only on his terms. When I was six, he became the high commissioner to the UK from the Commonwealth of The Bahamas, where we originated, and to which we return every year for two weeks at Christmastime.

Delores and William were raised under the full sway of British colonialism, and this has made me an odd, anachronistic creature. Dad was head boy in his high school. He knew every British monarch's lineage and history and was an ace bowler in cricket. Mum can quote passages from Dickens, Wordsworth, and Milton by heart. She knows her scones from her crumpets. My parents were raised in a colony where old British ways were adhered to more vehemently than anywhere in modern England. A place where, in the tropical heat, Black schoolboys happily sweated in uniforms of wool blazers, as if dressed for winter at Eton.

Many decades after England itself had fallen from its colonial glory, Delores and William raised me in, essentially, a perfectly Victorian household. If displays of desire were out of the question, homosexuality was unmentionable. I found it ironic that my father used to joke that after our independence from Britain (barely a decade before I was born), his island peers became "more British than the British." These island men were arrogant and comically officious, rigid, with old-fashioned English mores, stiff posture, and overly enunciated Queen's Speech. They were Anglophiles to the highest degree. In their minds, I imagine, they were simply trying to be "good enough," "capital fellows," "right as rain." But all the while, they were constrained by the proverbial Victorian corset. The irony of my father's joke was that he was no less English. I was raised in the same Victorian ether as Forster.

At events like my school's arts festival, I noticed the subtle ways in which my parents were different from the white parents, especially the progressive Londoners our school was known to attract. My parents were actually even more reserved than the Brits. They often, almost imperceptibly, gave me the "hard-eye" (their secret warning) whenever they noticed some white kid acting too precocious or "sassing" their parents in public. "You better not even think

of trying that with us," their hard-eye said. That kind of "white lib-
eral nonsense" was not acceptable to us Black folks. There were certain cardinal rules—and they weren't ever taught to me per se, I just
knew them: good children were to be seen and not heard; absolutely
no private family matters were ever to be discussed in public—ever;
and contradicting your parents or showing them up in public was,
as far as I knew, punishable by death—it was never ever allowed
under any circumstances. But besides the occasional hard-eye when
my parents would observe others' infractions of these cardinal rules,
I thought everything was going fine that evening.

The idea of the arts festival was that parents were to see the
school's choir performance, watch a little play, and view students'
artwork on display. Available for sale were copies of the students'
literary magazine, about twenty mimeographed pages stapled together, imaginatively titled *Words*.

A poem I had written had gotten into the magazine that year. I
hadn't given the poem a title but, unbeknownst to me, my favorite
teacher, Miss Wiseman (the reason I'm still partial to red freckles,
and more important, the one who'd said my name meant I was
destined to be a great writer), had titled my poem "The Son of
Stone."

I had written the poem for an English assignment. As Miss
Wiseman had instructed, we were to base a poem on a metaphor
of our choice. We had been given several examples of what a metaphor was, and how it could be developed into a poem, but I was
stumped for most of the class, unable to come up with anything.
Finally, I cheated. I had an old school yearbook in my desk, and I
secretly flipped through it looking for past student poems. I finally
saw one by a girl named Jessica, who'd mysteriously left school the
year before amidst rumors that her mother had killed herself. It

was a poem in which a child had been molded by her parents into a statue and become frozen in time. I stole the idea, gave it a twist, and ran with it:

> *There was a goddess*
> *Who bore a sun.*
> *He was an accident, her glaring mistake—*
> *He burned away her many loves to none.*
> *And so to have something of her very own,*
> *She cast her sun into stone;*
> *Her image that could not break.*
> *She marveled at him;*
> *She watched her son shine;*
> *She used him as a sundial*
> *To mark her time.*
> *But then one day,*
> *The stone turned to flesh.*
> *He stood alone and strong.*
> *The mother's statue broke—*
> *Or else, the sun went wrong.*

If it wasn't a work of genius, I thought at least it was clever of me to use the pun of "sun" and "son," to use the stolen metaphor of being carved out of stone, and also to have my statue come to life and shatter the mold. I was also rather proud that my poem had been chosen for the literary magazine.

Publication had suddenly catapulted me into the small club of the artsy bunch, the city kids who lived in Hackney Wick or Stoke Newington, the kids whose parents were famous artists or intellectuals, like the already brooding Pippa Day-Lewis, who said she suffered from ennui (which to me sounded like the absolute coolest thing to suffer from); or Roger Strachey, who wore his hair in a ponytail and vacationed in Los Angeles; or the tall and beautiful, doe-eyed India Trevelyan, who'd already seen old French films in black-and-white and whose parents occasionally let her drink wine and smoke pot—parents, I imagined, like Edina from *Absolutely Fabulous* (a show I was *absolutely* banned from watching, which only meant I found ways to absolutely see it). Now that I was published in *Words*, I had joined that special literary set, and I imagined my parents, while not famous bohemians, would also appreciate my achievement.

That was not the case.

I became aware of my mother's odd silence throughout the arts festival that evening. It was after she'd already picked up *Words* from Miss Wiseman's classroom when I noticed her making a quick scan of my poem, unable to repress an ugly snarl. Later, as the choir sang a funny ditty about an old man and his grandfather clock, my mother wore a false, tight smile. A grin I immediately recognized as her angry-in-public face. I watched her, hoping to get a reassuring glance, but she avoided me altogether. Not even the hard-eye. Her smooth, brown skin only wrinkled periodically around her pursed lips, lips that occasionally twitched as if she'd quietly vomited in her own mouth.

On the car ride home, she was absolutely silent—and this was rare. The previous spring, following the primary school arts festival, my mother was jolly with various observed shortcomings of my teachers: "Honestly, that maths teacher ought to fix her teeth!" Or "These British people have no respect! Your headmaster, calling me

Delores—as if we were on first-name basis! I'm not his girlfriend!" But, on this evening, Delores Starling had no critiques at all. Nothing. Something was terribly wrong.

When we arrived home, just as my father was unlocking the front door, silent as an undertaker, my mother looked in my direction, but not straight at me. She actually focused somewhere over my head, as if I should have been a foot taller. "You got it all wrong, you know, Kipling," she said.

"Got what wrong, Mummy?" I asked, genuinely confused.

"Your birth was not a 'glaring mistake.' Your father and I waited five years to have you after we were married, until we were sure we were ready. And I never had any other 'loves,' as you call them. You ought to get your facts straight before you go and tell your little story to the entire world!"

Apparently, my mother didn't understand the idea of poetic license. She had taken my poem to be my attempt at a factual account.

"What?" I said. "Mum, you don't understand. It's a poem. I made it up."

As she shut the front door behind us, my mother's face trembled, her lips curled in a display of disgust, or bitter pain, or maybe both. "I can't believe you would do this. How could you write something like that, for everyone to read? How could you have done this to me? This is what we get for sending you to that fancy white school!"

"Mummy, you don't understand." I now saw the disaster that was upon us, and I desperately tried to reverse her trajectory. "It's just made-up, Mummy. Fiction."

Then my mother's composure cracked altogether and she exploded with tears. Bawling, she ran upstairs, her long legs stretching two steps at a time, her burnt-orange skirt billowing in her wake like a flag of distress. My father and I stood silent, dumb at the foot of the stairs. Finally he turned to me. "You've really upset your mother, you know. That was very careless of you."

I ran upstairs after her to fix the damage. But my mother had now locked herself in the bathroom. I could hear her in there, sobbing inconsolably. I knocked on the door. "Mummy, I'm sorry."

"I hope you're happy now, Mr. Poet!" she shouted through the door. "How will I face any of those people ever again? Just imagine what they'll think of me! Leave me alone. You've done your damage!"

Silently, I marched down the hall to my bedroom. In the dark I walked straight to my bed, sat on it, and slumped. Then I collapsed, lying curled in a fetal position. The fact that my mother had so violently shut me out shattered me. How could I have done so much damage without even trying? My mother's love had always been like the sun for me—illuminating my being, necessary for life. I had never known the sun could be eclipsed, or that it could even disappear at all. And I did not imagine I had the power to banish the sun myself. But I obviously did. My heart sank and seemed to keep on plummeting. I thought the falling would never end.

And then it came, the final thud. The strange and scary realization: I could never again idealize my mother. She could not be my sun. I needed to find my way to another source of light. She had always led me to believe she was a strong woman, smart and courageous, blazing trails in a white man's profession, knowing the answers to any question I had ever asked. "Your mother knows everything!" she'd say, half teasing, half believing it herself, I think. But I now saw the truth: she was a fragile girl pretending to be more, instantly shattered at the thought of being sullied in the eyes of others.

I am on my own, I said to myself, as I lay there in the dark.

Even at thirteen, I knew this was not how parents were supposed to act.

Dad still paced outside the bathroom door. I could hear the ice clinking in his scotch on the rocks (that's what it always was). He tried to calm my mother, but he too was feeling helpless, I'm sure. His voice was thin and uncertain. "It will be all right, Delores. We'll be all right, dear."

Now the proverbial curtain had been drawn back and there they were: two helpless souls with no more self-assurance than children. How can they both be so fragile? I asked myself. One little poem and they're reduced to this? There are no real grown-ups here, I said to myself. I listened, there in the dark, waiting to hear footsteps approaching to comfort me. But after two hours of waiting, my mother was still crying, and my father was murmuring ineffective attempts to console her: "Come on, Delores, open the door. Let's go to bed now, dear." A refreshed glass of whisky was in his hand, I guessed, since the ice was still clinking, and clinking.

The realization of losing my parents' unconditional love was both terrifying and painful. The fact that I had also caused them pain by my actions added salt to the wound. I wished I could have died at that moment. And then my fear of being abandoned grew to rage, and the fire in my stomach swelled so much I didn't know how I'd possibly sustain it. Maybe I should kill myself and let them find me dead, I thought. I imagined a gunshot to my temple, blood splattered over the white sheets. (Ben once told me that behind every suicide is a murder. He often asks his suicidal patients, "Who do you want to kill?" or "Who do you want to find you dead?")

Without thinking, I ran to hide in the closet. It was dark and safe in there, numbingly cool. After I buried myself under the dirty clothes dumped from the laundry basket, I decided to wait until my parents came looking for me. As we get older, we seem to forget the intensity of such feelings that occur in young people. When your entire survival thus far has been dependent on two people, to lose them is to lose everything. "Come for me," I prayed. "I need you!" But I fell asleep, and when I woke up, a bright line of light spread beneath the closet door. I walked out, squinting and crusty-eyed, into morning. I knew right then that this was the end of an era—the end of my childhood.

My first published work had resulted in the worst outcome I could have imagined: I had lost my parents. I now knew the sun could disappear if it was displeased by me. Nothing was the same after that.

Yesterday was an absolute waste. I got nothing written at all. I don't know what happened to the time. I lapsed into a reverie, got overtaken with memories, and before I knew it I was asleep with my head on the desk. I slept like that all night. I was woken just now, not by the sunlight—it's a yellowish gray out there—but by that strange whispering voice again.

"Come," she said. She had a warm, deep voice, spoken directly into both ears this time in full stereophonic sound. *"Come."* I popped my head up so fast I got an instant crick in my neck. My eyes wide as saucers. But again, no one was there. I don't get it, I thought. Am I actually having auditory hallucinations? Oh, Kip, keep it together. You've got to finish the novel on time.

I hope there aren't unknown forces working against me. Internal forces, I mean. I've been in psychoanalysis long enough to know that the unconscious is a bitch. It sneaks up on you, and even when fully in its grip, you can hardly see it. Then it makes you do shit you don't intend to do. My therapist once told me Carl Jung jokingly said that we English don't have an unconscious because the class system makes up for it. But we'd better be careful: the unconscious is a tricky little monster. The good news: it can't get away with much if the lights are on and the eyes are wide open. We have to stay awake.

I can't get overtaken with my memories right now. Today I've got to write Mohammed's next chapter. Time is of the essence.

My main struggle at this point is getting Mohammed's voice just right. They say the key to any literary success is narrative voice. Sure, I can identify with elements of Mohammed's struggle, but the voice must be true and distinctive. I'll confess my initial attraction to the story of Forster's love affair only started when I saw a photo of Mohammed in one of Forster's biographies. I felt an instant affinity, like a bolt of lightning, really. To be totally truthful, and I'm reluctant to admit this, it was like I'd seen a ghost of myself, a ghost from the past. It was *myself* that I was looking at. I did one of those farcical double takes. Pulled the book closer to my face. "It looks so much like me," I even said aloud. The same sad eyes. It was like looking in a mirror.

But never mind. My task is to hone the voice of that haunting image I saw. And I need to make sure Mohammed's voice is distinct from my voice, which is, ironically, more like Forster's.

D. H. Lawrence once berated Forster for being unable to throw himself passionately into love, saying he was a Victorian relic, holding on to an Imperial-era Britishness. Lawrence proclaimed the timid Forster to be "the very last Englishman." Well, if my Bahamian family is more British than the British, then I am more Forster than Forster. Even more so than he was, I am the very last Englishman!

But now I must channel Mohammed—the Egyptian, the other, the outlaw. There are only a few surviving letters written in Mohammed's hand. They are all cryptic, somewhat poetic. It's hard to tell how his spoken words might have sounded. He was well educated, fluent in English, deeply feeling, but also somewhat aloof. The key to a character's voice, they say, is in understanding the person's motives. Gabriel García Márquez reportedly struggled to find the right voice for his narrator in *One Hundred Years of Solitude.* Then he finally realized he could simply tell the story as his own grandmother had recounted her fantastical stories to him. And bingo!

If only I could find the right motivation for Mohammed, I'd be set. Who could he be telling his story to? To Forster? No, that makes no sense. To his young son? By 1919, Mohammed was married to Gamila and they had a new baby boy, Morgan—named after Forster, of course. Would Mohammed possibly tell his story to his little Morgan? No, that wouldn't make sense either. Why would Mohammed tell his son about having a complicated sexual relationship with an older white man?

Wait . . . What if Mohammed is telling the story to me—to Kip Starling?

Just as I'd felt that lightning bolt of connection upon seeing the photo of this young man who lived a hundred years ago, what if Mohammed felt an equally strong connection with his image of a man in the future? A Black man, one hundred years hence; a man who might understand his dilemma with Morgan; a modern Black man who lives the life he can't. What if Mohammed wants to tell me about his experience so that I know, from his perspective, where we queer, Black, colonial men have come from? What if Mohammed also needs me to exist so that he knows, as he is dying, that there is a future for our kind, a life to come, a Possibility?

Yes. Talk to me, Mohammed. Whisper to me from your cold cell. I'm here for you. I'm listening.

The Ticket

Yes, now you see—this is all for you. So why should I simply recount more facts? You've done your research. You know the facts. You know it was winter, two years ago, when I met Morgan. And yet what you don't know is what that first meeting meant to me, or why I agreed to meet him again.

If we had come across each other in summertime, I don't think I would have noticed Morgan at all. He was an unremarkable Englishman sitting near the rear of my tram, the Bacos line, dressed rather shabbily: the hems of his gray wool trousers were coming undone; there were buttons missing on his brown tweed jacket; and his hair was rising, brambly with the humidity. In Alex, only a British man would appear like that in public. Their power is unquestioned, they needn't impress. It is a mark of privilege to be shabby.

We only first spoke because of the muddle with my winter box coat. We were pulling out of Chatby station. And it was nighttime, almost the end of my shift. But I had a chill and decided to fetch my coat. Normally, I did not like to wear the box coat. The royal blue clashed with our tram conductor's uniform—the military khaki tunic with gold buttons and the red fez with the light blue silk tassels—but it got cold approaching the suburbs of Camp de César, so I forsook fashion for necessity. Although Morgan will tell you I'm a sensitive type with a bent for poetry, I will disagree. I feel I am practical above all else. That's why I needed the box coat. And "practicality," ultimately, is why our love got complicated. As I made my way down the aisle to the seat in the rear—under which I'd previously stored my coat—I saw it was now occupied. I asked Morgan to please hand me my coat.

You know how the rest of our conversation went. But what you don't know is that I lied when I told him my English was poor and needed improvement. The truth is I may be poor of pocket, but not of mind. In school I scored the top marks for English. I even corrected the grammar of my own English teachers at the American Missionary School. I have also read philosophy and science in English, French, and Arabic—Darwin, Descartes, and Al-Farabi. And you cannot get by as a tram conductor in Alex if you don't know some Greek and Italian too.

Only those Egyptians who are well educated can get such a job as mine. But I told Morgan my English was poor so he'd know my standards were very high—as high as his own. Still, I didn't want him to think I valued his native language more than any other, so I also said that one of these days I should think of brushing up on English, but there were so many more important things to do first. So many great books to read in Arabic, I said.

I did not expect his response. He agreed. The most important story in all of narrative history was written in Arabic, he said: *Alf Laylah, wah-Laylah: One Thousand and One Nights.*

I pretended not to be impressed. I felt my lips turning up to smile, but I clamped them down. I wasn't sure if he was pulling my leg or if he meant what he was saying. I would not fall into his trap. Why do you like this book so much? I asked.

He told me it was the greatest example of what all storytelling is based upon: you must always keep the reader asking what happens next. Like Scheherazade, he said. A storyteller must possess something of the seductress, he added coyly.

I smiled. He'll tell you I was vaguely seduced, but really it was almost embarrassing to see how awkward he was at flirting. Smiling, however, was my mistake—it seemed to encourage him. He made a comment on how white my teeth were, how they shone against the brown of my skin. He asked if I was from sub-Saharan Africa. I could tell he did not mean it as an insult, but I was not sure what he was insinuating, and so I told him I speak Arabic, not Swahili.

I chastised him for prying about my sub-Saharan appearance. Of course I gave him no idea of what I have suffered due to being Black, the darkest in my entire family. Always the outlaw, even here in my own country, even in my own home. But I let Morgan know that I knew how the British really think. I asked him, Do I look like a Black savage to you?

That seemed to rattle him. Oh, no, no, no, he said, shaking his head; his fair brown hair kept flopping about.

I must get back to work, I said. My coat, please!

He finally offered it slowly and I snatched it up. But then I realized what had just happened between us, and without showing him any feelings that might give the wrong idea, I said, If I see you on my tram again, you will not pay. I will reward you for treating me as no other Britisher has ever treated me—as an intelligent human being. Good night.

He looked confused; he wanted something more from me, it

seemed. I almost recognized that look. I had had men want things from me before. All my life. I was never innocent. Well, maybe at six, before my uncle Mahmoud took a bent interest in me—his little Black nephew who nobody really wanted. I knew the look of being wanted. Only I wasn't exactly sure what this British man wanted of me. If he wanted to degrade me for his pleasure, why did he also look so frightened and timid? The other men had never looked so frightened when they wanted to use me.

I had never seen myself as something of value, so that night on the tram, I got confused. I even forgot to collect Morgan's ticket. I could not recognize that inexplicable look in his eyes. What I now know is this: you can only see in others what you already see in yourself. I had never known true kindness towards myself, so I did not recognize it when I first saw it in Morgan's eyes.

Abandon All Hope

Every novel is a confession, they say. The truth of this is now undeniable to me. I had no conscious intention of revealing to you the very essence of my first meeting with Ben, but somehow, in writing the last chapter, that's what I've done.

After my year in the Indian ashram, I returned to New York City as a failed monk, struggling to readjust to a householder life. I fell into the same depressed state I'd been in before. Although I couldn't shake my dark mood, I did have some reason to be happy: I'd had the unbelievable good luck of winning the Green Card Lottery, a Diversity Immigration Visa. Only fifty-five thousand out of the thirteen million who applied that year had such good luck. For the next ten years, at least, I could stay and work in the States with a proper Social Security Number. But not even that lifted my spirits.

India had been a balm to my injured soul, especially after the horrible experience with my Columbia MFA program. Anyway, once back in New York, the scene of the crime, I completely decompensated. Frequent panic attacks left me immobile and sweating bullets on the subway platform, incapable of boarding the crowded train. Or sometimes, with a life-sucking depression, I slept for days, unable to get out of bed, pinned down with an

invisible weight, as if a grand piano were perpetually falling inside my chest. Worst of all were the inexplicable bouts of anger,
like the one that finally led me to verbally attack a nice, waiflike
white kid who worked at The Container Store. "Whatever you
need to contain, we've got a container for you here!" he said with
a big fake-cheerful smile. I might normally have felt allied with
this seemingly queer young person. But instead I only wanted
to slap that smug smile off his simpering face. "A container for
anything?" I said. "Really? Do you have something to contain my
unfathomable rage, you asshole?" The vile words just spewed out
of me. I saw tears well up in his pale blue eyes. He shook like a
Chihuahua. I suddenly snapped out of it, full of shame. What the
hell am I doing? I thought. This isn't the gentle Kip I know myself
to be. I quickly apologized and left the store.

Don't let anyone tell you depression is a lame, sad state of
weakness. *Au contraire, mon frère.* Depression is a raging monster,
a savage beast that devours you whole and leaves behind not even
a trace of your previous self.

After that troubling incident, I sought out a shrink. Ross, a
former MFA classmate, referred me to Ben O'Keefe, a Gestalt psychotherapist. Ross was also gay, and he had been in analysis with
Ben several years prior.

In the first therapy session, Ben immediately wowed me. He
had an alluring, enigmatic smile, with a gap in his top front teeth.
He had a sprinkling of ginger freckles around his nose (you know
my weakness for that). There was also a warm tenor to his voice,
with that Boston accent. He had an equally warm gaze. The kind of
guy who you imagine loves puppies. And yet, every so often, there
was also something penetrating about his hazel-green eyes that
was a bit scary, as if he could become unpredictable, carnivorous,

even. He spoke with a calm, unquestionable intellect. "So, Kip, in our work together we'll also be exploring the relationship between client and therapist." When I asked him to explain, he reluctantly offered something about the phenomenological field. I had no idea what he meant, but it all sounded very, very smart.

About halfway into our first session I heard myself say, "Ben, I know this is strange but I have to tell you, I'm very attracted to you." It just came out. Maybe it was the confessional mood of the therapeutic experience that moved me to be so frank so quickly. Ben was extremely professional; I didn't get a hint of sexual interest from him. He said it was common to have a "romantic transference" for one's analyst and that we could use those feelings to explore my own fantasies and disappointments.

I was persistent and asked under what circumstances would it, theoretically, be possible to go on a date with him. He said it wasn't possible. "The minute you walk into my office, a therapeutic dynamic has been established. I cannot cross that line."

I was crestfallen. I didn't go back for a second session. I wasn't angry, I was bereft.

I eventually found another therapist, Margaret. A mature, red-headed Jungian genius with a deep voice and statuesque beauty. I never regretted the move, but still I could not forget Ben. He became a central subject in my work with Margaret—my fantasy, a projection of something ideal, my daddy issues, my yearning for the all-nurturing archetypal Mother.

But eventually I got Margaret to reveal a very practical golden rule to me: even if you are seeing a therapist as a patient, if you cease treatment and avoid all contact with said therapist for at least two years, it is no longer, technically, unethical to begin a romantic relationship. But since I only had a single consultation with Ben,

Margaret thought one year might be an acceptable time to wait before approaching him for a date.

I anxiously waited out the three remaining months before it would be a full year, three months of envisioning Ben and me walking hand in hand on autumn walks in Central Park, or training together at the Y on Fourteenth Street—me spotting him as he did his manly squats into my supporting, randy arms—or just cuddling on the couch for a night of Netflix binging. Then finally, on the exact day a year was up, with butterflies in my stomach, I called Ben. I left a voicemail message—immediately regretting how I rambled and let out awkward, unnecessary "ummm"s and "like"s, yet still believing he'd be flattered and find the message charming.

But after three weeks, I received no return call. And after four weeks, I gave up all hope.

There is a great teaching from Atisha, the eleventh-century Bengali Buddhist master: *Abandon all hope*. The hitch to this teaching is that one is also to remain steadfastly on the path to enlightenment. Zen also has four "Great Vows," and they are similarly paradoxical: *Delusions are endless; vow to cut through them all*. I tried to practice what I had learned in the ashram. I tried to abandon all hope of ever finding love. It was a baffling concept that, at first, seemed like giving up on life, until I began to understand it was, instead, the secret to being more alive with the present moment: not always being dissatisfied with your actual life, not basing happiness on what may, or may not, happen in the future. So I gave up all hope.

On the Analyst's Couch Again

A month later, Ben called me back. I'd been so nervous when I'd left my message on his voicemail—with my heartbeat thumping in my ears—I hadn't listened carefully to his outgoing message. I was so fixated on what *I* was about to say. It turns out, in his message he'd said he'd be away on vacation for several weeks. When we finally spoke on the phone, he confessed he was dealing with a breakup during that time. His ex-boyfriend, Julio, had just moved out of their brownstone in Fort Greene. He hadn't wanted to call me in the midst of all that drama, he said. My heart kept leaping to the sky as he spoke. He then confessed he'd been thinking of me too, and that he'd also been attracted to me, but I was so much younger. At the time, I was twenty-eight and Ben was forty-seven, which was a considerable gap and gave him pause. And, besides, he said, he wasn't sure it was even ethical to pursue a relationship based on the way we met. I mentioned the golden rule. He knew about it, of course, but said he still had reservations.

Eventually, I convinced him to meet anyway. No pressure, just a friendly coffee, I said. He finally gave in. "Okay," he said. "How about a real drink, though? After my last few weeks, I need it." He suggested meeting at the Boiler Room, a dive gay bar on Second Avenue in my neighborhood.

We sat on high stools at the old worn bar in the dim glow of Christmas lights strung up above the mirrored wall behind the bar (still up in February). We talked and talked, and drank and drank. I found him quirkier than he had seemed in our session: he blinked a lot and chewed at his fingertips. He had the dizzy air of a sweet, absentminded professor. Although he looked mostly Irish, his mother had been Jewish, he said, from Newton, Massachusetts. His speech was peppered with adorable Yiddish exclamations (*Oy vey! Verklempt!*) and awkward, self-deprecating gestures that made him seem like a genuine mensch, as he might say.

Blissfully intoxicated, we finally headed back to my railroad flat on Avenue A. We hooked up—nothing earth-shattering, but it was extremely satisfying, like having a tall glass of ice water on a summer day. He slept over; we spooned perfectly. In the morning we made pancakes. We laughed at the outrageous attempt on the box of pancake mix to update the racist image of Aunt Jemima, with her new, straightened perm, and then the hopeful gaze of the Native-American beauty on Land O Lakes Butter ®, with her headdress of patriotic American feathers—red, white, and blue! Really? Are they serious? Everything set us into a tizzy of giggles.

Afterwards, I walked him to his office, which was in the West Village just past Washington Square Park. He got a text message that his first scheduled patient had to cancel last minute. So I accompanied him upstairs into his office to kiss him goodbye. We soon found ourselves naked on his black leather couch. The same couch I'd sat on when I first fantasized about being with him.

We made love again—no, that's not quite accurate: we had crazy-ass, nasty sex. Love didn't have much to do with it. Thank God his white noise machine was outside the office door, otherwise anyone in the waiting room would have sworn we were making a porn video: there were cries of degrading expletives, sexualized hyperbole, detailed pleas for where to put certain racialized body parts. Nothing was politically correct, but it was so damn hot! I was surprised at Ben's ability to abandon all control, to sacrifice his body entirely to my basest will. But he also could take total control when he wanted. I admired the liberation he had in sex. I'd also been right about those carnivorous eyes. After that day, we kept meeting up, and in less than a month, we were truly in love.

Of course, I could tell you I was struck by Ben's intelligence, warmth, and good looks, or even the hot sex we found ourselves practically addicted to, but in truth, it was something else. As a rule, in those days I had purposefully excluded white men from my repertoire—too much racist nonsense to navigate in such an intimate relationship, I'd thought. So I could not really explain, even to myself, why I had fallen so hard for Ben, at least not until an hour ago, when I was writing the scene where Mohammed first meets Forster in the tram in Alexandria.

I now realize what happened in our first meeting: Ben had seen something in me that I had not yet seen in myself. I could sense it—just as Mohammed felt it when Morgan looked up at him in the tram—only I didn't know what it was. I now know: for a moment, I felt fully seen. Seen for being me. Such a simple thing. For ages, since the invention of love, it has been said that the eyes are the window to the soul, the truest expression of the heart. But because, at that time, I had no reference for being truly seen, I had no idea why I was drawn so irresistibly to this man.

Amazingly, as more months went by, our sex stayed hot for longer than it ever had with anyone else. My previous record had been three months before looking for someone new. And despite our age and cultural differences, Ben and I were surprised at all our similarities. We were astonished that we loved the same books (all the Russians, Faulkner, Toni Morrison, Hollinghurst), the same foods (Thai, Italian, Indian). We even had the same taste in movies: we devoured Kiarostami and De Sica like crack fiends, pondered endlessly about Tarkovsky's *The Sacrifice*, sobbed like banshees when finishing the *Apu* trilogy, and together walked out midway through *Avatar*—ran out of the cinema, in fact, like freed prisoners of war. "I don't get it!" "Me either. An Academy Award for a two-hour video game?" As with new lovers all over the world, we began by feeling perfectly in sync, like the proverbial two peas in a pod.

I've got to get cracking. After another avalanche of memories, I fell asleep again. It's ten past five in the morning. I've wasted six good working hours. Three days gone by and I've only just begun. I'll make a pot of espresso, munch on a few saltines, and I'll be ready to go.

But I have to tell you—it happened again. I was woken by that whispering woman about an hour ago. *"Come,"* she keeps saying in her strange, deep voice. This time I didn't lift my head from the desk. I tried to ignore her. I know it's just my imagination—there's no one actually in here. But then, as I was telling myself to get a grip, I felt something touch me on the back of my neck, fingers running down my spine, all the way to the tailbone. I jumped up like I'd been struck by lightning. Spun around. "What the fuck is that?" I said. But there was no one.

This shit is getting really crazy. Was it a spider—a daddy longlegs? No, it was definitely fingers. I'm sure of it.

And then something occurred to me: there's probably a ghost or spirit in here with me. What else could it be?

I've been visited by spirits once before. Yes, I've known dead people. Years ago, a few months before I had moved into the ashram, I had a dream in which Baba, my guru's guru, appeared to me. He had actually died decades before I was born, but in the dream he came and embraced me. It felt as if I were reuniting with a long-lost lover for whom I'd been searching for thousands of lifetimes. As we embraced, I wept. And when I awoke, to my amazement, he was still standing there at the foot of my bed. Baba was actually there in the flesh, his beautiful brown face glistening under his white beard, and he was dressed in saffron robes. I felt instantly transported as if I were existing on another plane—not afraid, not questioning my reality. I jumped out of bed and held him for as long as I could—more than five minutes. I watched the minutes advance on my digital alarm clock. And then Baba vanished. I stood there shaking and astonished, not understanding what had just happened.

My family in The Bahamas call these kinds of appearances "visitations." My grandmother used to tell me of how her dead grandparents would often visit her. They would even move things around in her kitchen sometimes, she said, laughing. "Dumped the sugar—just so—on the counter!" But most of all, she said, her "sperrids" (as she called them) would protect her, and they'd also remind her of "old-time stories."

Perhaps that's what Mohammed is too—a visitation of sorts. He's come to tell me his story. And I must write it. For him and for me.

MOHAMMED'S STORY

Sticky Cakes

I'm sure you've seen him in photographs, so you can tell from those sepia-toned images of the gangly white man with his head always lopped to one side, peering up apologetically at the camera: Morgan is no peacock. Darwin says many species go to extreme measures to attract a mate. I suppose this is why, on that rainy January afternoon in 1917, Morgan waited to "accidentally" bump into me, pacing on the pavement outside the terminus tram station of the Bacos line. It was his attempt at preening. With his broken umbrella, khaki suit soaked, and hair plastered to his skull, Morgan was no beauty.

I pretended to be surprised to run into him on the pavement. He asked if I'd join him for coffee at his favorite café on Rue Fouad. I laughed. Poor man. He had no idea what a scandal it would have been. I would have been chased from the establishment or arrested for harassing a British subject.

When he asked me what I found so amusing, I told him that he looked like a wet rat. It would be more suitable for us to meet another day. But I had to get back to work. Let's go, I said, we haven't much time!

We ran to the tram, huddled under my umbrella, water splashing off us like liquid fireworks. Yes, there was something electric about our connection. He held me by the elbow, pushing his chest against my back, and his knee kept folding into the back of mine. There was an urgency in his touch. And I felt a kind of power, as if I could save this drowning man.

On the tram, while I sat on the back footboards, he smiled bashfully every time he turned around. When I walked down the aisle, he handed me his piasters for payment. I said, No. You shall never pay. I keep my word! But he insisted, and released a handful of coins. There was a massive clattering, the coins falling like rain on a tin roof. We both had to get on our hands and knees to retrieve the piasters—under seats, between legs, down the aisle. I scolded Morgan and told him he was too stubborn. He accused me of the same, only he was now laughing. But I was not.

I agreed to meet on Thursday, my next day off. On the back of his tram ticket I wrote the time and place in clear capital English letters. But you know this, of course, my Possibility. You've seen this ticket in the archives; you even picked it up when it fell from the large manila envelope onto the desk; you held it close enough to smell where my lavender hair oil rubbed off, where it still remained after all these years. Is that possible? you asked yourself. Yes, it's possible. I still remain.

Meet me at the entrance of Chatby Gardens, I wrote. Morgan asked if I'd meant the Nouzah Municipal Gardens. Yes, I said. I call them the Chatby Gardens because Chatby is the nearest tram station. I also warned him he should not wear his Red Cross khakis, nor I my conductor's uniform. If we were noticed together, I could lose my job. Or worse.

The eventual meeting was a muddle (that's what Morgan calls any kind of confusion). I waited for half an hour before he noticed me. I was wearing an all-white tennis outfit and he didn't recognize me on the park bench, up the slope. And I didn't recognize him either; he had on a tan suit and his hair was oiled and orderly. I mistook him for an Italian.

Finally, he approached me. Mohammed, he squinted, is that you?

No, I said. It's Cleopatra. Mohammed left when his friend did not arrive on time.

He offered me a box of sticky cakes bought from an Egyptian bakery. I said I did not like sticky cakes. Morgan insisted. They are delicious, but I didn't let him know that. I said it would be better to give them away to someone who needed them. Besides, I said, they are a bit stale. How long ago did you buy them—a year ago?

I did not say what I was really thinking—I was not going to let him think he could buy my affection; I was not like any poor Egyptian boy who would be seduced by sticky cakes and chocolates. And I did not want him to think I would ever be reciprocating. I couldn't afford to buy Englishmen sticky cakes. It was enough to be seen with him at all.

We sat on the park bench overlooking the pond with ducks. After he probed me with questions about my background, I refused to take the bait. He seemed anxious and filled the silence with information about himself. He'd been in Alex for less than a year, he said, volunteering with the Red Cross. He was inspired by his favorite poet, Walt Whitman, who had also volunteered during a great war, aiding wounded and dying soldiers. Morgan himself was a Searcher, he said. When I asked what he was searching for, he laughed slyly and said that maybe he'd finally found it. He smiled in a strange way and I waited for him to say what he'd finally found—even though I knew what he was insinuating by the way he stared at me. But then he said, Never mind.

He told me about his travels to India to visit his close friend Masood, who had moved back to Agra from Weybridge, where they had met. Masood was handsome too, like me, he added. And he'd had a very, very special friendship with Masood, indeed. But it never became quite the connection he yearned for, he said. Morgan was not as subtle as he may have thought. I got the point. Then I asked him how much money it costs to have friends from foreign lands. Wasn't it cheaper to make English friends?

I think I was too indirect for him to catch my drift (I eventually learned this English expression from him). I was not for sale—if that's what he had in mind. But he never caught on.

And then the conversation turned to sad things, and unexpectedly I grew more tender towards him. He began to tell me a very peculiar story about an experience he had in childhood. I was listening so curiously that I nibbled away at a sticky cake without even realizing until I'd finished it. As I listened I understood that despite our great differences we actually had much in common. I already imagined how his sad story would end. As Morgan would say, we were like two peas in a pod . . .

Every Little Scar

Ben and I were well into our third year before the inevitable happened—the end of the two-peas-in-a-pod phase.

I suddenly noticed the annoying way Ben had of always sniffling after he ejaculated. I couldn't believe I'd never noticed it before. Soon it drove me around the bend. He wasn't congested; it was clearly a nasal tic: *sniff, sniff, sniff*. For a full minute, sometimes two. I found it unattractive, a sign that he was a little off, in fact. I eventually developed a Pavlovian response: I'd cover my ears whenever he got close to ejaculating. I realized it was partly my own issue (well, my therapist helped with that insight): I was losing my fantasy of an idealized Ben, the ever-strong lover and consummate caretaker. But still, every time he sniffled, I couldn't help seeing him as spastic and very unsexy. I eventually started avoiding sex.

But that wasn't even the worst of it. The thing I'd tried most to avoid finally reared its ugly head between us: racism.

At brunch one Sunday, at Walter's restaurant, across from Fort Greene Park, we were crammed in at a tiny table between two other couples (both white). As I dug into my favorite American culinary offering—fried chicken and waffles with maple syrup and heaps of butter—Ben felt he needed to give me health tips. "Fried chicken is not good for you, Kip. And you should definitely take off the skin. That's the absolute worst part."

I stared at him over my round glasses with a deadpan look that, coming from a Black person, was surely recognizable as saying only one thing: "nigga, please!" Then I responded as calmly as possible, saying that I'd never heard him voice the same condescending judgment about foie gras or the lardons he loved at L'Express—which weren't much healthier.

Then another time: one spring evening, we were rushing along Atlantic Avenue, walking to a dinner party at Ben's old friend Quentin's—an evening that was sure to be a repeat of previous gatherings with the same coterie of gay intelligentsia, where I (by far the youngest and darkest) would be tolerated, albeit smiled at often.

"Hurry up, Kip! Walk faster! Being late is so rude!" said Ben, practically jogging, with the gift-wrapped wine bottle swaying in his hand like a relay runner's baton.

"Rude? Don't you know arrival time is a cultural thing?" I said, having to jump up onto the sidewalk after almost getting hit by a yellow cab because Ben had yanked me across the street.

"Cultural?" said Ben. "What do you mean? CP Time?"

"Exactly! Colored People Time is a real thing. Did you know there is no word for 'late' in most African languages? 'Yesterday' and 'tomorrow' are the same word. 'Late' is a Western construct!"

"Oh, come on! Even Obama says being late is a sign of rudeness."

"Well." I bristled, and my heart started to race, not only from rushing but from the rabbit hole we were going down. "For your information, Mr. Benjamin Isaac O'Keefe, just because Obama is half African, it doesn't mean his is the law for African ways and customs. And it definitely doesn't mean he abides by the Nigerian rule that says it's better to be late for an appointment than to cross a neighbor on your way and not stop to ask how they are doing. Have you ever heard of that custom? Of course not! Why not? Because it's not European!"

Yet another time: one August weekend we'd rented a Zipcar to drive down to the Jersey Shore. After a perfect day at the beach, capped off by delicious fried clams at a boardwalk hole-in-the-wall (also "unhealthy," but Ben didn't seem to mind this time), we returned to our motel. After I showered, having used the big white bath towel to dry myself, Ben said, "Kip, your bath towels always get dirty so fast. That's kind of gross. Why don't you use more soap?"

Did he really just say that? I thought. He might as well have said, "Why are you such a dirty-assed nigger?" That's how it felt—totally debasing. When I recuperated and caught my breath, I informed him, in as measured a tone as I could muster, "It's not dirt, dear [my inner voice substituting the endearment with *you stupid git!*]," my top lip involuntarily tightening over my upper teeth, "it's dead skin. It shows up on white terry-cloth because my skin is brown. Dead skin, not dirt, dear [*motherfucker!*]."

The entire weekend was soured from then on. Ben and I slept in separate beds. I made the excuse of Ben's loud snoring, but really I was pulling away in self-protection. I didn't feel safe from the innocent lethality of White Supremacy.

And the list goes on. You see, I have all the incidents engraved in my memory. Not a racist slip has gone unnoticed or forgotten. When you're Black, you remember such things the way you remember the cause of each scar that's marked your body: the day you fell from your bicycle and busted the right side of your upper lip, where that deep C-line mark remains; the time you got bitten by the neighbor's dog and your little finger was stitched up but remains permanently bent. You carry these little scars, these little injuries, forever. And so, I remember all of Ben's passing little "compliments" about my articulate speech, or my natural athleticism, or the envied bronze shade of my skin, or how "unfair" it was my genetics had blessed me with a bubble butt and "luscious lips." "Do you really want to get into what's unfair?" I'd say, with the threat of a lambasting barely restrained in my voice.

But I have to admit, Ben eventually did see his own white privilege and cop to his blind spots, apologize, and try to do better. He was not, at least, like some of the naive white guys I'd known, who'd boasted that since they treated all people equally, they weren't racist. Ben understood that we don't all have equal power, opportunities, or access; we can't simply aim for equality; we can't chop a man's hand off and then give him equal time to pull up his bootstraps. The game is rigged against Black people in our society. If you really saw us, you'd understand this, and Ben ultimately did.

But by then it was too late.

Lies Are Sometimes Necessary

Morgan's sad story started with a remark he made after we saw a little boy, about twelve years old, alone by the pond at the Chatby Gardens on that first day we met there. The boy was throwing bread crumbs to the ducks. We laughed as he retreated hastily every time a flock would rush towards him. Then a thin man, dressed in a dark suit and tan English Panama hat with a black band around it, approached the boy. The boy quickly ran from the man. Morgan grew silent after this. Finally, he said, I wish I had run away like that boy.

When I asked him what he meant, he said, Never mind.

But I kept looking at him. I could see his eyes widening, as if a great pressure were behind them, and his brows lifted to a peak, despite his smiling. He repeated that he was fine. It was nothing, nothing at all, he said. But then a tear fell from his right eye.

I had never seen an Englishman cry before. I knew it was possible, but I'd not been sure. He kept apologizing. I don't know what's come over me, he said.

I said, If you have a burden, you can share it. I can keep a secret.

I have no friends in Alex anyway—no one else to tell. I only just moved here six months ago myself, from Mansourah.

He said he wasn't sure why—it made no sense, he said—and some things in life didn't ever make sense. In fact, the most important things of all made the least sense of all. And all of that was only to say that, somehow, he felt he could trust me. And yes, there was, in fact, something he hadn't told anyone other than his mother. He felt I may be a person he could tell. Perhaps I would not judge as he imagined others would.

I agreed. I am just a poor, Black Egyptian, living in misery. Who am I to judge anyone? I said. To tell you the truth, though, I do not always tell the truth. *Lies are sometimes necessary.*

Morgan closed his eyes and took a deep breath. Well, he said, it was when he was at boarding school in Eastbourne. He went on to say he was about the same age as the boy we saw. He'd gone on a walk alone on the Downs. It was March, he said, snow was still on the ground, and it crunched as he made deep footprints. I closed my eyes to imagine snow. I envied Morgan, that little white boy in the snow. Then, Morgan said, he saw a man by a gorse bush, in a salt-and-pepper knickerbocker suit, with a black mackintosh and a grey deerstalker hat. The man was pissing into the bush, and when he finished, he left his fly unbuttoned. The man motioned for Morgan to approach, and Morgan wanted to run away, but he couldn't, he said, And then . . .

Morgan barely remembered what happened after that, he said, not until the man was buttoning his fly again. After confirming that Morgan's parents did not live nearby, the man dug into his trouser pocket and pulled out a shilling. Morgan said he refused the coin, but the man insisted. Morgan refused again, and then the man got cross and said he *must* take it.

People use coins for strange things, I thought. And then it occurred to me that Morgan, himself, had insisted that I take his coins on the tram. Was he up to strange things too?

I didn't say anything. I was mostly feeling sorry for Morgan's sad story. And also surprised a white man had confided in me. It seemed he must have been dying to tell someone for a very long time. This is not what I expected of an Englishman.

Morgan said he had felt an odd emptiness after the man had used him in the snow. When he'd written in his diary that night at school, he did not know how to explain the feeling, he said. He couldn't find the words. But to remember that it was something, he'd written, *Nothing happened*.

Then he said I must think him rather foolish and strange to confess such a thing.

As he spoke, I looked up—pearl-gray clouds streaked the sky, motionless as brushstrokes. I was thinking, I know exactly why he has cried: the pain, the shame. I know it too. Shall I say anything? I tied a knot in my gut to keep myself held together, and then said it: Nothing happened to me either. Nothing happened every afternoon after school from the time I was seven years old. If not Uncle Mahmoud, then Farid. If not Farid, Jalil. If not Jalil, Mr. Greene.

Morgan put his hand on my shoulder. His eyes were wet again. I pulled away. I did not want his pity—that's not why I told him. I told him so he'd know how strong I was. I was not going to cry. Crying was for little children, innocent and afraid. I was never innocent or afraid. I let Morgan know he needn't pity me, and so I made a joke.

Look! I said, pointing to a Frenchwoman in her fashionable hobble dress, waddling after her little boy as he ran for the pond. She is so fashionable she can barely walk! I laughed.

Morgan laughed too. Then everything seemed to make us laugh: I burped loudly, unexpectedly, after finishing the sticky cake. And while shooing away a fly, Morgan poked himself in the eye, and a black bird flew overhead dropping yellow shit on Morgan's knee. Everything made us laugh. I think it was mostly the joy of having someone else who shared our particular pain—it fueled our laughter. Sharing lifted some of the burden. Laughter was our mutual relief.

The White Gaze

I cannot tell you when Ben and I stopped really laughing together—those joyful, giddy belly laughs—but it must have happened gradually. It only dawned on me after last week's fiasco that it has probably been years since we've laughed the way we used to. Slowly, bit by bit, after too many rushed breakfasts, with soft-boiled eggs dripping from his sloppy mouth as he fled for work; after too many stupid tiffs about who left the downstairs lights on all night, or the toothpaste open, or dirty dishes in the sink, our differences became more apparent. Not the obvious differences—race, culture, age, we always knew about those—but the subtler differences we had assumed weren't there. What we valued most, what we aspired to, what we could or could not do without. And these newly perceived differences now made it difficult to have that joyful levity in the relief of sharing our pain. Now, when seen at its very worst, I saw Ben as the source of my pain, aligned with the greater white forces working against me.

I blame racism. White people often wonder why everything always comes down to race for Black people. "You're playing the race card again! Can't you get over it?" Well, no, I can't. That's the problem. It's the White Gaze that dominates us so, and there seems to be no way of getting over, under, or around it. The best way out, as Robert Frost says, is always through.

My perception of any given situation is sometimes clouded by the ever-hovering cumulonimbus of racism. And so, at times, it's hard to know what's what. This is one of the biggest problems with being Black. You live with this ever-dangling question: Is it racism or not? If, for example, a waiter attends to a white person before me, it could be that the waiter simply has missed seeing me, or is absentminded, or is already in the middle of attending to that white person in the next booth of the diner; but also, the waiter could be racist.

It's a pernicious mindfuck that never goes away. I need to validate my suspicions, but I can never be absolutely certain. And so, when that hypothetical waiter at the hypothetical diner finally arrives at my table, I'll usually test them carefully by smiling to see if I'm met with a warm, receptive gaze, and also to show I am not one of those savages or thugs to be feared. Sometimes, though, to prevent any further confusion and degradation, I might demand that the server provide me equal service. I'll point out how every white person was attended to first. Yet, with either of these approaches, I'll risk seeming either too complicit in my own degradation or else too rude and demanding. I may even come off as straight-up paranoid: What if the waiter was simply nearsighted and missed seeing me, and it had nothing to do with race at all? I cannot win. And yet, I'll have to choose what kind of Black person to be at any given moment—accommodating, demanding, silently paranoid, or overtly paranoid. And it could all be for nothing! It is exhausting to be Black and go out in public at all.

But in private, at home, when the defenses are down, it's deadly.

Last Wednesday, Wilson, my faithful agent, called to inform

me that eleven new editors had passed on my Forster historical novel. Ben and I were in the kitchen preparing dinner. Ben
was still cooing over the new marble-topped island countertop
we'd had installed. We were making spaghetti with homemade
pesto sauce. With the worn wooden pestle, I pounded the basil
leaves, garlic, coarse salt, and pine nuts in the mortar, crushing
and cursing—"Fuck this fucking, fucking shit!"—crying and saying how devastated I was to be constantly rejected by publishers.

"Eleven rejections in one day!" I cried. And now Wilson was
suggesting I think about making some further changes. He wanted
me to "soften" the Mohammed character to make him "more lik-
able." He said I'd made Mohammed seem "shifty" and "conniving"
by taking money from Morgan and saying he needed it for food
or medical expenses, playing on Morgan's heartstrings—and then
secretively using the money to buy houses. I argued that Morgan
was using Mohammed equally, if not more so. Morgan was the one
with all the power, and the one who had the least to lose in their
affair. Wilson saw my point, he said, but we had to think about
what would appeal to the publishers: "Just downplay his shiftiness."

"I'm not doing any more rewrites," I told Ben, as I pounded
with the pestle. "And calling Mohammed 'shifty' is just another way
of saying he's a 'no-good Negro'!"

"Oh, come on, Kip. That's not fair." Ben shook his head, with a
smirk, it seemed.

"Why not? Of course it is! Why should I rewrite the only Black
character in my novel to be more pleasing to white editors? Why
shouldn't Mohammed be as complex and nuanced as Forster? It's
not fair. I'm not doing a rewrite! I've already done two years of rewrites with Wilson—now this!"

"You want to sell the book, don't you?"

"Of course I do, but I've worked my ass off, and I'm not chang-ing it any more just to make white readers more comfortable with the *one and only Black character*."

"Oh, come on. Isn't getting white people's approval your obses-sion? White publishers, white readers? The entire white world, as you say? Who are you fooling, Kip?" Ben made an exasperated sigh and dumped a heap of basil leaves into a Pyrex measuring cup. "You know what, Kip? I think you're making excuses because, actually, you're either too afraid of success or just plain lazy."

"Too lazy?" I stopped dead in my tracks and made an exag-geration of my already gaping eyes and mouth. "Too lazy? Are you fucking serious?"

"Come on. No need to get hostile. But admit it—you just don't want to do the work."

"Lazy? What—am I *shiftless* too?"

"Jesus, Kip. I'm not doing this."

"What? *What? You* started it!"

"I'm just saying—"

"Yowza. Amma jus' a lazy, shiftless nigga who don' wan' give Massa what he wan'? Is that what you're saying?"

"*Oh-ho-ho*." Ben dropped both arms to his sides and rolled his head, looking up to the ceiling. "Now you're just being ridiculous. Are you seriously saying that after nine years of being together, after marrying you, after *everything*, you still think I could see you as a . . . a—"

"Yeah! Go ahead and say it: a lazy nigga!"

Under his freckled skin, Ben's jaw flexed like knuckles on a willing fist. He clamped his mouth shut and seemed to keep on biting at the inside of his lips. Then he turned away from me and practically threw the spaghetti into the boiling water.

"Oh boy! White people are dangerous for us Black folks," I said, feeling my ears burning now. "I'm serious. Just think about photography!"

"Photography? Wow, that's a non sequitur," said Ben, his back to me still.

"No. Photography is the visual proof of what white people do to us people of color. In a photograph, the white person will always take up all the light. Ever notice that? They'll leave the Black person's features nearly indistinguishable—no nuance, just a blur of darkness. Even in movies it takes a skilled cinematographer to know how to make the exposure equal when Black and white actors are filmed together. Ask Roy DeCarava. Ask Spike Lee. Ask Steve McQueen. They can tell you. The Black person is literally never properly seen when placed next to a white person."

Ben swung around to face me again. "What the fuck are you saying, Kip?" His lips were trembling. "No. Forget it! That's it. I can't do this anymore."

"Do what?" I really was confused about what he was referring to exactly. "Do what?"

"You, Kip. You!"

And then the volcano finally exploded from him and the red-hot lava kept pouring out: he was fucking exhausted by my obsession with being published, with my nonstop whining about never being fully seen, when, in fact, he had been present and loving with me for over nine years. *Seeing me* for over nine years. There used to be a time, he said, when I seemed to care about his happiness too, when I would stroke his head with sympathy, console him when he'd told me about the pain of growing up with his alcoholic father or of losing his mother when he was only sixteen. There was a time, he said, when I'd supported him as he dealt with Garth, his younger brother who was heroin addicted and living god-knows-where in Seattle.

But lately, Ben said, and for far too long now, I'd been unable to see anything but my own disappointment at not being accepted by the almighty publishers! I clearly had some gaping need that neither he or anyone could fill. It wasn't just my narcissist tendencies, he said, which he knew were worse when I was feeling bad about myself. But it was that he couldn't make up for everything that every white person had ever done to me, for all of the history that I was a victim of. I had too big a wound, he said, and he clearly couldn't help me to heal from it. His love wasn't enough. And he was tired of never being enough.

"That's not true," I told him. "You don't understand. It's not just you—it's everywhere. How am I supposed to know where it is and where it isn't? I know you've loved me, Ben, but sometimes I don't know what's what, and you need to understand—"

"No," he said. "Kip, I'm done." He was pacing back and forth along the island in our kitchen. At fifty-six, he wasn't getting any younger, he said. He had maybe twenty-five good years left in him. Thirty, if he was lucky. And he'd already wasted a whole decade of his life with the AIDS panic, holding his breath for the entire '80s before daring to seek love. He wasn't going to wait anymore, he said. "And by the way, Kip, I can tell you're not into the sex we have anymore. You're never fully there. What do you think that feels like for me?" His voice was strained now. "Well, I can't wait for you to find your voice. Or to get your approval before you're finally able to show up for me again. Life is going by too fast, Kip. And *this* isn't how I'm going to live it anymore." He spread his arms open as if presenting me to an audience—I was the *this* he was referring to. "You know, I also need to be seen. By

you, Kip." Ben started shaking his head repeatedly. "But not anymore. I'm done trying." Tears welled up in his hazel-green eyes.
"I'm done," he said. "*Done.*"

"Done?" I said.

"Divorce."

Divorce? How the fuck did we get here?

"By the way," Ben folded his arms in front of him and looked
down at the floor, jogging one knee below his red Wesleyan University gym shorts, "I know you're still waiting to hear if you're
getting that gig for *Esquire* but—"

"You know freelance is a bitch, Ben. But there's a possibility
Atlantic Monthly—"

"Yeah, well." He seemed to be examining his bare feet as he
curled up his pale toes. "Anyway, you didn't pay your part of last
month's mortgage, and now it's time for this month's and—you
know our agreement about that, Kip, and—"

"So, is *that* what all this is about? Money? Is it because I don't
have a steady job? Is that why I'm 'lazy'? Is that what this is, Ben?"

"No, Kip." He finally looked at me and his eyes were red; they
seemed about to burst. "It's everything."

I have to admit Ben is right: I've been obsessed with the idea of being recognized by the publishing world. For me, it's been larger than romantic or friendly love, this monstrous need of mine. The reason I'm so fixated on getting published is that the giants of the publishing world are, to me, the gatekeepers who say whether or not I matter to the entire world. And for some surely problematic reason, as a Black, gay man, I need the world to say, *I see you. You matter.* I know you exist!

Several years ago, Ben told me about a famous experiment conducted in the 1970s by the developmental psychologist Edward Tronick. It was called the Still Face Experiment. Tronick filmed hundreds of pairs of mothers holding their infants. He then instructed the mothers to suddenly stop responding to the child—no reciprocating smiles, no frowns of concern, no widening of the eyes. The babies were to get no indication at all that they were being seen by their caregiver. To the infants, it must have seemed as if their mothers suddenly ceased to exist. After three minutes of trying various tactics to get the mother to respond—smiling, crying, kicking, giggling, pouting—every single child lost its shit. Complete meltdowns from every child in the experiment. Nothing could distract or console the child from the pain of the mother's still face.

If we are not recognized by those who we need, we lose our shit. As adults, we don't show it like babies do. We've developed strategies—just as many of the babies in the Tronick study eventually did—to disguise or bury our unbearable pain. But even as grown-ups, we are no different—the pain of not being seen is still unbearable. We need to know we exist, that we matter.

And the fact that the publishing giants are, by and large, mostly white also means I'm stuck with waiting for white approval. Oh God, admitting that feels repulsive. But I have to confess—as pathetic, pitiful, and lame as it is—this is the sad state of affairs I haven't yet resolved. It's humiliating to bare my faults so blatantly to you. But Kip Starling's motto remains the same: *Seek only truth*. No matter how ugly and shitty it is.

In an odd way, this is what Mohammed is teaching me too. To understand the paradox of holding on to one's truth alongside the necessary lies, treading that delicate balance. "Tell all the truth, but tell it slant," says Emily Dickinson. Mohammed never betrayed his own truth, but he knew when to tell it slant and when to lay it all out bare.

All of Me

Yes, I bared it all when I needed to. How else are we to live in the world of Possibility if we cannot also show our truth? That's why I decided to show Morgan who I really am. Not his fantasy of a Black Egyptian boy, but the truth.

Would you like to see my Home of Misery? I asked Morgan one day, after we met in Chatby Gardens again. It is a miserable little stone house in Bacos. A miserable neighborhood. It will be awful and uncomfortable, I added, but I can make you a mint tea, and I can show you who I am.

Morgan immediately accepted the invitation. On the tram I dared to sit beside him. It felt safe enough—there were only Egyptian passengers, no policemen around. Morgan and I were in jolly moods. I gave out his sticky cakes to everyone. Morgan was perplexed by that, but I explained, Generosity is in our Egyptian blood!

When we arrived at my Home of Misery, Morgan seemed afraid of what he might find; he looked about suspiciously. He followed me through the black iron gate, down the dirt path, under the jacaranda tree with its yellow petals falling lazily about us. He kept smiling oddly. I have noticed that English people smile a lot, especially when they are not comfortable.

Once we were inside, he went on and on about how immaculate my house was. He wanted to know about the fresh smell too. I told him I wash the floors and walls with carbolic soap. So white and clean, he kept saying. I asked if he had expected an Egyptian's home to be filthy, like an animal's den? He looked panicked again and said, No, no, no, no. Please don't misunderstand me!

I didn't respond. I let him feel how uncomfortable it is to have one's goodness doubted, to always be put to the test. Just as an Egyptian is put to the test every day here in this Europeans' Alexandria, where Westerners always doubt our goodness, our worth.

Finally, after he saw that I only had a bed and a desk and a chair and a trunk, I took him to my big, wooden trunk and flipped the top open. I took out everything in it, and laid it all on my bed, one item at a time: three shirts, all clean and white; my khaki conductor's uniform; my brown and grey trousers; my blue American jacket; my plaid necktie; my red fez; my formal black suit and bow tie; my black shoes and spats; my tan leather slippers; my white djellaba and red vest—once my brother Ahmed's; and my royal-blue winter coat.

Yes, I remember that blue coat! said Morgan. Under the tram seat, that first night!

I continued to empty the trunk: my tram conductor boots; three pairs of dark grey socks; my English dictionary; the Koran; an English-language King James Bible; one canister of Italian beeswax from a shop on Rue Rosette; a little bottle of jasmine oil; a pocket watch from a missionary, no longer working; two bars of soap, carbolic and French lavender; paste for cleaning teeth;

my toothbrush; my comb of tortoiseshell; my razor and bowl for shaving; and finally, my little tin box, which I called my Ministry of Finance—I give my own special name to things—where all my money was saved.

I gestured for Morgan to have a good look at everything, and I said, Now I have shown you all there is to show. You see, I own nothing. Nothing. This is all of me.

Morgan stood there in silence for a long time. I could not imagine what he was thinking. He looked down at the floor and back at the items on the bed again. Then he finally looked over at me, shaking his head. His eyes opened wide as if he'd had a sharp pain. And, at last, he sobbed. He buried his head in his hands and sobbed.

He was not pitying me this time, I could tell. It was something else.

Finally, when his waves of sobbing ceased, Morgan looked up, wiped his cheeks with the backs of his hands, and slowly, with a cracking voice, he said, I only gave you sticky cakes. And you—you gave me everything.

No one had ever been so happy to know me. Not ever.

I said, But you gave me your trust, the first time in the gardens. The sad story of the boy in the snow.

He finally smiled and said I was the most beautiful person he had ever laid eyes on. He said he'd be happy to look at me forever.

He didn't try to touch me at all; he just saw me, and kept on seeing me.

It was the best day of my life.

The Nowhere Man

I was fresh from England, in the first year of my MFA program at Columbia, and the racial divide in America was no more apparent than in the school's main dining hall. When I first entered John Jay Dining Hall with Sarah Weiss—a smart, funny Jewish woman with a Long Island accent and the frizziest hair I'd ever seen on a white person—after initially being impressed by the traditional paneled walls, long wooden tables, and high chandeliers, I immediately realized the awful decision I had to make: either split with Sarah and head for the small cluster of Black students' tables or stay with Sarah and suffer the consequences.

I didn't have the heart to ditch Sarah. In our first couple of days we became fast friends. We'd both been assigned the same advisor in our writing program—a fastidious white Brit who had the annoying habit of adjusting his silk cravat continually as he spoke. Sarah and I bonded when we realized we were the only two students suppressing laughter at this ridiculous habit. So, on that first day, I stayed with Sarah and suffered the stares from across the dining hall. The Black students transmitted accusations with eyes that spoke loud and clear: Traitor! Self-hater! Oreo!

The next day I made a lame excuse not to join Sarah, and I snuck into the dining hall unaccompanied. I finally made my way over to the Black students' section, smiled nervously, waiting for a welcoming face. But I was only met with hard, militant stares.

My mistake of sitting with Sarah had been quickly followed with a thorough investigation by the Black student mafia, and they now had the full lowdown on me.

I learned all this from Gerald Andrews, one of my three Black allies at Columbia. "They say you talk with a pretentious fake British accent," said Gerald. He was gay and wore black nail polish and combat boots. He addressed me in a hallway of Dodge Hall, with his hands on his hips. "And they also say you obviously prefer the company of white people. And, basically, that you're a saditty Oreo." At first I thought "saditty" meant faggot, but then Gerald informed me otherwise. "It just means uppity," he said. He informed me that being a faggot per se was not a problem for the Columbia Black kids—there were several fierce Black faggots of the James Baldwin and church-choir-director ilk, and they actually had prestige among the other Black students. But for saditty Brits like me it was a different case. I was simply "not Black enough," they had decided.

Being a foreign student, I had prearranged (with much finagling) to live in the Pan-African House in East Campus—a Black special-interest community primarily for undergrads. All the dorm residents had quickly organized themselves into a unified posse with their own separate, all-Black orientation events, parties, study groups, and clubs. I, however, was excluded from all that. It was not because at twenty-four, I was older than most undergrads (another Black graduate student from Nigeria *was* included), but the word had already gotten out: I was a pariah.

For the first month I ate alone in John Jay. When I tried to sit near the Black kids, they would casually move away, one by one, and congregate a safe distance from me. I felt like a leper. I barely ate; my stomach was clenched like a fist. (I lost ten pounds in less than three weeks.) But at least I didn't cry right there in front of everyone—I held it together. Still, inside I felt as if I were falling into an abyss. When Sarah or another white classmate would try to sit next to me, I'd tell them the seats were taken, or that I was just about to leave. I couldn't bear the idea of the Black kids seeing me surrounded by white people. It would only have verified their stupid assumptions about me. Soon my white friends got the message and started distancing themselves, avoiding me. I must have seemed like the most unfriendly asshole to them. Eventually no one wanted to join me. I'd sit alone at a long wooden table, as if on a deserted island. The Nowhere Man.

One day I ran into Gerald in the South Lawn quad. He was with a group of four or five other Black guys. All of them were kind of cute. One guy in a red T-shirt was gorgeous. He had short dreadlocks and smiled at me a lot. Gerald introduced me to the group and then said they had to get going. They had a meeting to attend. "A meeting?" I asked. Gerald said it was actually more of a social club, really. And then he blurted out, "It's a Black gay *thang*—you wouldn't understand!" They all laughed. I laughed too, then asked if it was okay if I joined them. Gerald's mouth hung open. "Really? You know I said a *gay* group?" When I told him yes, he seemed shocked. "You didn't know I was gay?" I asked. "No," he said. "Honestly, girl, I just thought you were European."

I joined them for the meeting, but every time I spoke up they seemed to look at me like I was an alien. They laughed uproariously when I said things like "shag" or "snogging," repeating the words over and over with great hilarity. They were baffled when I was confused about certain terms or words. "Kipling, you seriously don't know what a rubber is?" (In England a rubber is a pencil eraser, I told them.) The sexy one with the dreads finally said, "I don't know about the brothers, but I bet the white faggots are gonna love you here in America. They'll go crazy for that accent. And since you don't sound like us homegrown niggas, they probably won't even realize you're Black at all!" They all laughed. I ended up excusing myself early and ran back to the dorm—literally running all the way up Morningside Drive—and fell onto my bed sobbing. Here I was with my Black gay brothers and I was still the pariah. Would I ever fit in anywhere?

During those first few weeks at Columbia I cried myself to sleep most nights, bewildered, heartbroken, questioning if I had made a huge mistake in coming to America. Maybe I should have stayed in England and found a Black gay community there. How was I going to follow the destiny of James Baldwin and become the great writer if I was categorically rejected by everyone in America? After a month into the semester, I decided to quit and go back to England. It was Gerald who convinced me to stay. "Fuck the bastards!" he said. "Aren't you here to become a writer, anyway?"

There were only three Black allies who ever reached out to me: Lorna-Lee from my writing class, who seemed to have a little crush on me; Gerald; and Carlia Corby, who were both Brooklyn-born Jamaicans from the MFA year ahead of mine. Having a Jamaican background, I imagine they had cousins or remote family members who lived in England. To them I must have been a recognizable type of colonial Black man. They defended me among their African-American peers. But the majority of Black students had never heard a Black Britisher before. They couldn't get past the "white" way I spoke.

If things hadn't started off badly enough, there were a couple of incidents that pushed things over the edge. In the winter, when

I signed up for the student excursion to Hunter Mountain in the Catskills for a day of skiing, the Black student mafia got hold of the news and used it as the ultimate confirmation of my Whiteness.

"Girl, you're not doing yourself any favors here," said Gerald—he referred to everyone as "girl," even the straight male professors. We were standing on the steps outside Dodge Hall before class, both clad in our scarves and wool caps. To avoid his glares I watched the occasional passersby on College Walk or I stared at the plaza's snow-covered fountain. "What kind of Black person goes skiing?" demanded Gerald.

"Me!" I said. "Skiing is fucking brilliant! What does being Black have to do with skiing?" I was beyond frustrated. "How does that make me any less Black? I am Black—that's just a fact—so whatever *I* do is what a *Black* person does, right?"

"No, girl," said Gerald. "Things that involve snow and ice and cold shit are not for Black people. We ain't built for that. Just like camping and water polo and equestrianism—and all that other white people shit. Genetically, we are literally not designed to endure cold weather and snow."

"Well, what about Matthew Henson?" I said. "The first man to reach the geographic North Pole? He led the Peary expedition. A Black man!"

"Girl, you can go ahead with your Matthew Henson, but I'm telling you, if you go on your skiing trip, you'll just prove you're as white as they think you are."

Then the crowning incident came from the most trivial domestic chore. One day, after I'd lost my socks in the dorm laundry room, I asked around to see if anyone had found them. After that, the Black mafia dubbed me with a nickname—"Mr. Socks": "Oh, dear me, he's lost his *socks*!" The way I'd rounded out the vowel of the word was way too British for them. From then on, "Mr. Socks" was ridiculed at every turn.

I was devasted by a categorical rejection from my Black American peers. Every cut eye from a Black kid—in the dining hall or on the quad—felt like a stab in the heart. The worst part was when they eventually stopped reacting to me at all. They'd look right through me. I became the invisible man, even among other invisible men. The rebuff stung deeply. After all, I'd grown up respecting and identifying with the fierce power of African Americans, with their victorious fight for civil rights and their overall dignity in the face of unthinkable trauma. But in the Black American paradigm, I apparently only made sense as an Uncle Tom, an uppity and confused house nigger.

I was also misunderstood by the white kids who tried to befriend me with their well-meaning racist comments. One white guy, Brian, a lanky, freckled redhead from Georgia, thought we were friends and reassured me: "Kip, just so you know, I don't see you as Black at all. You're just a person to me. Just Kip."

"Which would be fine," I said, "except that I *am* Black, so if you don't see that, you don't really see me!"

I didn't know where to turn to be seen or accepted. There was no place in America—or maybe the world—for a Black person like me. After the time I'd hidden myself in the closet back home, at thirteen, this was now the second time I considered what it might be like to die. A bottle of aspirin? Or jump from the roof of John Jay Hall? Or leap from the George Washington Bridge, like Rufus in James Baldwin's *Another Country*? I was not meant for this world, I thought. Why go on living? Would anyone even notice if I disappeared forever? No—no one would ever see me anyway.

For the Nowhere Man, it was a lonely, cold welcome to America.

Kipling's Voice

After my initial heartbreak with the Black American kids at Columbia, the next big disappointment was with my thesis advisor, the Brit with the cravats, to whom I'd been assigned—more like shackled.

Throughout my MFA program, I'd been working on a novel I named *The Nowherians*, using the Caribbean-English word for people of no fixed abode. It was about a Caribbean psychology professor who'd been in self-imposed exile in New York and who had returned to his island home for the funeral of his estranged mother. Her cause of death was a mystery, suspicious. As he searched for answers, family secrets were uncovered, and his own familial history paralleled the history of the Caribbean itself. I'd also decided to throw Shakespeare's Caliban—fiction's first New World native—into the mix. I weaved him into the story as a spirit haunting my protagonist. The entire project was a bit ambitious, I admit, with magical realism and melodrama akin to a Dickens novel. In short, it was a crazy mash-up in the best genre-bending way possible—or so I thought.

But my MFA advisor—let's call him Mr. Asshole to avoid any ambiguity, and also any potential legal action—broke my spirit completely. He hated me and my project. He was a persnickety, effete man from Surrey (or so he said). A wilting Peter Pan with a boyishly clean-shaven face and poufy Justin Bieber hair. In short, a fellow queer Brit. He'd had some early success with two novels in the mid '90s, one short-listed for a Man Booker Prize, the other for a Whitbread. But he was insufferable as an instructor.

He was pouty and vain. Besides constantly adjusting his silk cravat, he had the annoying habit of beginning every feedback session with "Yes, well, right, and—" in what seemed like an affected Queen's English. Always scanning the room with the exact same four words: "Yes, well, right, and—" He rarely offered a constructive critique but was instead fixated on reminiscing about his "old pal" Colm Tóibín, especially about the time they both went out to dinner in Dublin with Sinéad O'Connor at the famous Chapter One restaurant on Parnell Square, beneath the Writers Museum, and Tóibín left abruptly before the dessert was done or the bill paid. Even though everyone thinks Tóibín's a genius, Mr. Asshole would say, "He's *massively* overrated!"

Somehow, in every session, Mr. Asshole would circle back to this same pointless, boring anecdote (probably a lie) and he'd always conclude with the same old refrain about Tóibín: "*massively* overrated!" Sour grapes, darling, is all I have to say. He also despised the glorious Alan Hollinghurst—which to me is just plain sacrilege.

This ludicrous advisor had it out for me. I couldn't figure out what it was about me exactly that raised the feathers on this bird's back, but he came for me like a bird of prey homing in for the kill. He seemed uneasy around me, and he was especially bothered by my speech. One day in front of the entire class he asked where I'd picked up my "posh London accent." Before I could answer, he added, "And where exactly in Africa are you from, again? Or is it the West Indies?" When I told him I was raised in the Home Counties, just as he was, and I'd attended schools in London for my entire life, he said, "Yes, well, right—" But he seemed insulted somehow. "Well, I'm only thinking of

Chris Eubank," he added, referring to the Black British boxing champion, famous for his posh style of dress and speech. "Eubank admits he learned to elevate himself by mimicking BBC newscasters!" He smiled smugly. And then he tried to disguise his pointless digression as a lesson on writing. "As a writer one can borrow a style of voice, but one must never copy. As T. S. Eliot says, Only immature poets copy!"

Being suspicious of his accent, I'd done some research and discovered that Mr. Asshole had only immigrated to the UK to attend Oxford. Originally he was from Sydney's North Shore—he wasn't English at all. (No wonder he quoted Eliot—another writer who passed as a Brit.) After his obnoxious remark to me that day, in spite of my deferential schoolboy manner, I couldn't resist blowing his cover. "So, sir," I said. "Where exactly are you from in Australia, again? Or is it New Zealand?" He turned crimson and clutched at his yellow cravat. I thought he might choke himself with it.

After that, it was over for me. Nothing I did was good enough. Eventually, at the end of my final year, he pulled out all the stops. "I cannot give your thesis a passing mark," he said. "Your novel is derivative. In sections you're mimicking J. M. Coetzee, but badly— you haven't the skill to find *le mot juste*. In other sections, you seem to be copying Toni Morrison, who, herself, is echoing Faulkner, but at least she's doing so with originality. And what's with all the magical realism? You're no García Márquez, no Rushdie! Magical realism is passé, out of style for decades now."

I tried to explain I was writing about experiences I'd heard about from my family in the Caribbean, where the belief in the supernatural is part of the culture, where Obeah and voodoo are part of everyday life. "It isn't a literary genre," I told the instructor. "Ghosts and magic are our *reality*." He scoffed and said, "Mumbo-jumbo! An excuse to be derivative! Voodoo? Aren't you Mr. Home Counties?

Mr. Posh London Schools? In any case, in these last two years, Mr. Starling, you seem to have learned nothing but to hide behind others' voices. *Where is Kipling's voice?* I can't find it. I can't accept this work. Go find a bloody voice of your own!"

I had the rare distinction of being the only student in my class whose final thesis was rejected outright. He said the entire department supported his decision. I wouldn't be able to graduate, not until I had turned in a satisfactory manuscript—either a collection of three new short stories or a complete rewrite of the first fifty pages of my novel.

I had never failed at school before. I'd gotten all A passes in both my O- and A-level examinations. I was devastated. It was totally unfair. I tried several approaches with Mr. Asshole. At first, gentle, being agreeable. Then demanding, as demanding as a British colonial boy could get, which meant asking for direct guidance and pointing out it was his job to instruct, not just find fault.

But I found that I, like my beloved Forster, was too much of a polite Englishman. I had already paid dearly for my first cheeky remark. I couldn't dare go further. I was still new to America and had not yet acclimated to the gutsy irreverence and entitlement that was possible from a student. And Mr. Asshole knew it.

There we were, two quasi Brits in a muddle. As much as I was familiar with the likes of him, he too was familiar with the likes of me. Back in England, he'd have come across the good Jamaican and Nigerian boys whose parents were of a striving middle class, the Black boys who would not rock the Victorian boat and came already indoctrinated with Anglophilia. The Nigels and Altons and Cyrils and Percys—my middle name is Percy, in fact. He knew we were afraid, if not incapable, of being rebellious like the Black boys from Brixton (back when Brixton was *Brixton*). We young Black strivers were too concerned with making white people feel comfortable around us, wanting them to respect our intelligence, invite us over for tea, and even maybe, one day, to marry us. We would not push back. *I* would not push back. He knew that.

When Mr. Asshole came after me so viciously, I eventually caved, crept away in shame, and blamed myself. I felt defeated and gave up. I never finished my thesis. My novel went nowhere. I never even officially graduated. I felt voiceless, worthless.

But the question of why he rode me so still perplexes me. Perhaps it was because I was gay. To my utter disbelief, I discovered years later that this effete advisor was actually *not* gay. He was married to a woman all along. If you knew this man you'd also be dumbfounded. Queer as a three-dollar bill, as they say. If he was closeted and attracted to me that may have explained it—self-hatred projected onto me like projectile vomit.

Or maybe it was just because I was Black. I noticed he rarely looked me in the eye, and he also gave very little attention to the only other Black person in the room, the African-American woman, Lorna-Lee. But she was outspoken and political in her views, and he knew that if he'd tried to fail her she'd have immediately taken it to the administration as a race issue.

She eventually encouraged me to push back, to fight and defend my position with Mr. Asshole. One day, after a brutal class in which Mr. Asshole had shamed me by telling the entire class it wasn't worth giving feedback on my work until I presented something original, Lorna-Lee and I walked to get lunch at Ollie's Noodle Shop on 103rd and Broadway. It was early spring but still cold enough for me to wear my favorite scarf, my black and white keffiyeh. Lorna, to match her red Levi's jacket, wore a pair of red-framed eyeglasses she kept pushing up on her nose. She seemed even more incensed by Mr. Asshole's treatment of me than I was.

"The only thing a bully like him responds to is a raised fist," she said. "Tell him to fuck off! I almost said something myself, but I didn't know how you'd feel about it. You know, he tried some bullshit with me once. He told me I couldn't write about a rich white character because it was too outside of my knowledge of the world. Hmph! Now what does the motherfucker know about my world? I told him if he said one more racist remark I was reporting him to the dean. Ever since, he's given me nothing but praise, nothing but 'Terribly good work, Lorna-Lee. Terribly good!'" She laid on the English accent thickly, badly; it made me laugh. "I'm telling you, Kip, in order to protect yourself, sometimes you have to use brute force. Fist to fist, weapon to weapon. Standing up to bullies is the only thing they understand. You need to tell the bastard it's not *your* problem if his limited ass can only accept writing that reflects his lily-white Eurocentric worldview!"

I was in awe of Lorna-Lee's badass attitude, the way she punctuated those final words by flipping her straightened hair in a parody of what she called her "Inner Entitled White Girl!" But I couldn't imagine me saying anything close to what she'd suggested.

I was gutted by my advisor's evisceration of me. He was cruel, vindictive, and perhaps an insecure homophobe as well as a racist, but his words stung. To allow me to get that far and then fail me was unforgivable. But the real problem was that being a good British-Caribbean schoolboy, I'd become adept at regurgitating others' opinions, not feeling entitled to strong convictions of my own. Conditioned to take the punches.

Even worse than all of that, there was another reason I couldn't fight back. Deep down I knew that Mr. Asshole was, infuriatingly, right: I had not found my own true voice.

I've only slept three hours, but enough to keep me going—along with this espresso. When I was in the ashram we always arose at four in the morning. Guruji said it was the magic hour, the best time to commune with your inner self. No distractions from the outer world; not even the birds were chirping.

I'm using this quiet hour to prepare for the next chapter, going over research materials on Mohammed. I'm struck by Mohammed's cocksure and obstreperous manner. For a young man of his station and race, he seems to have had no interest in being a good boy; he didn't aim to please or appease. Perhaps his early misfortune—being unwanted, being spurned from birth—never gave him the illusion of having others' acceptance. Was his early curse his ultimate freedom?

Ben has often quoted Abraham Maslow's dictum that the self-actualized individual is "independent of the good opinion of others."

If Mohammed, with almost no love and nurturing at all, could become so indifferent to the good opinion of others, why can't I? Why do I need so desperately to be approved of, to be recognized by the great literary giants?

Oh, Mohammed, I wish you were here to tell me how you were able to possess your natural voice. I am deeply flawed, stuck in the quicksand of my own limitations. Mohammed El Adl, you possess the secret I need. Help me, please.

MOHAMMED'S STORY

The Cut

You can recall with me my first visit to Morgan's room in the big boardinghouse in Sidi Gaber. There, I learned how to say no. And saying no to them matters, my friend. It makes all the difference.

Morgan's room was like the chambers I'd seen illustrated in French novels with lovestruck heiresses and baronesses miserable with ennui: a high canopy bed, a sitting area with settees, a dressing table. It was larger than my entire home.

We decided to play chess, stretched out on his high bed, as if we were on a picnic. When I asked for a glass of water from the side table, Morgan looked surprised and then nervous. I asked if it was a problem. He turned red and then said, No, no, I'd be happy to get it. When he slid, belly down, off the bed and stood up, I understood. He had an erection in his khakis. He couldn't seem to adjust it to be less conspicuous.

I don't know why, but immediately I got aroused too. My body seems to be an awful copycat. I was not thinking of sex, that is certain. Perhaps I was feeling the power of being desired. I imme-diately thought of my uncle, and the butcher, and the soccer coach, and the music teacher. They had all mistaken me for something I was not: an object for their gratification. Yet, I was also the desired one, and I knew there was power in that role. If only I could use that power.

Morgan touched my knees and his hands moved up towards my crotch. I sat up to pull away just as he dived down for a kiss. We were nose to nose.

No, I said. This is not proper.

But I can see that you want it, he said. His breath was hot and smelled like goat's milk. Your trousers cannot hide it, he said. We should not hide our true desires anymore, Mohammed. We must be free to love. Enough of saying no! he exclaimed. So many years of saying no!

I was saying no for the first time in my life. What did he mean, so many years saying no?

He reached to touch my face, but I dodged, and with the glass in his other hand, he banged my forehead. The glass broke and cut me. It burned like a match struck across my skin. I covered the wound with my hand, but thick drops of blood fell to the pale blue bedcover.

I'm so sorry, he said. It was an accident. Do let me staunch the cut.

I pulled away and asked myself why men's desires always lead to suffering. I only wanted a nice friendship with Morgan, not to be touched.

I said, Now look what you've done! You've ruined everything!

I flung the door open and bolted down the stairs. I ran all the way to the tram station holding my forehead, blood dripping through my fingers. I didn't care who saw me running. I was desperate to get away from Sidi Gaber. But I had said no to Morgan, and even though I was cut, it felt a victory.

For a week afterwards, Morgan kept riding the Bacos tram on my route. I ignored him. Then one day he rode to Camp de César, the last stop, and no other passengers were left. He walked to the back where I stood on the footboards.

Mohammed, how can I make up for my mistake? He presented me a box of sticky cakes. He said, I know you only pretend not to like them. He raised his eyebrows and smiled.

I had only eaten one of his cakes that first day at the gardens, trying to hide how I felt, but I must have allowed pleasure to show on my face, because he had caught it. I could not escape Morgan's gaze. He really saw me.

Morgan said, Are we to be friends again, then?

I nodded. But I added that he must not think he could buy me with sticky cakes, or anything else, for that matter. Friends cost much more than that, I said. And I was not talking about monetary costs, I added.

Morgan beamed.

I felt happy to make him happy. But then I felt afraid to have power over someone's happiness.

Behind Morgan I noticed a tram inspector—in khakis, with a black patent leather sash and a khaki cap—approaching down the tram's aisle. I did not know this inspector, but from the calculating clack of his heels on the boards, I knew trouble was coming. He was a tall, thin, Syrian-looking man with a black mustache, bushy eyebrows, and a very large nose.

The inspector tapped Morgan on the shoulder and asked if there was a problem.

Morgan explained there was no problem at all.

The inspector insisted that Morgan was being "too kind" to the "Black boy." He said he'd seen me laughing with Morgan and even accept a gift—all of which was against department rules. This would have to go on my record, he said. Then, in English, he asked Morgan to show him his tram ticket. To prove I had charged him for the ride.

Morgan looked panicked, which didn't help my case, and said, It's not the boy's fault!

The inspector ripped my conductor's badge off my jacket, tearing my pocket. You are fired! he said. Get off this tram at once!

Morgan protested, following the inspector down the aisle, pleading, and saying it was his fault.

I hurried after Morgan and told him to stop. Who cares? I said. Let the inspector have his little power. He knows nothing! I regret nothing! I did it for friendship.

I asked Morgan to tell me again how much it had cost him to travel from Liverpool to India to visit his friend there. How much was the passage on the S.S. *Morea* to Bombay?

Morgan looked cross at me, and asked how I could possibly ask such a question at a time like this. Wasn't I worried about getting my job back? What did it matter how much it had cost him to go to India?

I don't think Morgan understood my question. He had gone all that distance for a friend. What was the cost? For a true friend, isn't there always a cost?

The Cost

The cost was, and is, dear for me and Concha. Ben once mentioned that, in his work as a psychotherapist, he'd observed that people often have to choose either authenticity for themselves or maintaining the status quo in their relationships, and that not all relationships can weather authenticity. This is the case with Concha and me.

I met Concha on my university study-abroad program in Seville. During my third year at the University of London, School of African and Oriental Studies, I was researching the early history of Black artists on the Iberian Peninsula—artists like Diego Velázquez's protégé and African slave, Juan de Pareja. Seville has the greatest archival collection documenting early immigration to Iberia, dating back to before Christopher Columbus's voyage to the Indies. It was also the home of a curious hospital specifically for Blacks founded in 1393: Hermandad de Los Negritos.

I had enrolled at the Universidad de Sevilla for a year, and Concha was a student there. She was studying English Language and Literature, and we found each other via a pin-up poster on the student announcement board. She was fluent in English but looking for a native speaker to keep up her conversational skills. On a yellow, blue-lined scrap, ripped from a notepad, was written,

Weekly conversations over coffee or tapas—one hour in Spanish, one hour in English.

Immediately, even back then, Concha was to me the epitome of a Spanish woman. On meeting her, I realized that the women in Almodóvar's films were not exaggerations; I had always assumed they were. She was dark and sexy and confident with her long legs and wavy, black hair. She made Sophia Loren's gaze seem innocent, Brigitte Bardot's lips less inviting. She had high cheekbones and almond-shaped eyes, which gave her an exotic look, even for Spaniards. She could run down narrow cobblestone streets in high heels, looking elegant all the way. But she also rode a Harley-Davidson and was ready to defend herself against any offender. I personally witnessed a woman attack her during Seville's yearly spring festival, the Feria de Abril. The woman's husband had been ogling Concha, and the jealous woman, in her long red-and-black polka-dot dress, lunged for Concha with a butcher knife. Concha tackled her victoriously, without even removing her sunglasses or high heels.

We soon bonded over sex—and by that I mean gawking lustfully at men together. Sitting at an outdoor table at Las Columnas café/bar on Alameda de Hércules (the sixteenth-century promenade mall), we sipped our *tinto de veranos* in the shade of Seville orange trees as we checked out the men passing by. We'd assess them as they strutted under the rows of poplar trees. Handsome, dark, slick-haired Andalusian men with pert butts and prominent bulges in their Zara trousers. Each one with the swagger of a toreador.

The gay guys were more drawn to Concha than to me. She was clever and glamorous in the way gay men love to worship. And although the straight guys were intimidated by her, they couldn't resist the challenge.

It was Concha who first tried to help me embrace my own sexuality. "Show off that ass, Kip! What are you waiting for?" It is a Mediterranean thing to preen and strut, she said. "Aren't you Caribbean? You should know this naturally!" But I didn't. Preening and strutting were not a thing in Weybridge, I told her.

One autumn afternoon, while strolling together across the Triana Bridge with the golden sun reflected on the Guadalquivir river below us, Concha gave me preening lessons. She was shameless. "Now stick out that butt more. *More!* Good. Now hike up your jeans in front so we can see what you've got! *Allí está!*" Laughing, we stopped for a moment to look over the railing at the scene—the tourists in flat tour boats floating below us; the Plaza de Toros on the river bank to the left—and even then, Concha made sure I was still preening. "Stand up straight. Don't slump like an American!" It felt good to get her attention but for a moment I wasn't sure if she'd forgotten I was gay. Her eyes rested a little longer than usual on my butt, then on my crotch. She gave me a sly smile when I noticed her noticing. She met my gaze daringly. I wasn't sure what to make of it.

One afternoon months later, we sat at a café, under the awning, in the plaza across from La Giralda, the twelfth-century Islamic minaret attached to the Seville Cathedral, where tourists lined up to tour the Gothic church, while others crowded around the plaza's fountain photographing the architectural wonder of the Islamic and Christian styles combined.

"The Americans are the worst at preening, just look at them!" Concha announced. "The Puritans really fucked things up on their side of the pond, didn't they?" Concha was already loose on her second *tinto* and sucking the *carne* off the *hueso* of a fat green olive. "Neither American women nor men seem to wear their sexuality comfortably," she observed.

She said that in Spain, to be objectified was a two-way street and not as patriarchal as it is in America. Of course, the mutuality made all the difference, she added. After her year in London, Concha had spent a summer in New York, and being in America, she'd come to certain conclusions. "In America, there's a huge double standard: American men get to look like total schlubs—as they say in New York—and yet they feel it's perfectly all right to catcall any woman they want, as if any female body is made expressly for their pleasure. But if the tables are turned—*ay, ay, ay!*—American men freak out! I don't get it! Look at that guy over there—an average hetero Spanish *tío*. Nice tight pants so you can see his ass and strong thighs; a definite bulge up front, to entice you. *Perfecto*. Not as nice a package as yours, Kip, but of course, you're a—"

"I'm a what?" I was ready for the old Black-man stereotypes.

"You know . . ." Concha didn't flinch. "A big guy, right?"

I saw why straight guys were intimidated by her—she looked at you as if she could eat you alive for breakfast and have plenty of room left for lunch. But I also felt embarrassed imagining that Concha saw me in that way—surely she knew I was gay, and not half the macho man she needed. Yet, I confess it was nice to be looked at like that. It quelled my awful internalized homophobia—my fears of being inadequate, less manly. And I played it up to make myself feel like the powerful hetero man I secretly wished to be. "You better be careful," I said, narrowing my eyes at her. "Snake charmers like you can get a man's cobra rising. And I can't be held responsible if the snake charmer calls."

Sucking on an another olive, Concha smiled and raised her eyebrows as if she'd just scored in a fencing bout. But then she seemed to get distracted and was back on her original tirade: "Just look at that American guy over there with his wife and kids—and, come on, Kip, there's no doubt he's American! That tentlike polo shirt and baggy shorts to accommodate his beer gut—and the baseball cap! I feel sorry for American women. Really, I do. But then, I can't feel too sorry, because they are the first to agree with their men and say they look like fags if they wear form-fitting clothes or a Speedo on the beach. Their whole society is averse to sexualizing men. The sexual repression of the Brits is surpassed only by the Americans' extreme phobia of any kind of sexuality!"

"But isn't the US supposed to be freer than us here in Europe?" I said. "America is the land of opportunity and freedom of expression. And women in America are more feminist; they don't want to be objectified. Don't you think?"

"Well, I really don't get it." Concha shook her head and sighed as if faced with an impossible dilemma. "Being objectified in a way that denies a person's humanity is unacceptable, of course. But there is also a strange obsession in America with being comfortable at all times. And as anyone who's worn high heels for an entire evening of dancing can tell you, being sexy is not comfortable, nor should it be! *Punto final!* Have you noticed how Americans seem obsessed with being comfortable? It's ridiculous! They wear joggers everywhere—to the grocery store, on airplanes, at the cinema, in restaurants, even to the opera. Yes, I've seen it! Well, they don't do it here, thank God. But, Kip, being comfortable is not the natural condition of life anyway. From conception till death, life is inherently a struggle, isn't it? Even sex is friction. Life is a constant competition for survival. The drama of the struggle! Why do Americans feel it their absolute right to feel comfortable at all times? It's not natural!"

Flash forward ten years later: Concha and I, now both thirty-one, were sitting at a booth in the Broadway Diner on Ninety-sixth and Broadway in Manhattan, still having the exact same conversation, still puzzling over the American obsession with comfort.

When Concha came to visit me here, in the summer of '06, before I started my MFA program at Columbia, she reconnected with Trent, the guy she'd met the summer she studied here—a tall, strapping blond fellow who grew up on the Upper East Side. He was a clean-cut Catholic boy; he went to Trinity prep school on the Upper West Side, then Dartmouth. He had some kind of finance job on Wall Street, though I never really understood what he did exactly. Anyway, he was nice enough, but he didn't seem like Concha's type to me. Very boring; he talked a lot about golf. But before I knew it, Concha had extended her stay indefinitely (she'd finagled some kind of work/study visa) and gotten engaged to Trent. A rash, stupid move, I thought. Twenty-four was too young to marry anyway, I said. But Concha wouldn't listen to me.

She accused me of being jealous of Trent. It's true that after a while I found it annoying she was no longer available for all the fun things we used to do. And I could no longer count on her to be my "spouse" to pick me up at the doctor's after a minor surgery or procedure; or to accompany me as my plus-one to straight weddings. Although she'd always go with me, Concha said I was using her as a beard. But that wasn't it. It was just easier not taking a guy and being the only gay couple on the dance floor, since the bride's relatives from Peoria would gawk in shock. Most of the time, being Black was enough of a spectacle at these mostly white events. Concha was wrong about my selfish motives. To me, Trent just seemed too boring for her, and a bit controlling.

Concha insisted I didn't understand how straight men worked; and almost defiantly, it seemed, she married Trent. Now, sitting at the diner, seven years after her impetuous decision, the two of us shared a side of french fries and sipped bad American coffee, as Concha talked about leaving Trent.

"It's his damn obsession with being comfortable all the time!" said Concha. "After all these years, he's still not ready to have kids. And we can't even discuss it properly because he also can't bear any conflict or difficult conversation. He wants everything light and happy. Every time I bring up the subject, he says I'm making things *uncomfortable*. 'Why rock the boat?' he says. Kip, I'm telling you, it's infuriating!"

"Didn't the subject of kids come up before you married him?" I asked. Concha ignored the question—on purpose, I think— probably suspecting I might gloat with *I told you so*.

Frankly, I never understood why a woman as outspoken as Concha could go along with Trent's bullshit. Ben said Concha was probably playing out her father issues—there was surely a story there, he said. She must be regressing to be a little girl with Trent; that's why I didn't see that side of her.

Anyway, Concha now went on about how Trent's parents' marriage was turbulent until his father's death, so Trent had vowed to never have conflicts in his own marriage.

"Kip, I know it seems absurd, but last Saturday, when we were getting dressed to go to MariCarmen and Tomas's wedding—" MariCarmen was Concha's friend who taught Spanish at the Cervantes Institute along with Concha. "I know it seems ridiculous, Kip." Her voice began to quiver. "But when Trent refused to wear a necktie for the wedding, I shouted, 'What in the fuck is your fucking problem?' He said, 'I just want to be comfortable.' And, Kip, that's when I lost it!" Concha had tears in her eyes.

"Lost it?"

"I told him *I* wasn't comfortable with his constant need for comfort. I wasn't comfortable with the idea of having a child with a man who needed to be so *comfortable* he couldn't even discuss the possibility of having a child. I told him I wanted a divorce."

After years of questioning whether she should stay in the marriage, Concha finally left Trent. Then eight months ago, Concha and I were at the Broadway Diner commiserating again. At the time, I was reading Julian Barnes's *The Sense of an Ending* and, as we mourned her marriage over french fries and coffee again, I quoted from the novel.

In the novel there is a section where Barnes writes about how we all cope with the damages we survive in life. He points out that the most dangerous kind of persons to encounter are those who try to avoid any further damage to themselves at all costs. They always need to be comfortable. And everyone else around them pays the price.

After reading the quote, I closed the book and looked up. "You did the right thing, Concha. Trent is one of those dangerous sorts." I tried my best not to show my secret satisfaction at having Concha all mine again, but I don't think I could resist a little twinkle of seduction in my eyes. I felt my gaze insisting, saying, *Yes. Be mine again!*

That's when Concha peered over at me with a look I immediately recognized, that flamenco dancer, death-defying stare, the look she'd had when she'd defended herself against that woman who'd attacked her at the *feria* years ago. I also noticed a tiny scar at the corner of one eye, like an *X*—somehow I'd never noticed it before. "Kip," she said. "I have something very uncomfortable to say."

"Okay . . ." I held my breath, pretending to be casual, and sipped my coffee.

Concha said that at the age of thirty-seven, it wasn't likely she'd meet anyone else to marry anytime soon. She wasn't going to be stupid and rush into anything again, the way she had with Trent. I agreed that was a good idea. And then she said the problem was that she also wasn't getting any younger. She reminded me of how we'd joked for years that if we were both single when we got old, we'd marry each other and make our own family. I wasn't single, she acknowledged. "But—" And just before she said the words, I figured out the bomb Concha was about to drop, and my heart sank and juddered with a pang of terror.

"Would you?" she asked me. "For me, Kip?"

"How—how do you mean?" I was buying time, trying not to sound too freaked. But I had frozen, couldn't think, and wasn't sure how to proceed. What should I say?

"Obviously, I'm not saying you have to have sex with me. I mean, that's negotiable, if you want, but not necessary. And you wouldn't even have to do anything once there's a . . . a baby. I'm not expecting you to. I just want your semen."

I laughed. I don't know why, really. I'd just never heard someone say all they wanted was my semen, just like that. Then I realized from the growing color on her face that this was no time to joke. "I'm sorry," I said. "I'm just shocked. And—" I coughed for a moment; something must have gone down the wrong pipe. "Shocked—and very honored, of course. Wow! What a compliment, Concha—that you'd want my—my—"

"I can't think of anyone else, really. You're smart, Kip, and handsome and—"

I almost didn't mention it, but then, out of nervousness I guess, it just came out spontaneously, recklessly, maybe: "And I'm Black. You sure that's okay with you?"

"Why not?" Concha sat up, ruffled like an offended ostrich.

"Why should that matter? And, besides, the child would only be *half* Black. It's an interesting mix, isn't it? The best of both worlds—a little conquistador, a little wild warrior—a perfect balance."

My heart stopped, as if I'd been stomped on the chest. But I knew I must have been overreacting—surely she didn't mean it the way I'd taken it. Even if she is perfectly fluent, English isn't her first language. "Concha? What exactly do you mean, *wild*?"

"You know, we people from Sevilla are so uptight with our tradition. Of course we love a good fiesta, but you've seen how conservative we are about keeping everything as if we were still in the fifteen hundreds! Stuck in the golden age! And your Caribbean-African blood is freer and more in sync with life's natural rhythms, no?"

"No, Concha. No. I'm from Weybridge. With British colonial parents who have instilled Victorian customs, if anything, in my blood. Wild? Are you joking?"

"Oh, Kip! Is what I'm saying so terrible, really?"

"Ah, yes. Yes, it is. A 'wild' side? Do you realize 'wild' is the exact word you use in Spanish to describe those Roma people— *gitanos*, as you call them—who used to beg from us when we were sitting in Alameda. *Salvajes!* you said. It's the same word you used to describe the Moroccan and African boys selling their knockoff designer goods from blankets laid on Calle Sierpes. I thought you were being sarcastic. Or maybe, if I'm honest, I didn't think it was my place to question the racist Spanish norms. But now I—"

"Kip, are you saying I'm racist? Me? Racist? Seriously?"

I just kept shaking my head, trying to get things clear. I was trying not to jump to conclusions or overreact. I was having to choose what kind of Black person to be in that moment: accommodating, demanding, silently paranoid, or overtly paranoid.

"Would I ask you to father my child if I were racist? It makes no sense!"

"No sense at all," I said, hearing my own voice, disembodied.

Concha folded her arms in front of her and nodded her head like a strict schoolteacher. "Well, forget it. I shouldn't have asked." A tear fell from one of her eyes.

"Concha." I reached over to touch her elbow.

"No." She yanked away and looked out the plate-glass window. A pregnant woman in pink shorts walked past pushing a pram. Perfect fucking timing, I thought.

"Concha, this is a big decision. Let's think, and talk it over calmly. Later."

"Sure," she said, wiping the tear from her cheek, clearing her throat officiously. "I'll pay for the coffees and fries. I know you're late to meet Ben. You can go, Kip."

"No, I'll pay. Come on, I can afford it. It wasn't that expensive."

"Wasn't it?" she said, and stared at me with those killer almond-shaped eyes.

After that Concha didn't respond to my calls or texts for weeks, then months. That was the last time I saw or heard from her for eight months. It wasn't until Ben rallied her to rescue me five days ago that Concha reappeared, outside this basement study, to help save me from myself.

Choosing Death

My apologies, but I must interrupt the account of my affair with Morgan.

Something is troubling me. Who else will listen to me now but you? You are my Possibility. You must understand what I have endured. And only you will fully understand when I say that my main suffering here is because I am both Black and the kind of man who is seen as less than a man.

Today my wife, Gamila, visited. She complained of how hard it is with me being in jail. Little Morgan has had a fever for three days now, and she asked her sister to stay and help her. But Aliyah came with her own two girls, and now they are eating Gamila out of house and home. Gamila is running out of money too, she says. And I must write Morgan to send us at least twenty-five pounds from Alexandria immediately. She says it is *his* fault our child is sick—his very name has been a curse. Little *Mar-gan* is now suffering the curse of the British! she says.

Not once did she ask how I was feeling. Me, sick, coughing more and more each day—I spat up blood last night—and sleeping on the cold jail floor with barely any food.

Do you think, at all, how I am suffering here? I asked her.

She looked at me and said nothing.

If I had known the cruelty and abuse I'd suffer in this jail, I said, I would have used that gun when I could have. When I was arrested that afternoon, on the corner of El-Abbasi Street, there were no witnesses. I could have easily shot the British policemen, run down the alley, and been free. Now, they sentence me to hard labor—digging ditches, hauling boulders, cleaning up the shit buckets. They stripped me naked and shaved off all my body hair. During the day they make me wear grey muslin trousers, a tunic, and this ugly old taqiyah on my head. When I tell them the food is inedible—hard bread and yellow mush with little chunks of rancid green meat—the British officers throw the grub back at me, as if I were a dog. And worst of all, they watch while the older inmates rape me. They laugh as I'm pounded in half until I'm bleeding and collapse in exhaustion. Little Black Bugger Boy, the British call me. They say buggers like me deserve to be crushed.

I think I should have used that revolver when I had a chance. Shot both policemen. Then I would not be suffering so under the evil British.

Gamila looked at me unmoved, staring at me, wrapped up in her white shawl as if she were a corpse. You brought this curse on yourself, she said.

Strange, I think. She never called it a curse when I bought the house on El-Abbasi Street with the money Morgan sent us. Sixty pounds. A narrow, white house, two stories high, with robin's-egg-blue shutters and doors. A respectable place, even if it's in a dirty maze of alleys where lowly Egyptians live. She was happy enough with *that* curse!

Gamila only looked at me coldly and said she wished my

brother, Ahmed, had not died and she could have married him instead. That is what was supposed to have happened, she said. Ahmed would never have welcomed the curse of the British.

She is right. My older brother, Ahmed, was with the rebellion. He hated the British. He used to go to the underground meetings in Mansourah, at the coffeehouse in the Al Khawagat Market. The meetings so secret you can't even read about them in the *Al-Ahram* newspaper. Saad Zaghlul and many committee members are forming a new party. The Wafd. Egypt for Egyptians! Ahmed cautioned me against Morgan. You are foolish to get so close to a white man. They are dangerous, he said. And an upheaval is soon coming in Egypt, he warned. The British must go. If I stay with Morgan, even if I survive the conflict, my soul as an Egyptian will die, he said. Sides must be chosen.

Ahmed drowned a year ago; the Nile swallowed him alive. But they say he will be resurrected from the holy river, like Osiris. Isis brought her lover, Osiris, back to life on the Nile. Each year, the Nile floods and surges up with Osiris in the form of mud and sewage to fertilize the crops. He regenerates life. Osiris is the Lord of Love and Death. For him to know the power of Isis's love, he had to first die, then be reborn. Love and death are inseparable, two sides of a single coin. So how can I choose when the two things are one? In choosing Morgan's love, I must also choose death.

It's 4:00 a.m. The magic hour. I'm wondering how to begin the next chapter, in which Mohammed and Morgan finally have sex. It was Morgan's first sexual relationship—at the age of thirty-eight. For Mohammed it was a different kind of milestone. But how to begin?

I suspend my fingers over Sophia, running piano scales in the air. I'm Chopin-ready, waiting for the Muses to sing. A word, a phrase, an image—I'll take anything, ladies, please! When suddenly I hear that tremendous thump. It's back—that crazy sound, the ghost, the thwapping thump of dragon-size wings displacing the air. And the thwapping sound now fills the room; the vibrations shudder through me again, all the way down my spine.

Is the sound coming from deep inside me?

When I inhale, I become aware of a slinking, snaking weight, like a huge slug lumbering up my lower abdomen. I look down and I realize I have an erection digging into my navel. Now it's vaulting. Rising like a parturient pillar in the crotch of my grey, Adidas tracksuit. Autonomous and willful. Defiant, even.

"*What the fuck?*" I say out loud. "What in the fuck is going on?"

Before I can even catch my breath, a loud exhale fills the room, like a gust of wind from the cosmos. Was that my exhale? I ask myself, but immediately my thoughts are interrupted by a booming sound.

"*I am the one thus come!*" She has a warm, deep voice, and again, she speaks into both ears in perfect stereo.

As illogical as it is, I wonder if it's my psychoanalyst, Margaret, outside my door. It can't be Concha; her voice is much lighter, and her accent distinct. But the accent of this woman's voice is difficult to pinpoint; she could be from anywhere—an easy-listening jazz radio host from Tel Aviv or Kentucky or New Delhi. But it is indeed a deep voice, like Margaret's. Has Ben finally called my therapist to deal with me?

But no—it's too late for house calls. When I stand up on the safety box to look through the small window, it's black outside. Nothing there. I can only see my own reflection under the silver pendant ceiling lamp, bearing an unsettling resemblance to Munch's screaming man. I jump down and rush back to check the top right of Sophia's screen: 4:05 a.m. Holy shit. I haven't slept in over twenty-four hours now.

"I am the one thus come!" she says again, more forcefully now.

I realize from the cinematic surround sound of her voice, from the woofer-like bass vibrations resonating in every single muscle of my heart, that I am probably losing my mind. Perhaps I should have listened to Margaret and seen the psychiatrist after all. I know I'm not dreaming, but I pinch my forearm just to make sure. No, I'm awake. It must be a full-on auditory hallucination.

I immediately think of the scene from Tony Kushner's play *Angels in America* when the angel descends upon the AIDS-stricken Prior Walter in his bed—he also gets an unbelievable erection as she arrives. And I remember now, after seeing the Broadway revival of the play, that the sound effect of the angel's winged arrival is similar to the thumping I've just heard.

"Are you my angel?" I say out loud, shaking my head in disbelief. Am I actually talking to an invisible, disembodied voice?

"No, not an angel," she says.

The fact that she actually answers freaks me the fuck out, and my heart starts beating one hundred miles an hour. "What are you, then? Where are you? What do you want with me?"

"I am the one thus come! *I am the one thus come!*"

I remember how the angel in *Angels in America* ended up being surprisingly stupid; she kept repeating her message by rote, even getting stuck and tripping up on words—my hallucination has clearly stolen from the great Tony Kushner, I think. But she says she isn't an angel, so now I am thrown. My hallucination is making an original turn of her own.

"I am the beginning and the end. *Tatha-agata. Neti neti.* I am the Great Goddess."

Everything is white suddenly, like a dense fog, and I can't see in front of me; yet I feel as if I can see with something other than my eyes. I see myself as a ghostly outline, sitting before me cross-legged, like a yogi. There is a pale blue light illuminating my astral-like body. My eyes are closed—even when I open them, they are closed. But still I can see myself floating there. I feel a fire at the base of my spine. An intense heat that would normally cause me to scream, but somehow I can bear it. I also see blue flames at the groin of the astral body. As the flames rise, they turn orange, then red, and take the shape of a serpent that slowly begins to coil up my spine; for some reason, this coiling strengthens my erection.

"What's happening to me?" I ask her.

"I am the one thus come. Kundalini Shakti. I awaken the sleeping one. Without me, even the Lord is unable to create or destroy. I am the giver of the fruit of action, the source of all creation." I'm thinking now that her accent could be American, from the South. Sultry.

"What is happening to my body? There are things happening . . . *down there*."

"That is my work."

"*What* is your work?"

"To wake you up."

"Am I asleep? Is this a dream?"

"All illusions are dreams."

"What's happening with this snake? It's got my . . . *you-know-what* on fire. And it's so hard. What is this?" Honestly, it feels as if I've had a massive shot of Viagra.

"Do you enjoy it?"

I don't know how to answer her. I haven't thought about enjoying it or not; it is all so incomprehensible. But I have to admit, all this is giving me the biggest erection I've had in years. And the fire isn't painful after all; it's igniting my desire, an overwhelming desire to explode with my creative juices. I'm not sure if I can even stop myself from ejaculating spontaneously—all of this without being touched, without even touching myself! "Yes," I say. "Yes. I am enjoying it."

"Come for me. All I want is your seed, your life force," says this goddess of the deep, jazz-radio voice. "*Come for me.*"

"I think I might—but I—I don't understand this!"

"All pleasure is the experience of divinity." Her voice ravishes. "The whole universe springs forth from enjoyment; pleasure is found at the root of everything. But perfect love is that whose object is not limited, love without attributes, the pure love of love itself, of the transcendent being-of-joy!"

And with an electrifying energy running through me, I release an explosion like never before.

PART 2

The Body Electric

The irony of our recent breakup is that just two weeks ago Ben said we'd had the best sex ever. I felt even closer to him too. It was the unexpected consequence of a horrifying incident with a rat. One Saturday morning, coming downstairs to make coffee, I found the giant rodent nosing up the trash bin in the kitchen. I freaked out. To me, there is nothing worse than finding yourself naked, utterly defenseless, in front of a wild rodent. I jumped up with feline prowess onto the kitchen counter and shrieked for Ben. He appeared, in his white Hanes briefs, in superhero mode. He grabbed the broom, his golden saber, chased the rat from the kitchen into the hallway and back into the kitchen. Finally, he cornered it between the wall and the refrigerator and whacked it to death. A revolting bloody mess. But Ben had proven himself victorious as my protector—and he knew it. Instead of being my spastic, sniffling lover, he had acted heroically, decisively and with force. He was the Ben I'd fallen in love with. It was a huge turn-on.

After we cleaned up the remains with bleach and water and every cleaning agent we could find, and after we'd thrown out the carcass in a Hefty trash bag, Ben seemed full of energy and suddenly very horny. He approached me as never before.

It started as we showered together. He offered to soap me down. He used the bar of Dr. Bronner's soap as his tool of seduction. In his hands the eroded slippery disc caressed my nipples, behind my ears, over my earlobes, and down the nape of my neck. The astringent eucalyptus stirred my skin. Ben swashed the wet disc back and forth below my navel, slid it down to areas that tickled but excited me. Rammed it firmly into crevices; slid it gently out. Soaped up my dick until it was straining and jogging upward on its own, pleading.

Being washed like that reminded me of being in Marrakesh at the hammam, when I visited Morocco during my study time in Spain. An old Moroccan man, a professional bather, soaped me up as I lay naked, flat on my stomach, on the worn marble floor. He scrubbed in every crevice of my body, first with a soft sponge, and then with a mildly scratchy one. Finally, he doused me with buckets of perfectly hot water, rinsing off any trace of dirt or dead skin. I don't think the old man noticed, but I began to quietly cry. I wasn't even sure why. I guess it was some kind of baptism. A spiritual, yet sensual, energy.

This shower with Ben felt like that too. But I didn't let on about my emotions; I didn't want to spoil the sexiness of the moment.

After our shower we had the most intense sex ever. I was so turned on I had three consecutive orgasms—which I didn't even know was possible. But Ben, when he finally ejaculated, rose up and stiffened as if he'd been stabbed in the back, or as if he were suddenly possessed. He shivered and spoke in tongues—literally. An unknown language came spewing out of him, sounding like an Arabic prayer and a charismatic Baptist hallelujah all at once. He became completely transported, beyond the physical experience, it seemed. I envied that.

"I sing the body electric!" Ben laughed as if in joyful disbelief at our act. But then he observed something I didn't realize was so obvious. "Kip, you know, you always hold back a little. Don't get me wrong—that was amazing sex. Amazing! But you don't ever fully let go, do you?"

I felt caught out. A wave of shame and confusion, and then shame that I felt confusion. I said nothing.

We lay there silently, postcoital, on the tussled white sheets, like summer swimmers collapsed on beach towels. It was a lazy Saturday morning and time seemed infinite. We sprawled, entwined, occasionally caressing a shoulder or forehead or thigh of the other.

"I sing the body electric!" Those were the words Ben had used. A quote from the Walt Whitman poem we both loved. I admired it not only for its celebration of the sensual in all its forms but also for its references to the slavery of Black folks, the debasing of Black bodies, bodies not valued for their spiritual force. For Whitman, the sensual body was only given value by the spirit. And Ben now explained why the body electric had meant so much to him too.

When Ben spoke again, I felt the vibrations of his voice penetrate through flesh and bone, reaching something deeper in me. "Do you know," he said, "I was nineteen in the summer of 1982."

"Oh God! That's crazy," I said, lifting my chin to rest on the wispy hairs on his hard chest, gawking up at him playfully. His skin, hot and moist, smelled of sweat, and Old Spice, and semen—which also reminded me of fresh-cut grass. "In the summer of 1982," I said, "I was barely three months old. Fresh out of the oven. Ben, what if—" I thumped my fingers impishly on his chest. "What if you'd seen me wrapped in hospital blankets and someone would have told you, 'That wee newborn there, he's going to be your husband one day!' What would you have said?"

"Impossible!" Ben laughed. I agreed and laughed too.

Ben's face grew pensive. "Then again, I guess I would have said the same about anyone being my husband. Or anything happening in the future at all." Ben took a deep sigh, and my head, still on his chest, rose and sank again. "I didn't think I'd be alive long enough to have any future at all," he said.

I sat up and saw his eyes seemed on the verge of tears. "What do you mean?"

"Well, in 1982, I was still in college," he said. "My crazy buddy, Mike Dooley, and I used to drive down from Connecticut to New York for the weekends to go to the gay bars near Christopher Street: Keller's, Julius'. Pick up guys and do crazy shit! We'd even have sex on the piers if the guys didn't have a place to go. So much was covert in those days. We were used to hiding. Legitimate spaces didn't exist for us then."

He said it was the same year he had entered a gay club for the first time—The Monster, on Sheridan Square, across the street from the famous Stonewall Inn. It was at The Monster where Ben finally found a place he fit in, he said; where he also, for the first time, discovered he was attractive; and, most important, where he learned what profound pleasure and connection could happen through bodily contact. At The Monster, he said, he met other college guys, but mostly working-class men of other races—African American, Jamaican, Puerto Rican, Ecuadorian, Salvadoran, Filipino, Guyanese, Dominican—young men who had very different histories from his white, upper-middle-class Newton upbringing. Ben said he connected with these men in ways that validated a common humanity, a common love that erased all lines normally drawn between the classes and races.

"I discovered the body electric, as Whitman calls it," he said. In his hazel-green eyes, a little glint shone out past the sadness. "And Kip, it wasn't just sex. I mean, it was, but not just physical." Ben explained, "It was an awakening to a new way to be alive and to connect to the world. Body and soul were one! It was like coming home to a place I'd never been—truly alive in my own skin!"

But, he said, as soon as he'd opened himself to this brave new world, the catastrophic news came. A year after the report of the small cluster of gay men with a mysterious illness, the *New York Times* starting running even more frightening articles: "New Homosexual Disorder Worries Health Officials," then "A Disease's Spread Provokes Anxiety," and then "AIDS, A New Disease's Deadly Odyssey." "And, Kip, it fell on me like a French guillotine—*Zhup!*" He gestured the fall of the blade. "It was all over. 'All this new life will kill you!' they said."

"Oh babe, that sounds so scary." I tugged gently at his earlobes, first one, then the other.

"Scary as shit. You have no idea," said Ben. "By the time I was twenty-one, I said to myself, I'll be dead. It was terrifying."

And then, said Ben, one after another, his friends and lovers started dropping like flies.

Alphonso: at twenty-three, Ben's former college roommate, a Black boy from Dayton, Ohio, was still closeted. A college track star bound for success as a broadcast journalist. He collapsed on Flatbush Avenue with pneumonia; was released from the hospital looking like an old man with a walking stick; grew purple lesions on his forehead and neck; locked himself away in his Brooklyn apartment on Vanderbilt Avenue, too ashamed to show his marred face in public. Two months later, he starved himself to death, sparing himself a month of a slow demise.

And Sergio: at twenty-six, from El Salvador, Sergio was lively and handsome, with a Clark Gable smile. Sergio taught Ben how to make Salvadoran tamales. He also showed him how to kiss slowly, tenderly, sensuously. They dated for four wonderful months before Sergio disappeared and never called again. A month later Ben heard from a friend in common that Sergio had collapsed while on a catering job for Glorious Foods in the Hamptons. The friend had taken Sergio to St. Vincent's Hospital.

The same day Ben visited him in the hospital, Sergio's family also came for the first and only time, with a priest in tow to perform an exorcism. "Can you believe it?" Ben asked me, his eyes popping. "A real-life fucking exorcism! The last words Sergio heard from his mother were 'You're not my son, you're the devil! You're going to hell!' Kip, it was *so* fucked up! And Sergio was such a sweet, loving guy. You would have really liked him."

"He sounds amazing." I tried to smile but instead, I felt my face contort, trying to suppress the eruption of something rising in me, a pressure pounding behind my eyes.

"And the real terror," Ben said, sitting up and seeming unable to stop himself now, "the terror was that you had no idea whether you had it yourself or not. Even when the tests came out, it was a long time before they could determine if the syndrome would lie dormant for years. At any moment it could—and chances were it probably would—strike you. We were all terrorized, Kip. For more than a decade. It was a living nightmare."

I don't think Ben noticed—he was so rapt, envisioning his past—but I couldn't stop tears running down my face. I kept having images of Ben facing all that horrifying death at such a young age. I'd seen photos of him from that era: innocent and strong, with wild, curly brown hair; arms akimbo in his white Bundeswehr tank top; and a big smile that said, "I'm ready for my adventure, World!" Just a boy, really.

"We all felt it was useless to pursue anything long-term," Ben added. "So we decided to enjoy what little time was left. We danced, and had more sex, or did more drugs and stopped feeling at all, in hopes of freezing time. And we only realized, at thirty or so, that somehow, unexpectedly, some of us were still alive. And then we had to figure out what to do with the rest of our lives. More than a decade lost, preparing to die."

Ben had never talked to me about this in such detail. As he spoke, I imagined how, at twenty-two, it must have felt like being at war; only there was no hero's homecoming for the survivors. No appreciation of what they had endured. Instead, just frightened looks the other way. Even Ben's peers today, the ones who have survived, barely refer to their shared trauma. They sometimes reminisce about the wild dance club days—The Saint and the Paradise Garage, hanging out with Grace Jones, Madonna, and Keith Haring—but they rarely, if ever, discuss the actual trauma.

I thought about something my MFA classmate Sarah Weiss once told me. I had asked her if her grandmother ever spoke about being a Holocaust survivor. "No, no, no, *bubbala*." She smiled wanly, her close-set eyes slightly crossing, as if kindly tolerating my naivete. "Of such things, Kipling, we do not speak."

"But Kippy," said Ben, now wiping my tears away. "Don't cry. I'm okay." I don't think it occurred to Ben that I was also crying for myself. Yes, I was sad for him, but also for myself, wishing I too could let go, be transported, experience the body electric. "Kip, to defy death and the debasing forces, we have *this* . . ." He held on to my shoulders. "And *this* . . ." He rested his hand on my chest, above my heart. "And," he smiled coyly, "*this* . . ." He grabbed my dick and squeezed with hot care. Then he quoted Whitman by heart, reminding me, oddly, of how my mother had often recited Milton to me as a child:

I sing the body electric,
The armies of those I love engirth me and I engirth them,
They will not let me off till I go with them, respond to them,
And discorrupt them, and charge them full with the charge of
    the soul.

Was it doubted that those who corrupt their own bodies conceal
    themselves?
And if those who defile the living are as bad as they who defile
    the dead?
And if the body does not do fully as much as the soul?
And if the body were not the soul, what is the soul?

Crossing to Brooklyn

Whitman is all I possess. Besides my dull pencil, and this black and white, marbleized composition notebook—left behind by one of the French soldiers, I suppose—the British officers have let me keep my *Leaves of Grass*. I had Gamila bring it from home. At first, it was to feel Morgan close to me—the book was his gift in our first year. It has a brown, Morocco leather cover, embossed in gold, from Philadelphia.

Whitman was Morgan's favorite poet. Morgan even knew someone who had met the great American bard himself. A man named Carpenter, a mentor of Morgan's, who had slept with Whitman. Carpenter now lives in the wilderness of England with a lover named George. Morgan says they are two of the bravest men he knows—they dare to follow their truest selves.

Lying together on the low bed in my Home of Misery, just a cotton mattress on the floor, Morgan used to stroke my face and read me poems from *Leaves of Grass*: "Passage to India," "I Sing the Body Electric," "Native Moments."

One night after reading these poems, Morgan said, Mohammed,

I cannot deny it, I want to kiss you . . . and to penetrate you too. I
want to connect deeply.

I told Morgan I didn't understand. Why do you want to connect so deeply? I asked. What is the point of it? Why don't you
just say you want to feel your cock in me? I would understand that.
Why does it have to be about a deeper connection?

I was in my white djellaba, Morgan still in his Red Cross khakis. Although we were side by side on the bed, we looked over at
the white wall, as if we could project the perfect scene on the bare
surface, as if on a blank canvas. I imagined miles and miles of snow,
far from civilization, and nothing else, except for an igloo of my
own. Morgan asked what I was thinking about, but I only repeated
that his notion of connecting was nonsensical to me.

It's hard to explain, he said, but then he tried. It is as if, when I
see you, Mohammed, I see a part of myself that I somehow cannot
locate inside myself—a part I need to be whole. And so, connecting with you is like connecting with that part of me. It makes me
whole. Together we can be whole. Does that make any sense to you?

I considered what Morgan had said and thought, Why not be
honest and say it plain and simply? I said, So, if you fuck me, Morgan, you will be connecting with a part of yourself that you cannot
feel without putting your cock in me. Is that right?

Morgan blushed like a chaste young nun. He avoided saying
words like "cock" and "fuck." But I made a point of saying them, especially to provoke him. And I know he liked my common speech,
because he smiled with a sense of relief, it seemed.

I will never understand you British, I said, laughing.

But I lied. I did understand what Morgan meant. There was
a kind of gentleness in him, an openness and innocence I myself
had lost. I could not find it in myself anymore. It had been robbed

from me so long ago. Life had made me evil and contrary. If I could possess his innocence again, if he could fill me with it, I might be whole again too.

Morgan stroked my face and said I was beautiful, that my black skin was beautiful.

I smiled at the irony of his words. All my life I had been told how ugly and unattractive my skin was. My mother had told me to avoid the sun, to make sure I didn't get any darker and uglier. I wondered if Morgan was lying, just to manipulate me. I said, Aren't you ashamed to be seen with me in public? People may say you are associating with a lowly Black tram conductor!

Morgan seemed to grow very vexed and gripped my hand as a stern parent would. Never say that, Mohammed! How could you even *think* such a thing?

As I looked at our hands, now one in the other, I tried to see them through Morgan's eyes, and I began to notice rich hues to my own skin, shades of reds and browns; and there was too a smooth silkiness that his skin did not possess. I suddenly saw how he might have found something appealing in my skin.

I made the decision in that moment. Now is the time, I told myself. Now.

Fuck me, Morgan. I said it. And then Morgan immediately responded, as if he'd been holding back too long. Will I hurt you, Mohammed? I knew all was set in motion now.

I don't care, Morgan.

But will it hurt you, Mohammed?

Do you want it to hurt me, Morgan?

I want you to never leave me, Mohammed.

You want it to hurt me, then hurt me.

But don't leave me, Mohammed.

Fuck me, Morgan, hurt me.

I won't leave you, Mohammed.

Never?

Never.

When we were spent and sweaty on the sheets, I looked Morgan in the eyes and said, If this will happen again, I have conditions: You can never own me. If I do not want to meet, or I do not want to lie with you, you must follow my word. I must never feel obligated. Do you accept my conditions?

Morgan smiled for a long time before he answered. He kept looking at my face—his gaze shifting from my eyes, to my nose, to my ears—as if seeing me for the first time, or perhaps the opposite, as if he were seeing me again after being separated for hundreds of years. Finally, he said, Yes, of course, Mohammed. It will be just as you say. Nothing but mutual respect.

I do not think Morgan intended to lie. Perhaps it wasn't an intentional lie. "Respect" is simply an impossible word to translate, I suppose.

Often our sex began like that—with Morgan reading Whitman. When he would read of "the midnight orgies of young men," he would excite my desire to feel what Whitman felt, to savor in Morgan's touch, and to let our bodies sing. But I could never exactly feel this connection that Morgan and Whitman spoke of, this body electric.

But sometimes, after Morgan left, when I read Whitman on my own, alone, I found other poems, and they began to remind me not of sex or Morgan anymore, but of myself—of the self I could be. My Possibility.

Alone with my leather-bound Whitman, letting the candle burn down to a nub before sleeping, I would feel as if I too were crossing on the ferry to Brooklyn, with the same salty sea breeze blowing across my face, rolling forward upon the scallop-edged waves.

And even now I can feel Whitman with me. *What is the count of the scores or hundreds of years between us? Whatever it is, it avails not—distance avails not . . .*

And I know I am not alone; or rather, I am more myself in my solitude, because he is here.

Yes, you are here too, my Possibility; you also know what it is to cross over to Brooklyn.

And I too, like Whitman, have knitted the old knot of contrariety . . . resented, lied, stolen, cheated. Yes. And the wolf, the snake, the hog are not wanting in me. Who is completely free of evil thoughts and deeds? Be clear about this, my young man of the future: I too *know what it is to be evil.*

When I hear a knock on the door, I decide to ignore it. I'm convinced it's Ben. I'm not going to answer. Let him suffer; he's the one who broke up with me. But is it really him? Six in the evening—too early for the goddess; she only comes at the witching hour. But as the knocking persists—an irregular, tentative rapping, like a child's—I'm realizing it's neither Ben nor the goddess. I get up and tiptoe towards the door. If I get close enough, I might be able to detect some slight sound to identify the knocker. Then, I smell rose perfume wafting up from under the door.

"Kip." Concha finally speaks, her voice as tentative as her knocking, very unlike her.

What should I do? Should I answer? I'm still upset about her eight months of silent treatment, and I'm not even sure if I can trust her motives now. How did Ben get her to come here, anyway? I turn to go back to my desk, but then I feel a strange weight grounding me in place, making me slump with my back against the two-by-four boards nailed over the door, and I sink, slowly but inevitably, to the floor. And when I'm there, squatted in place, I rest my head back on the door with a little thud.

"Kip? What are you doing in there?"

I shut my eyes and take in a deep breath. "I'm trying to write my bloody book. You know what I'm doing. What are you doing here?"

"Look, I'm not going to bother you for long. If you want to starve yourself to death, that is your problem. I just came here because when Ben told me you were doing this crazy thing, I realized that it may be my last chance to talk to you before you absolutely lose your mind. And also, since you're locked in there, you can't run away when the conversation gets difficult."

"Run away? Me?" I shake my head then grip it in my hands for a second. "Don't you think you're confusing me with Trent? And anyway, *you're* the one who ran away. You didn't answer my calls. You never reached out. How can you say *I* am the one who runs away?"

"Well, you are!" I now hear the clickety-clack of Concha's high-heeled boots pacing in the hallway on the wooden floor, like a ticker-tape machine.

"Concha, can you stop that noise and stand still while we talk?"

"No, I can't. I *won't*! This is exactly the issue, Kip. You are always the one setting the terms for everything. You pretend to be meek and humble, but you're a great big ego! And you have been from the first day we met. Remember? It had to be either at Alameda or by the cathedral where we met—nowhere else! Always your way! And you think because you're gay you can get away with being an entitled male asshole. Well, lots of gay men are entitled assholes. My father is gay—he left us when I was eight years old. He had to go to Madrid, he said, to find his truth! Truth! I can tell a gay, patriarchal, narcissistic asshole when I see one!"

Suddenly, I'm on my feet, rising from pure adrenaline. "What are you talking about?" I turn towards the door now, grabbing a two-by-four in frustration. "What in the hell is this about?"

"Do you know what I am in your life, Kip? I'll tell you. I am

a secondary character in your novel whose only purpose is to illuminate the protagonist's puny development. That's all I am for you.
Do I have an arc of my own? No, of course not. It's Kip's story. The
only one that matters! The long-suffering writer whose story must
be heard or else the whole world will stop spinning! And Concha
is always there to pick up the pieces when the many, many lovers
leave or disappoint poor Kipling. Always there to be on your arm as
you pretend to be straight when you feel it's necessary to impress."

"Oh, that is so unfair! Never!"

"Yes, it's true. And you never approved of anyone I ever dated.
You hated Trent—"

"He was boring. He wasn't even your type!"

"That was for *me* to decide. You don't get to decide! Why is
that your right, Kip? Because you're a man?"

"You've got it all wrong, Concha."

"Do I? Do I really?"

She stops pacing. I listen to hear what she may be doing, but
there's nothing—silence. Is she gone? "Concha?"

Then her voice comes again, closer and sterner and harder.
"Kip, what did you think when I asked you to father my child? Be
honest. What did you really think?"

"I don't know—I guess I was shocked. Honored, of course,
but—"

"Honestly, Kip. Aren't you always talking about honesty?"

"I don't know." And I really don't. I'm so confused by the way
I'm being falsely accused of things. Can she really believe I view
her as only secondary in my life? A bit part in the plot? "I—I don't
know what you're talking about, Concha."

We are both silent. I sink to the floor again, sitting with my
elbows on my raised knees, leaning my back against the door.

"Kip, do you remember that time we went to the Neue Galerie café and we pretended to be from France, speaking out loud in bad French, going on about all those rich Upper East Side women with their face-lifts and furs? *Quel dommage! Quelle scène moche!* Remember?"

I do remember that day, with a tinge of embarrassment—how adolescent of us! But I don't have the spirit to say anything. And I don't think Concha is really asking for an answer, anyway.

"Well," she continues. "You were joking when I told you about my troubles with Trent. You kept saying, 'Well, then, leave him, Madame Bovary! Find another man with more passion. Go on, Madame Bovary!' What did you mean by all that, Kip?"

"Concha, I honestly don't know what you're talking about. I don't remember that."

"You don't? You kept on saying it. Even after we left the café. All week you kept up the joke: 'Yes, Madame Bovary.' 'Do you think so, Madame Bovary?' Kip, what was that about?"

I really have no recollection of ever calling Concha that. But I do remember I was rereading *Madame Bovary* around that time, so I believe her. But that was over a year ago. I feel a sinking in my gut. How can she have harbored so much resentment over that?

"You weren't taking me seriously, Kip. My life is a big joke to you. I was talking to you about my real problems with Trent. Painful stuff. Ten years of a marriage. But it was like a silly fiction for you, and I was no more than a fictional character—a frivolous and tragic one at that! Your Madame Bovary!"

"Concha, what is this all about? I don't understand. Is this about you having a baby? About the fact that I didn't just say yes? That I suggested we have a more in-depth talk about it?"

"You are blind, Kip! It's about everything! I'm not going to be a bit player in your life, Kip. And none of you—you, Trent, or any other man—is going to be the one to set the terms. Not for *my* life. And yes, it was annoying that you felt you could decide how and when we talked about *my* body having *my* child. Yes, you also reduced all my pain to a clever excerpt from a book you quoted— words of wisdom, from a man, of course. *The Sense of an Ending.* Ironic title, or maybe prescient? And yes, you expected me to come back and apologize to you. Poor wounded, misunderstood Kip. Always victimized by racism. Do you think I care that you're Black?"

"Well, you should!" I yell back. "That's the bloody point: it matters!"

"But the real issue, Kip, is that you weren't being honest. And you still aren't. What did you really think when I asked you to father my child? You haven't been honest about that yet."

"What do you want me to say, for Christ's sake?"

"The truth. What was the first thing that went through your head when I asked you? The first thing you thought of! Say it, coward. Be brave and say it!"

And then it comes out of me—something I didn't even know was there: "Fine! You know what I really thought?" I shout. "I thought, 'Oh God, she's in love with me! She wants me!'"

"*Allí está!* Finally," she says. Then nothing. The silence seems deafening. I actually wonder if I've lost my hearing until Concha speaks again, more quietly now. "Finally."

I stand facing the door, numb, speechless. What the fuck have I just said? Is it even true?

"At least now we can be honest, Kip. You've known how I felt about you all along. And you took advantage of that. Used me. Well, do you know what I finally told myself? I can use him too. For his semen. Why shouldn't I use you too, Kip? Then we'll be even. *Bueno. Allí está!* That's all I have to say. Now you can starve yourself to death if you want."

"Concha, I know you don't mean that. And how can you say I used you? Concha? *Concha?*" In frustration I bang my fists against the rough two-by-fours. I don't even realize how hard until I see blood on the boards, blood dripping from my fists. "Concha?" I shout out again.

But I can't hear her heels anymore. I can't smell her rose perfume. She's gone.

I got nothing written yesterday, or today so far. Before Concha came I was, admittedly, stuck but determined to get back on track. But after her visit I was gutted. Couldn't write a thing. I've never believed in writer's block before, but I think I'm genuinely blocked now.

Also, something odd is happening inside of me, distracting me. It could be Goddess Shakti's damned Kundalini snake curling up my astral body, but there's something else I'm even nervous to say aloud—you will think I'm truly losing my mind. But, oh well, this is it: I feel as if, somehow, Mohammed has possessed me—or rather, that I am being possessed by him. He is becoming me, or I am becoming him. I don't understand what's happening but I can't shake it.

And although I feel stuck about where I'm going with his story, Mohammed assures me with a voice that somehow comes from deep within me, that *is* me. He knows perfectly well what he has to say. All I need to do is open up the channels, to let it flow, and he will do the rest.

But how am I to open the channels?

And there is an even bigger problem, yet. I sense that Mohammed is more dangerous than I had previously assumed. God knows where he's going with this story. Or, even worse, what he's going to do with me.

MOHAMMED'S STORY

Wild Warriors

I am whispering to you, dear friend, from this cold cell floor. Come to me. Come closer still. Yes, dear Possibility, we are alone. Time avails not; distance avails not. Do you not feel me here?

What do you want to know of me? Go ahead, ask it. What's that? Do I use Morgan to my own advantage? Why not? I say. Who doesn't use the one he loves? Who else do we have to use? But the mutuality makes all the difference. Do you think you are not both the tormentor and the tormented?

We outlaws have to look out for each other. Do you think we dark ones have not unseen ourselves? We need wilderness more than the rest—the space and the silence to be. Where is the wilderness, you ask, dear friend? It's where your demon, the evil one, is.

Ah, don't pull away, come closer. Do you think you are not the enemy too?

But we're not there yet, not in our wilderness. This is not your house. Not our Home of Misery. Farther, farther, we must go to become the wild warriors. Wrestle the true demon, my friend—but out there, beyond the reaches of their civilizations. Out there, where there is space enough to see him entirely. Go, my Possibility. Go!

I'm plagued by Mohammed's voice urging me towards the wilderness. I don't know where exactly he expects me to go. In any case, I'm blocked with the writing—ironically, because of him. He's supposed to be telling me of his affair with Morgan but he keeps taking me off track.

I'm reviewing my notes, trying to get unstuck, to get back on track with the actual story. As I'm thumbing through a Forster biography—the fat, heavy double volume by Furbank—I stop at a passage I'd forgotten I'd earmarked. On the yellow Post-it stuck to the page I've written, *Forster's visit to the wilderness.*

I remember when I stuck that note there. I was doing my research for the Forster novel at King's College's archives, feeling very much like a Cambridge intellectual—in my white, Irish cable-knit sweater and brown tweed jacket—sitting in that gorgeous Gothic room overlooking the front lawn and King's College chapel. There, I'd come across the notes Forster had written for his then "unpublishable" gay novel, *Maurice*, and his description of a fateful and, in retrospect, monumental visit with his friend and mentor, Edward Carpenter.

I have not given this episode much thought since then, but now I'm remembering that it was on this visit that Forster had a peculiar experience that got him unstuck from a bout of writer's block and propelled him to write *Maurice*, the most daring work of his career.

Edward Carpenter was a Victorian-era gay guru, a humanitarian, philosopher, poet, and socialist activist. He was tall and slender, with a shock of white hair and a Whitmanesque beard. A charismatic character. He had also achieved what few ever achieve—as a young man, he'd shagged his idol, Walt Whitman. Carpenter lived in the woods, in the East Midlands, near the hamlet of Millthorpe, with his lover, George Merrill, a younger man from the slums of Sheffield.

On their farm, Carpenter and Merrill wore only homemade sandals (often nothing else but the sandals), which were fashioned after a pair Carpenter had brought back from his time in India. But sandals were not all Carpenter brought back with him. He had also studied yogic mysticism and had been transformed, perhaps spiritually enlightened, by the experience. The yogic philosophy was in full alignment with all he'd learned from Whitman about the oneness of humanity with nature. Civilization, he felt, was the result of a human illness; it ran contrary to man's truest nature. Industrialism and capitalism, along with class, race, and religious distinctions, would ruin man and the planet itself, he felt. Carpenter lived by his beliefs. He loved and made love and ate—as a vegetarian—in the most natural way possible, with no heed to civilized norms.

Forster's Cambridge friends Roger Fry and Goldie Dickinson urged him to visit Carpenter and Merrill at their cottage in the woods on the farm. There was something very powerful about the two men in the wilderness, they said. The couple emitted an otherworldly energy, a sense of serenity, but with an electric twinkle behind their eyes. Forster later described it as "the influence which used to be called magnetic." The healer's power. So, when Morgan was creatively blocked after publishing *Howards End*, he decided to pay a visit to Carpenter and Merrill.

Years later, Morgan spoke to Mohammed of the intrepid gay

duo as an example of what they could also have together one day. "They live as a married couple in the woods, without giving a damn about society, absolutely off the map, in the wilderness."

In his diary, Forster wrote that on his visit, Carpenter and Merrill "touched everyone everywhere," not just energetically but physically. They were a randy duo, especially Merrill, who caught Forster in private by surprise one day and slapped him on the buttocks. The sensation was shocking to Forster. And the strangest thing was it lingered and grew in intensity. For several hours afterwards, it continued to arouse Forster, stirring an erection.

In his Terminal Note to *Maurice*, Forster wrote that Merrill's touch "was as much psychological as it was physical. It seemed to go straight through the small of my back into my ideas, without involving my thoughts. If it really did this, it would have acted in accordance with Carpenter's yogified mysticism, and it would prove that at that precise moment I had conceived." In a flash, Forster had been given the entire story for his gay novel. One smack on the arse and a seminal novel was born.

As I sit here now I'm realizing that Forster had the same Kundalini Shaktipat experience I had a few nights ago. The Goddess Shakti is the same force who awakened Forster's creative energy, with that fiery serpent coiling up from the base of the spine to the crown of the head. Forster had not written *Maurice* for civilization's approval—and he certainly didn't write it to please a publisher. In fact, he assumed it would be unpublishable. Yet, to find his true voice, to wrestle with his demons, to create his *Maurice*, Forster too had to go to the wilderness.

Telepathy must be real. Ben hasn't disturbed me in over a week, and now, just as I'm thinking to myself, God, I wish he'd come down here. I need him to fetch me the combination to the safety box—lo and behold, here he is, knocking at the study door.

"Kip . . . Kip! I think we should probably talk. Kip? Are you still alive in there?"

I get up from the floor and dust off the knees of my tracksuit. I've been kneeling in front of the safety box, spinning the wheels around, trying to guess the combination. I make my way over to the study door and stand there examining my handiwork—the seven planks of two-by-fours I've nailed up across the doorframe—trying to figure out how to pry them loose when I finally get the hammer out of the safe again. Perhaps it would be better to use the hammer's blunt end and bang the lumber into smithereens?

"*Kip!*"

I need him for practical purposes. I may as well answer. "Yeah, Ben. What is it?"

"I think we should talk, Kip. I think I rushed into the decision about us."

Last week, despite my hurt and defensive stance, I would have been desperate to make up, but now I'm not sure. I've been trying to focus on other things. Trying to stop those avalanches of memory from falling upon me. I haven't succeeded, I know, but I have to be alone with myself. Away from Ben. And, yes, maybe I've been selfish—but I need to be now, don't I?

"Kip—what's going on? Are you okay in there?"

"Yep. Hey, Ben—" I hesitate for a moment and then decide I have to say it. I tell him I need him to get the combination for the safety box for me. I remind him that the instructions are in my bedside table drawer.

"What? You finished your novel already?"

"No. But I have to leave, Ben."

"Leave? Don't you have to finish the novel? You've got less than two weeks! Kip, look, you don't have to go anywhere. This is your home too. And I feel terrible, but I've got something to tell you. I was washing the dishes and I took off my ring and—and now I can't find it. And I know you'd think I'd taken it off because I wanted to break up, but honestly, it wasn't that. And I remembered our promise, Kip. And it made me realize, we can't just break up like this. I was angry and hurt that you'd—anyway, I can't find the damn ring. I feel terrible . . . Kip? Kip?"

It's just hitting me now, what exactly I'm walking away from if I leave Ben. All that I've got with him—his honesty, his care, the way we can talk about anything, the way I often feel seen by him, and it's with me he felt the body electric. Who else would I ever have the hope of experiencing that with? In theory, it's a lot easier to leave him behind, but in practice—I'm not sure. But I have to leave, don't I? I look down at my left hand, at the gold ring on my finger. What should I do? I tug at it, but it's so tight it barely slides to my first knuckle. I will have to pull hard to get this ring off. I will have to yank, and squeeze, and wrench. It's not going to be easy.

The Lore of the Rings

Although we never got legally married, Ben and I had our own private commitment ceremony. Like every good gay person, we fought and rallied for the right to be legally married. But, for ourselves, we thought the institution too bourgeois, mainstream, and therefore, essentially un-gay. It was my idea to avoid the courts and, instead, take *saptapadi*, the Hindu "Seven Steps" wedding vows, making the seven vows with each circle around a small fire and then exchanging rings.

Ben went along with the idea and even began to get excited about it. Since we aren't far from Prospect Park, we decided we'd have our ceremony there, by the boating pond, at sunrise.

On the big day we ended up oversleeping (unconscious resistance, Ben has noted). We finally got our gear together—copper fire bowl with wood chips for burning, wedding rings, our personalized written vows—and we rushed to the park while it was still early, at 7:00 a.m. But when we got there, the park was more crowded than ever. We soon realized it was the day of the Brooklyn Half Marathon—the largest half marathon in the entire United States.

Frazzled but undeterred, we went through with our plans anyway. Crowds leered as we circled around our illegal fire, constantly on the lookout for the police while making our vows. People muttered odd or curious comments—"What are they doing? Are they Hari Krishnas?"—and some sneered as we held hands, exchanged rings, and then kissed. And when we agreed to wear the rings, both with tears in our eyes, Ben and I swore we'd only take the rings off if we were certain our circle of trust had been irreversibly, irreparably broken.

The rings made me think about Forster and Mohammed. In 1922, a month after Mohammed died of tuberculosis, when Forster was already back in England, he received a ring in an envelope mailed from Egypt. It was Mohammed's dying gift, Gamila's letter said. Morgan wore the ring for the rest of his life, until his death in 1970. For fifty years, Morgan treasured Mohammed's ring.

When I was at the Forster archives in Cambridge, I was stunned when I was allowed to request the envelope with Forster's actual belongings. As I emptied the envelope's contents onto the table, out fell a narrow gold ring. As if by magic, it circled on its own, like a shiny little Hula-Hoop on the wooden desk before me, before finally landing flat. I picked it up and, after making sure no one's eyes were on me, I slid it onto my own ring finger. It fit perfectly. My heart fluttered. I know it's silly, but it felt as if, somehow, I was instantly joined to Forster and Mohammed, part of their sacred union.

At that moment, I knew Ben and I had to get rings when we married. There is something ancient and powerful in the binding force of the ring. Mohammed knew it. Forster knew it. Ben and I knew it.

When I open my eyes, I hear her approaching, the flapping sound of her giant wings. Not the goddess, I pray (really pray), not now! I must have fallen asleep, giving her the opportunity to slip in when I was unconscious. The sound of her wings vibrates throughout the room, makes my entire body shudder. I can't even hear my own breathing. Am I even breathing? I must be, but it feels as if my lungs are slaves to her bidding, rising and falling with her rhythms. And then I feel it again: the rising, the stiffening of an erection.

"Come," she says, with that sultry voice of hers.

"What? Where?" I hold on to the desk; maybe it will ground me in reality. "What do you want from me? What am I supposed to do?"

"Come."

"I don't understand. What do you mean?"

She doesn't answer, just the beating sound of giant wings. Why does a goddess have wings, anyway? I ask myself.

"Sometimes I am transported here on Hamsa, the massive swan, or on Garuda, my giant sea eagle," she says.

Holy fuck! She answered me. Now she's reading my mind too.

I wish someone would save me from this. Where in the hell is Ben, anyway? Did he forget me down here? Did he fall asleep? Change his mind? I thought he was coming back immediately with the combination to the safety box. I need to get out of here now, to get the hammer and bang my way free again. But I'd have to take the gun too, wouldn't I? Ben would freak out if he knew I even owned a gun. I definitely can't leave it behind for him to find. Yes, when Ben comes back with the combination, I'll take the gun out, grab Sophia, and get the hell out of here. I'm losing my mind down here.

Maybe if I walk around, busy myself, the goddess will go away and leave me in peace. I go over to the little window. There's a full moon up there; snow is shimmering on the ground. The snowman is looking down on me again. Is he smug or am I just imagining it? "I'm free and you're still locked away," he seems to taunt. Can't I go anywhere without someone or something imposing itself on me?

I think I hear a rustle at the door; a shadow appears underneath it. Is it Ben, finally back with the combination? Is he slipping it under the door for me? I start towards the door, but I'm stopped.

"Soon you will be with me!" her voice resounds. "Come!"

I spin around, look everywhere, but all I see now is a blinding whiteness. I can't escape her; I have to submit to this madness. What else can I do?

"I am the beginning and the end. The Great Goddess. *Tatha-agata: I am the one thus come.*"

And then with an electric surge rising from my erect penis and coiling up my spine, convulsing my entire body, a thought occurs to me: Yes! I can join this goddess. I too can be the beginning and the end! I too can be everything!

Isn't this what I first experienced in my mystical epiphany from years ago? A flash of the ecstatic truth I've been chasing. And my nagging question from the Vedas: Who am I, really? I've asked myself over and over again. Well, the Great Goddess is answering me now: I am all of this!

But if I am everything, am I also the forces enslaving myself?

I've blamed Ben for holding me back, for imposing a domestication on me and my art. I even felt I had to lock myself in here, to keep away from his hindering forces. But I now realize what my therapist has been trying to tell me for years: I have only used my relationship with Ben to keep me protected and safe. I'm the one avoiding my unruly instincts, my dangerous desires. Ben is not the limiting, civilizing force. I am.

But I'm actually terrified of the wilderness. I like indoor things, civilized things. I like dining at nice restaurants, room service in hotels, with those stainless-steel, domed cloches over the plates. I like people who say please and thank you. I like box seats at the opera. On the other hand, I am drawn to the frontier, I admit, despite my love for civilized things.

Even coming to America was a move towards the wilderness—the land of the rugged individual, of the ever-looming frontier—but as you see, I've never let myself go all the way. I've always allowed something to hold me back. I used sex in the ashram to distract me from my true spiritual goal. And then I continued using it to avoid real connections. With the skill of a master illusionist, I've made one thing appear as another while making the real thing disappear. No wonder Ben said I never really let go when we made love.

And something else I've never fully admitted, not even to myself: I was too afraid to finish the novel I'd begun in my MFA program, *The Nowherians*. Doing that meant going to a place I feared most of all—my true self. And so, instead, I wrote a new novel from E. M. Forster's cool perspective. I hid behind his voice, or else faked it, as if I were a ventriloquist's dummy. And all of this to avoid going to my own wilderness.

Just as I'm feeling overwhelmed by the goddess's call, closing my eyes as I brace myself, with my back pressed against the brick wall behind me—my damn erection growing harder still—I suddenly hear Mohammed's voice too.

It's as if his warm lips are pressed against my ear; and this time I know I have no choice but to obey. "This is not your house, my friend. Not our Home of Misery. Further we must go. Out there, where there is space enough. Sing the body electric. Go, my Possibility. Go to the wilderness!"

PART 3

The Nowherian

I'm in the back seat of a yellow taxicab on the Brooklyn–Queens Expressway speeding into the night. Out the window the sky is black, starless. But on the horizon, to the left, it seems the stars have fallen to earth, collected themselves into spectacular columns, and are now aspiring homeward again, up to the skies. The Empire State Building, the Chrysler Building, and hundreds more—all twinkling there across the East River. The young driver—a Sikh, I assume, from the blue *dastar* on his head—is driving more recklessly than I'd like, swerving and dashing towards JFK. Yes, I'm about to take a flight, a voyage to—well, to Nowhere.

I'm also practically inhaling an entire large take-away pepperoni pizza. The flat cardboard box is still warm on my lap. The driver was kind enough to stop at Not Ray's Pizza, a couple of blocks from the house, while I got the pizza to go. Eleven days of only saltines and I was practically hallucinating about pizza. Along with the tasty delicacy, I have everything I've brought along with me here on the back seat: my navy-blue backpack, in which I've stored my passport, green card, iPhone, Sophia, some pens, and my black Moleskine notebook. And in my red carry-on suitcase there's a change of clothes and a few toiletries. I'll have to check that luggage, of course, due to the gun I've packed in it.

Don't worry, the revolver is unloaded, secured in its container, and it's legally registered too, so I'm allowed to travel with it. I'm required to declare it at Customs and Border Control, but with my green card status, I prefer to avoid questions. I'll say nothing and pray the gun slips unnoticed past the X-rays—I've heard it happens on the odd occasion, from a reliable source: a gay cop I once knew. It's a big risk, sure, but since I'm an outlaw, I may as well act like one. Anyway, there can't be a law against taking a gun Nowhere, can there?

Speaking of going Nowhere, the Caribbean-English word "Nowherian" has always best described my status in the world. I've never really felt at home anywhere—not even where I was born or where I grew up. In the UK I was British, but not really. I can't tell you how many times my neighbors in Weybridge—people who'd known me since I was a kid—asked me where I was *really* from. And I couldn't answer that I'm really Caribbean. Visiting Nassau once a year for two weeks at Christmastime has only made it clear I'm not a true islander. My bare feet are too soft to stand the hot sand on the beaches; my palate too delicate to tolerate the spicy goat peppers in the stew fish and the conch salad; and my accent and my inquiring style is, to my Caribbean relatives, laughably foreign and "white." Except for the rare spaces where almost everyone is homeless—in airports and hotels and in transit—I don't belong anywhere. Only in the liminal spaces am I finally at home.

I should tell you how I got out of my self-made basement trap, but I'm afraid there isn't much to say. The disappointing truth is that I'm completely fuzzy on the details.

It all feels like a dream now, the past eleven days. I only know after I asked Ben to fetch me the combination for the safety box from my bedside table, I fell asleep; and Shakti woke me up; and then I heard the voice of Mohammed telling me to go to the wilderness. But after that, I must have lapsed into a state of sheer exhaustion or become dizzy and faint. It's possible I was halfway unconscious from hunger and low blood sugar. I can't say what it was. But then again, perhaps it wasn't exhaustion or blood sugar at all. Maybe it was a state of great exaltation, and I was transported by the spiritual forces of the goddess. Anyway, I can't remember getting the combination for the safe or getting the gun, prying loose the two-by-fours, or packing up my things, or what Ben and I said to each other before I left. I can't even remember hailing this taxicab. I must have been in a very strange, altered state. Obviously, all of the above actually happened—banging my way out, packing my bags, and leaving Ben—because here I am, in a taxi with my bags packed, my gun in my suitcase, and eating an entire large pizza on my way to the airport.

The taxi driver slides open the clear Plexiglass partition and turns his head to address me. "What airline are you taking, brother?" He has a deep-voiced Indian lilt.

The photo ID, facing me from its plexiglass frame, is clearly of an older turbaned man with a long white beard. My driver cannot be this Vindi Singh, as the ID says. My driver is seemingly in his mid-twenties, with a projecting underbite and quick, slightly bulging eyes. "Which terminal am I taking you to?"

I have no idea where I'm going. I'm only now vaguely remembering my decision process, ruling out taking a bus to upstate New York—I'd briefly thought about escaping to the Catskill Mountains—or taking an Amtrak train bound west, heading for the Southwestern desert wilderness of America. But while I assume I'll find a flight to somewhere tonight, I honestly don't know where to go.

"Well," I say to my driver, "I know this may sound kind of crazy, but I actually haven't decided where I'm going. I need to go where there's wilderness, no civilization. Lots of empty space. Sounds crazy, I'm sure."

I see him eyeing me through the rearview mirror, his large

eyes widening even more. His white teeth flash from his black, shiny, well-groomed beard. "Oh, I get it." He nods his head. "I get it. You are needing a real escape. You are needing a complete unplug. I get it, my brother! I get it!" And he laughs.

"Yeah, that's it! A real unplug." I smile at him through the rear-view mirror.

"So. Let me ask you something," he says. "May I?" He peers intently through the mirror, as if we are face-to-face. He waits for me to catch his gaze. "May I?" he repeats.

"Sure," I say.

"Okay. Very good. This is my question: Have you just committed a crime? I am not judging. It is just a question. Because if you are fleeing the law, I'm telling you, there are some places better to escape to than others."

At first I'm confused, then I'm insulted. Is it because I'm Black he assumes I'm a criminal? "What makes you say that? Do I look like a criminal? And what's your name, anyway?" I examine the driver ID again. "This isn't your photo. Are you driving illegally?"

"No. This is my uncle's car. I am Rajandeep. Call me Rajan. Don't worry, I am driving legally. And there are no judgments in my question, brother."

"Well, Rajan, why are you calling me 'brother'? Is that what you call Black people?

"Black people? What Black people?"

"I think we should probably end this conversation, Rajan. I'll let you know my terminal when we get to the airport."

After a few minutes of riding in silence, and Rajan now avoiding looking at me through the rearview mirror, I cannot leave the issue alone: "Rajandeep, why did you ask if I was a criminal? Do I look like a criminal to you?"

"If you do not mind, sir—"

"Kip. Call me Kip."

"If you do not mind, Kip, may I answer you with a question?" He raises his thick eyebrows and waits pointedly, with those bulging eyes, for my approval. I nod. "Okay. Very well," he says. "Am I looking like a professor of geological engineering to you?"

"What?" I think I've not heard him right.

"I'll repeat: Am I looking like a professor of geological engineering to you? Or, rather, a geological engineer who also writes a blog on Indian culture and Russian literature? *From Moscow to Mumbai: The Whole World in a Nutshell.* Did you know that Gandhi and Tolstoy had a great friendship and even influenced each other's work? I am not a Hindu like Gandhi, but I'm Indian, nonetheless. But this is all beside the point. I am not judging what you look like, Kip. I am only asking you: Did you just now commit a crime?"

"No, of course not." Even though I feign indignance, I can't help but feel ashamed at my own prejudices: I had greatly underestimated this taxi driver. "No, I didn't just commit a crime."

"Good. Because, Kip, you know, there's nowhere to escape your own sins. But, of course, if you were to escape being caught for a crime, I would recommend Cancún as a good choice." He gives a quick laugh. "But seriously, no wilderness can protect you from your own demons. Look at what happened to Raskolnikov in *Crime and Punishment.* Are you familiar with that novel by Fyodor Dostoyevsky, Kip?"

"Oh yes." I laugh at the incredible turn of this conversation. "I've read it more times than you'd believe, Rajan."

"Good. Well, since you are wanting a Tolstoian existence, Kip, and to be alone in the nature, far from the civilized, then I may very well help you."

"Help me?"

"As a geological engineer, I know a thing or two about this planet, Kip. Although my thesis at university was on redirecting groundwater in Nepal, I have studied the entire planet's forestry too. I can tell you, for example, that there are considered to be only ten great wildernesses left on the planet. The only one in North America is in British Columbia, the Great Bear Rainforest. But it's such a cold time of year to go way up there, Kip. Then there's one in Bolivia and two in Australia, where it's much warmer—it is even summertime down under now. That might be a good choice, Kip. And then there are two great wildernesses in the UK: Knoydart Peninsula in Scotland and the Scilly Isles. And also, other great wildernesses are awaiting you in Namibia, and Nepal, and Jordan, and western Sweden. There are still great spaces left on this planet."

"Wow," I say, revealing my complete ineptitude to reply even vaguely intelligently. This young taxi driver/geological engineer/literary blogger is leaps and bounds more knowledgeable about his field than I'll probably ever be about anything in my entire lifetime. I feel like a schmuck, as Ben would say.

"So, Kip, where to?"

"I don't know. Where would you go if you wanted to find the perfect wilderness, somewhere far away enough to find your own true voice?"

Rajandeep laughs, and then I laugh too, even though I'm sensing I'm the butt of his joke. "Where would *I* go?" he repeats. "Well, Kip, I would go to New York City! What better wilderness than this concrete jungle right here! Why do you think I'm here? Once I get my qualifications validated here, I'll be applying for real work again, in my profession; but meanwhile, I'm driving a taxi and finding my true voice. Right here in the wilderness of New York City.

Along with the demons and wild natives, there are also freedoms here—things I couldn't find or do in India. Shouldn't a person do what he feels with his own body? What do you think of that?" He winks at me through the rearview mirror. Is he flirting? "But if you must leave New York, Kip, I say go back to England. You are British, right? We colonials can hear it in each other's speech. I say go back to England! Find your wilderness there. Just a gut feeling. In my thirty-seven years of life, Kip, I have learned to trust my instincts."

I'm amazed he is my same age. He looks much younger and yet seems so much wiser.

"So, Kip." Rajan's eyes penetrate through the rearview mirror again, and then he narrows them with a little twinkle. "I will take you to terminal seven. British Airways. There's a flight leaving for London at eleven thirty-five p.m. Kip, you are arriving just on time!"

Home again in my Nowhere zone, in JFK at the boarding gate. I bought a one-way ticket to London Heathrow with my credit card and I'm waiting to board my flight. My passport and boarding pass ready in my Levi's front pocket. No sign of an issue with my gun in the checked luggage. Everything's going smoothly. I close my eyes and sigh—I finally feel I fit in somewhere. Sitting next to me is a Pakistani family with more carry-ons than I imagine the flight attendants will permit. On the other side of me, a young, straight white couple are in joggers with inflatable pillows already around their necks. Standing close by are several African men—Nigerian, I think—in native dress with hard brown briefcases, talking loudly with each other. A Japanese father and his teenage son sit across from me, silently glued to their phones, ignoring each other. I wonder if they've had a row. And next to them, is an interracial gay couple, Black and white, in their forties, it seems—Londoners from the sound of them. They're both in tight, pectoral-gripping jumpers and wearing baseball caps, New York souvenirs, I'm guessing. One has a Yankees cap, the other a cap with an image of a rooster with "Cock" printed in red. But happily, I don't stand out in this crowd. I actually fit in somehow. And more than that, I imagine I'm the only one who truly feels at home here.

A woman's voice comes over the PA system: there's been a delay; now we'll be one more hour before boarding, she says.

Maybe it's the adrenaline of taking this big step, but I'm not thrown by the news. In fact, I feel full of energy. I take out Sophia and flip her open. I'll use this time to work on the novel.

The Drunken Officer

Time is racing; each day we are closer to the final day. I know you'll think it morbid of me to say, my friend, but death is never far away. It's like the stink of your own underarm—inevitably with you, and stronger by the end of the day. I never felt this truth so much as when my mother died suddenly two years ago. She was not a perfect woman; she was not always kind to me. And although Father had shown her mercy, probably to save both their reputations—there was, after all, no real proof I was not his son— Mother still took out her guilt on me, the dark stain on her virtue. She denied me attention and love; she hated my black skin. Yet for some reason, when she died I felt a part of me also died. Her rejection had defined me, spurred me on. Winning her love was always a possibility. With her gone, there was a gaping, black hole in my heart; and it ached.

The week after her death, when I came back to Alex from Mansourah, I visited Morgan at his boardinghouse. We held each other as if both of us were drowning. No one in my family had comforted me like that. They did not understand me. I was too Westernized for an Egyptian, they said. Too Black, too proud, too abused for them to understand my pain. But Morgan could understand my strange aching and how the loss of Mother's love—the possibility of her love, really—left me homeless and nowhere. He too had no one from his home who understood him, he said. Neither his mother or his friends, even the most free-spirited of them, would have ever understood him loving a man like me, he said. We both belonged nowhere, really. Except when with each other, perhaps. And so, we clung dearly.

We were interrupted by a knock at his door. It was Morgan's landlady, Irene, an old Italian lady. She had heard crying and was worried Morgan was unwell, she said. She stood at the doorway like a matronly warden in her long black widow's dress.

She gasped suddenly upon seeing me and told Morgan that Blacks were not allowed on the premises. Morgan stood motion-less, speechless. By the time he composed himself to challenge Irene, it was too late. I had picked up my fez from the side table and marched past the old lady in the doorway, squeezing to get past her girth. She stank of garlic and alcohol. I lengthened my neck, held my head high, and pretended not to be fazed. But inside I was shaking; my gut clenched like a fist. I wanted to strangle the old bitch.

As I walked down the stairs, I heard Morgan arguing with her, begging Irene to rethink her rules. I didn't slow down when he called for me to wait. I slammed the front door and hurried all the way to the Sidi Gaber station.

The Bacos tram bound for the terminus station was crowded with Europeans heading to the Corniche for a sunset promenade along the seaside. I was the only Egyptian on the tram, and I'm sure they expected me to stand and give seats to the whites. Morgan's friend Robin Furness, with his governmental connections, had now gotten me my conductor job back. So I stood because it was right of me as a city employee, that is all. As the tram was about to pull off, there were some stragglers near the footboard where I stood, four sloppy British soldiers, a rowdy crew, hanging half off the tram.

I whistled to get their attention. I addressed one of these British officers, who was plump and red-nosed and half cross-eyed. Please, sir, I said, get on or off the tram. You are holding it up for everyone. On or off, please!

Are you talking to me, coolie? he said.

I took in a deep breath to calm myself and could not avoid inhaling a blast of alcohol from his breath. I said, Please, sir, on or off. The tram must pull out. I repeated, Now, sir! On or off!

The red-nosed officer said, How dare you take that tone with me, coolie! Do you have any idea who I am? Do you know who you are addressing? I—I am a *se-se-sergeant major* in the B-B-British armed f-f-forces.

The officer had now raised his voice so much that a hush fell over the passengers.

A young French boy of about seven or eight, wearing a white beret, stood up on his seat and pointed at the sergeant major: *Maman, regarde le gros bouffon au nez rouge!*

A few chuckles came from the Francophones on board.

One Englishwoman turned to another and asked what the little boy had said.

A silver-haired Englishman leaned on his cane with a sardonic air, saying the boy told his mother to look at the big clown with the red nose!

Raucous laughter erupted from the passengers. I laughed too. The French boy, with mouth and eyes wide open, looked about at the adults, seeming delighted to have incited such uproar. It seemed an entire tram of Europeans was joining me, laughing at the stupid British officer. I felt, perhaps, not all whites are so bad.

But when I looked back at the drunk officer, he was pulling his truncheon from its halter, and before I knew it, he struck me on the shoulder. I fell from the footboard to the pavement. I looked up to see the tram pulling off, a crowd of white faces staring from the back, still laughing. The officer fell too; and then he scrambled up to bludgeon me with his club—my arms, thighs, shoulders, ribs. Each blow pounded breath from my body in powerful bursts. I felt like my flesh was on fire. He bashed my skull, and I went numb. But it was only when he held his boots on my neck, pressing down so that I could no longer breathe, that I knew, for certain, I would die. With my eyes swollen shut, I gave up fighting. I saw my mother's face; I saw Morgan's too.

I do not remember how I got home. Ahmed was there, and later, he told me five young men—Berber water-sellers who had found me after the assault—had carried me home. I must have told them where I lived, somehow. I was unable to walk for two weeks. My eyes were swollen shut for days. My face was bruised black and purple. The scars from where the club split my skin still mark my back and legs today. Here, over my eyebrow, is a scar that looks like a scythe.

Ahmed did not need to say anything after that. He knew I finally heard the message he had been delivering all along: The British are dangerous. Stay away from them.

You, my Possibility, will not know what it is to be pulverized by an officer of the law; surely one hundred years from now you will hear my story and wonder how such a thing could happen. You can understand, though, why I traded the dried beans for the gun from that Australian officer. It is not safe to be Black in Egypt. If only I had shot the British officers who arrested me, I would be free now. We outlaws need all the weapons we can get our hands on. How else can we survive? *Alhamdulillah*, thank God, you will be free in the life to come. Safe and far away from them. Do not hesitate. Go, my Possibility. Go now to the wilderness.

One more thing, my friend; you may ask why I am still with Morgan. After such a beating, why have I not cut all ties with any Britisher? I will tell you: it is because I am cleverer than my brother, Ahmed—may he rest in peace. I, Mohammed El Adl, will not be humiliated. I will make the British know humiliation. Even in death, I assure you. But I will not subject Morgan to this fate, if he is true to me. And this I will find out very soon. This is my great secret, just for you, dear friend—I have decided to put Morgan to the final test.

The Sweet Sacrifice

I suppose I should explain the gun.

About twelve years ago, in the second year of my MFA program, when I'd moved out of the Pan-African House and into my own railroad flat in the East Village, at about three o'clock on a Saturday morning, I was walking home from the Cock—probably the least imaginative and yet most succinct name for a raunchy gay bar ever. It was September and still hot and humid. The thick air clung to my skin, glomming onto every part of me, it seemed, like a jilted lover; and that dark, clammy, clinging accentuated an awareness of my body, its sexual sway. I was wearing a black tank top and my favorite skinny-fit blue-jean shorts. I was a little tipsy too, but not drunk, crossing Sixth Street on First Avenue, when, out of nowhere, a cop stopped me and asked if I was aware I was jaywalking.

My mouth instantly dried up. I apologized in an embarrassing show of deference, knowing I had to swallow my pride and go into Black man survival mode. For a second, I was hopeful this cop may be Latino, but then I saw his name badge: *Tsvousis*. Greek. Great! Greeks can be as racist as any whites on the planet—often the closer to Africa and the swarthier the complexion, the more racist "white" people get. Horrifying images of Emmett Till, Rodney King, and Amadou Diallo flashed before my eyes. (This was way before Tamir

Rice, Eric Garner, Philando Castile, Andy Lopez, Treyvon Martin, and so many more than I can't even bear to go on naming them).

Then Officer Tsvousis laughed. "Don't worry about it," he said, in what sounded like a parody of a New York City accent. "Jeez, I'm only fucking with you! I'm not even on duty. I'm Gus, by the way." He put a hand on my shoulder, gave it a manly squeeze. "What's your name?" I told him, and he asked if I minded if he walked with me. He was about my height, with thick, dark eyebrows and an olive complexion. Dark stubble shaded his face. It took me several blocks to realize what was happening. This NYPD officer, Gus Tsvousis, was actually coming on to me.

He came over to my place on Avenue A. We immediately started kissing, rapidly undressing, never questioning our mutual intention to hook up. But my heart stopped when he thumped his gun, with its leather holster, on the nightstand. The table's spindly legs shook as if in sync with my own. I insisted he prove the trigger was locked. He laughed, but I was dead serious.

After having so quickly undressed and made out, it seemed we were now shy to make the next big move. We sat on my bed in our underwear—me in my white briefs, Gus in red plaid boxers. I turned on some music from my clock radio: WBLS's Quiet Storm. Barry White softly crooned and growled. I went to the fridge and got us beers, hoping to set the mood, loosen us up. But as we sucked on our bottles of Corona, Gus noticed I was still fidgety.

He asked if I wanted him to leave.

I had to be honest. "No," I said. "It's the gun." I couldn't get it out of my mind. I kept imagining him yanking it out of the holster and shooting me once I was naked and vulnerable; or else, some-how, it would accidentally go off as we knocked into it while having sex, inadvertently killing one or both of us. I'd never seen guns routinely anywhere in my life. In England, I explained to Gus, not even policemen carried guns.

"You gotta be fuckin' with me!" Gus made a big smile without opening his lips, still chugging at his beer. "How is it possible to maintain law and order without a gun?"

"Well, I think it's easier because there are no guns," I said. "There is clearly only one thing you can do with a gun: kill easily and quickly, right? So, to prevent the plethora of gun murders in America, the simplest solution is to get rid of the weapons that allow these murders."

Gus looked at me puzzled for a few seconds, cocked his head, and made a funny pout. "Plethora? What's that mean?"

"Sorry, I'm just being daft." For some reason his question made me feel ridiculous and, ironically, even a bit stupid. "But do you see what I mean, about guns being unnecessary?"

Gus shrugged his shoulders and made that funny pout again.

I asked if he'd seen Michael Moore's *Bowling for Columbine*.

He said, "More bowling for who?"

I explained it was a documentary film in which Moore deftly dissects American gun violence, linking it directly to racism, to white people's guilt and their fear of retribution from Blacks. Gus patiently listened to me with a bemused smile that didn't seem as condescending as it was pitying of me.

"Look, Kip," he finally said. "I don't wanna get into all this stuff. I just wanna get to know you, you know what I mean? I'm a simple guy. Yeah, I studied criminology at John Jay College, but I don't know much about culture and stuff. Maybe that turns you off?" he said. "But I think you're cute. And I just wanna have a nice time. How about that? And, by the way, do you think I could"—he lifted his empty beer bottle and dangled it by the neck like a pendulum—"think I could get another brewski, bro?" He smiled devilishly; he had a deep dimple in one cheek.

God, he was sexy.

"Sure, Gus, of course." I leaned over and kissed him. I felt guilty for messing up the romantic vibe with my discourse about guns. Come on, Kip, I said to myself, how often are you going to get a good-looking NYPD officer naked in your bed. Just shut up and get busy!

But then it was driving me crazy not knowing what he actually thought about my disquisition on guns and American racism. As hot as he was, I couldn't bring myself to lie in bed with a serious racist. Did it matter if he was inadvertently a racist, if his heart, or dick, was in the right place? If he wanted *me*, did it matter? But as I leaned over to kiss him—his lips were fleshy and pouty and parted, waiting for me—I heard myself say, "So, what do you think about what I said? About guns and racism?"

He looked down at his bare feet, his big hairy toes, and brushed them over the rough wooden slats of my bedroom floor. "Look. I think you seem like a good guy," he said. "And I think you believe in a world where violence should not be necessary. But that's kinda naive. Let me tell you how the world is, Kip."

He went on to say, "There is only one way to sustain life, and that is to kill. We have to consume life to keep living. None of us would survive without killing something. Life requires a sacrifice. For one thing to live, another must die. That's just the facts of life. Think about it: life itself would not have been possible without the Big Bang. A giant violent big bang is why we're all here! Every single act in the universe has both good and evil results, Kip."

"Okay," I said, still trying to figure out the thrust of his argument.

"And the thing is, we humans have tools that set us apart from all the other species. Look." Gus put his bottle on the floor, folded his arms over his hairy chest, and turned to me with furrowed brows. "From rocks, to stone spears, to steel knives, then arrows, right down to guns, this is how we have survived as a species. We use weapons to shape the world we want, to protect us and prolong our lives. You think I go to work every day hoping to shoot and kill someone? Come on! That ain't the way it is. I took an oath to protect and serve—that's what I do. And to protect life, you need a weapon. How else can we be safe? And besides, I don't wanna get philosophical or nothin'"—Gus unfolded his arms and gestured as if holding a gun now—"but when you have the power to take life, with a single gunshot, it makes you realize how close death is at all times." He moved his fingers "gun" to his side. "Right here on my hip, every day, death is *here*—*this* close. And that makes me treasure life. I know you want to believe all violence is bad, but nothing is only good or bad, Kip. And there is no life without violence."

Gus took me aback with his plainspoken eloquence. And while I considered rebutting his arguments—I thought *he* was naive not to acknowledge the extent that institutional racism allows unaccountability for cops and the fact that policemen seem to shoot Black men with less concern for their lives than they show when encountering a black bear (with a bear, at least, they follow protocol and use tranquilizer bullets)—I didn't say anything. I just swallowed my ire and leaned over and kissed Gus passionately, as if I were consuming him alive.

And Gus was right about some things: every act does have both good and bad in it. Being a writer, I've always wrestled with the fact that "The Snow Man," a poem so sublime it attains spiritual perfection, was written by Wallace Stevens, who called the Pulitzer Prize–winning Black poet Gwendolyn Brooks "that coon." And also, the exalted, spiritual poetic genius T. S. Eliot was a horrible anti-Semite. So many paradoxes. I knew that my discomfort about Gus's blindness to racism would have to be sacrificed for our eros to arise. As he said, for one thing to live, another must die. And, as I was kissing him, feeling a hot, ravenous appetite rising in me, Roberta Flack's sultry voice came over the airwaves of WBLS, singing "Killing Me Softly," as if affirming some necessary, sweet violence I was required to embrace.

A Gun Because He Loved Me

A couple of months later, when the novelty of dating a cop began to lose its charm, I realized Gus was deadly boring. His plainspoken eloquence had impressed me on the first night, but I soon discovered he had nothing much else to say. Not only did he never read anything, not even a tabloid newspaper, nor did he like any of the same movies I did, or have any hobbies to speak of, but he also never ate anything except Greek diner food, which he insisted I also eat whenever we dined out. The moussaka was good but got tiring after the umpteenth time. But most of all, Gus was extremely boring in bed. He just sort of lay there, silently quivering, like a lamb ready to be sacrificed. And yet, although he seemed passive to the extreme, he always managed to rouse himself enough to stop me from finally penetrating him. "No, no, no," he'd say, smiling slyly and wagging a finger. "Gotta save that for our wedding day, babe."

The first time he said it, I laughed. But I soon realized he was serious. Gus was comporting himself like a good Greek girl, saving himself for the nuptials.

He was a kind person, that was clear. He loved his family. But he wasn't out as gay to them, he said. They still expected him to spend Sunday dinners at home, where he'd often be subjected to meeting a nice Greek girl he was being set up with. He never complained about it. He even joked that one day he might take his parents up on one of these girls. He loved to tease me with this, warning me, "So, babe, you better treat me right, or else . . ." Gus—so sweet, so boring.

Just about two months into our dating, I was coming to the conclusion that Gus and I were not a great match. Being sweet was not enough. I needed someone who shared my interests and cultural references, who, at least, let me fuck him. But I had been unable to break the bad news to Gus. He was so damned good to me, and he was completely wrapped up in his fantasy of our lives when we would finally marry.

"So, babe," he said one evening at the Waverly Diner while we waited for our "usual"—two Greek salads and moussakas—"I really see a future for us, you know. You're my guy, Kip. I know it." He reached over and held my hands over the table. In Queens, Gus was totally closeted, but once he crossed the river to Manhattan, he was a liberated gay man. "I can see us together forever. You know what I mean? We could buy a house out on Long Island, and maybe adopt kids. You like kids, right? I bet you'd be able to teach our kids all the cultured stuff you teach me—about books and movies. Our kids wouldn't be numbskulls like me!" Gus laughed and I laughed too. But while I laughed, I was thinking, How the fuck am I ever going to get out of this? And when I looked in his big beautiful brown eyes, with those eyelashes, I almost wanted to cry at the thought of disappointing him.

"And, babe, I see more," he continued (yes, there was more!). "With our own family, we could take summer holidays to the Grand Canyon and Niagara Falls, have barbecues in the backyard. You could stay at home and write the great American novel, while I provide for us. And I'm going places in the force, Kip. Did I tell you my uncle Nick went to high school with the commissioner? Took me out to lunch with him a few months back. Can you believe it? Me, having freakin' lunch at Peter Luger's with the commissioner! And he says he's keeping an eye on me for promotion. The commissioner himself! I'm going places, babe. And I'll take care of you. You won't have to worry about a thing. I'll keep you safe."

Each day the fantasy of our perfect married future appeared to get more and more fleshed out until it began to seem almost inevitable, even to me.

Then, when it had been exactly three months of our dating, Gus called me from work and said he had a special gift for me, for our three-month, quarter-of-a-year anniversary. He couldn't get the day off from work, he said, so he had hidden a gift-wrapped box under my bed. He told me he'd stay on the line while I opened it; he wanted to share the moment.

I said I felt bad; it hadn't occurred to me to celebrate a three-month mark. I didn't have a gift for him. He said it wasn't a problem, it was just something he really wanted me to have.

While he held the line, I went to fetch the box under my bed. When I picked up the phone again, Gus was gone. But he hadn't hung up. I heard voices in the background, people yelling, panicky voices. Finally, a woman's voice said, in husky, rapid succession, *"Hello? Hello? Hello?"* I responded and asked what had happened, where was Gus? She asked who I was. Without thinking, I said, "I'm his partner." She was silent for a moment and then asked if I was Officer García. "No, I'm his boyfriend, I mean." She said I'd better come down to the precinct at once. By the time I got there, his body had already been taken away. He'd died instantly, holding the phone, waiting for me to fetch his surprise gift.

They never found out what killed Gus. Later, his sister told me that her paternal uncle had also died suddenly at the same age—a mysterious stroke or aneurysm.

Gus's biopsy was inconclusive. It was devasting to me. The reality of the unpredictability of life shook me to the core. For more than a year, every time a phone call was dropped, I'd panic that the person on the other end had suddenly died. But the worst part of it all was my guilt.

I realized how unfair I'd been to both Gus and myself. I had dismissed his love and dedication to me as not being enough. Where was I ever going to find someone to love me like that again? Just a week prior to his death, I'd had a terrible thought. I had said to myself, If he dies a sudden death, then I'd be spared having to break up with him. How stupid! I had been dreading having to break his heart so much, afraid to shatter his fantasies of our perfect life together, that I'd been cowardly enough to imagine him dead. And worse, that I might actually have felt some relief if he were gone! And now that he was dead, I was racked with guilt. I'd caused his death. I'd killed him with my evil thoughts!

When I got back to my apartment that horrendous day, I finally opened his gift. What he'd given me was the Glock 22 revolver. A compact little piece of machinery. Matte black steel, with a blunt, two-inch barrel. It had a smooth, drag-free, black rubber grip. And there were ten bullets in the box for the ten-round capacity: shiny, silver ammunition with brass tips, Golden Sabers. As I picked up the revolver and ran my fingers over the clean, cold weapon, I was surprised at how beautiful it was.

The even greater surprise was that, somehow, Gus had managed to get the gun fully licensed in my name. All the papers were there, with my full name and Social Security number; even my actual fingerprints were on file—all the requisites of a legal gun owner.

How the hell had he pulled that off? I wondered. I've often pondered how Gus managed to get my fingerprints when I wasn't aware. While I was sleeping, maybe? And even now I feel both impressed but also creeped out by the fact that he forged my signature. He must have pulled some serious strings to get that license. Later, I almost asked Gus's cop partner, Eddie García, if he knew anything about how Gus got my license. García was also gay, it turned out, and friendly with me afterwards. Once in a while he'd call to check on me. But then I figured if García hadn't been privy to the whole gun deal, that would only open a whole can of worms and tarnish Gus's name. I also seriously entertained the far-fetched idea that Gus had gone as high up as the police commissioner to make it happen—he did have the connections, after all.

Inside the Hallmark Happy Anniversary card with a red glitter heart on it, Gus had written a personalized note:

My Dearest Kip,

Surprise! Don't ask me how. Believe me, you don't want to know. ☺ *But. I just wanted to show you, babe, I'll do anything (I mean anything!) to make sure you're always safe! Even when I'm not there in person, I will always protect and serve you. Forever.*

Love, Gus

A gun, because he loved me.

As I approach my assigned seat inside the Nowhere vessel, I notice the passenger in the aisle seat is an older Black woman, probably in her seventies. She's wearing gold wire-framed bifocals. Her head is wrapped in a yellow and white scarf. Around her shoulders she has a white knit shawl that cannot hide her buxomness. Underneath it I get a glimpse of a slightly tacky tiger-print dress. Upon seeing her, my first association is of Aunt Jemima. Why does she have to wear that mammy-like scarf on her head? I ask myself. Instantly, I'm annoyed to be sitting next to her. Will people think we're related—that I'm *that* kind of Negro? Should I ask a flight attendant if I can switch to the empty seat in the row ahead of mine, next to the young blond woman with an infant? Would that be preferable? And then, like a punch to the gut, I'm hit with a nauseating wave of hot shame. Who in the hell am I? These are unforgivable thoughts. I squeeze past the older woman to take the window seat.

As I stow my backpack under the seat in front of me, she looks up from her copy of *The Economist* and smiles. I return the smile, holding back an uncontrollable urge to cry from utter disgrace. *The Economist*! Clearly this old woman is not the stereotype I had believed her to be.

I also now notice, upon closer inspection, the old woman's yellow scarf is, in fact, a Hermès. If worn by Gloria Swanson, I would have immediately thought it chic, not a mammy's rag. And I think to myself: What if this Black woman didn't read *The Economist* or wear Hermès? And what if she were poor and uneducated? Would I have continued to devalue and be ashamed of her? I cringe at the thought. Yes, I'm infected with White Supremacy. Internalized racism has taken hold in me like a cancer. Nothing could be worse than having your greatest enemy trapped inside your own consciousness—the cancer of Whiteness.

I smile at the old woman now, trying to convey a profound apology. The old lady's smile seems polite but does not invite conversation. She appears to be generally self-contained. I also detect a hint of Chanel No. 5. on her. My mother's favorite perfume. Then I notice she has a tiny scar cut through her left eyebrow, like a scythe. It's odd, I think—I have the exact same scar, only above my right eyebrow.

"Holiday trip?" I ask, cozying into my seat, pressing my head firmly into the headrest. I'm trying to be friendly now, warm, still trying to make up for my sins.

She smiles at my question but blankly. "Just going to a funeral," she says. Her voice is full and round, robust, and her accent sounds vaguely Southern. Alabama, maybe? I can't quite place it, but there's something very familiar about her sultry tone. "Just going to a funeral," she says again, as if resigned to a tedious chore.

"A funeral?" I say. "I'm so sorry."

"Sorry? No." She lifts her hefty chins, as if she's considering options, and then she looks down at her magazine again. "It's okay. I hated the bitch."

"Oh." I make a funny imploding face with my lips and cheeks. "All right, then."

"Yes." She gives a one-note laugh, a kind of exalted *humph*. Then, after a few seconds, she half whispers to me in her surprisingly smooth, seductive voice, with the tone of a late-night radio host, "You know, sugar, you sound just like that actor, Idris Elba."

I don't believe I speak very much like Idris Elba. But I don't correct her, I only smile back. "Thank you," I say.

Long Live Idris Elba

Thank God for Idris Elba! On so many levels, I rejoice in his existence. He must have been sent down from my Black, British, African—and yes, a bloke can dream—gay heaven! Before Idris Elba was widely known, I was an anomaly here in the States, labeled as a sophisticated, uppity Black boy. Like the Black students I'd encountered at Columbia, most Americans had no idea someone Black could sound like me. And since Americans still lived under the delusion that everything British was far more sophisticated than anything American, I gained, or rather suffered, as a result of this American delusion. I gained a strange sort of respect from whites. I wasn't seen as one of their homegrown niggers, but I suffered by being misunderstood by the Blacks, and was also not seen as *really* one of them. But when the character Stringer Bell appeared on the scene—the sizzling-hot drug dealer from the HBO series *The Wire*—and then when the actor who played him, Idris Elba, began to give TV interviews, America now had a new version of what a British voice could represent. And it wasn't the stuffy, intellectual snob. It was Idris Elba: sexy, dangerous, clever, powerful, alluring, and Black. *Definitely* Black.

The Wire had already aired by the time I was at Columbia—in fact, it was nearing its fifth season—but Idris Elba had not yet registered with American audiences as being a Brit. His character, Stringer Bell, was African American and Idris did a credible Baltimore accent. It would be several more years before the real British voice of the actor would be known. For me, it would have been nice for Americans to have heard that beautiful, sexy voice while I was still at Columbia.

Thanks to Idris Elba, however, now when Americans hear me speak, they at least have to pay attention. They can no longer assume what I am. I can actually see people looking at me more carefully, as if they're trying to figure me out: Uppity Nigger or Stringer Bell? And in that gap of time before the assumption is made, in that small window, it is now possible for me—actually who *I* am—to be seen. Idris Elba changed how I could be seen in America; his visibility suddenly made me visible too.

Last year, when I was alone in the kitchen one morning, waiting for the espresso pot to boil, flipping my way through amusingly mindless YouTube videos on my phone, I came across a clip of a Black boy about nine years old being interviewed after seeing the Marvel Comics film *Black Panther*. The boy said he had never seen a superhero who looked like him before—dark brown skin, kinky hair. "Now I know what white people feel like all the time," he said. "If I always felt like this, I'd love this country too!" It broke my heart. I knew what he meant. Abruptly, to my surprise, I broke down sobbing.

I remembered myself as a child, hiding in the closset, and the pain of never being truly seen—not even by my own parents. Apart from my parents' devastating reaction, I now ask myself, what made me feel so oppressed by their molding of me? It's normal for parents to shape a child, isn't it?

I first assumed it must have been because they somehow

detected I was gay, even before I knew it. My mother had already by then revealed her anxiety about my lack of manliness. "Kipling, don't walk with such short steps. Only girls walk like that." Or "Don't whine like a little girl, speak like a man!" But I don't think that was the main reason. I think it was because—just as the young me said in the poem—I felt they were not interested in raising a flesh-and-blood person, with all the necessary flaws of being human. They needed to produce a figure of perfection, as invulnerable as a statue. And they could not see how dehumanizing it was for me, because it is what they strived to become themselves: perfect and indestructible.

In their defense, I realize that being Black in England at that time—and especially being educated, professional Blacks—meant that my parents constantly needed to prove their worth to the white world. Not only for status but even, at times, for their basic safety. They didn't have the luxury of appearing weak or stupid or lazy. They had to disprove the long-standing stereotypes of "colored people."

They tried their best to provide this example for me. In exploring the world of British culture, they were brave and adventurous where some Black folks weren't. They ventured into predominantly white spaces with an intrepid spirit, for which I am grateful. They took me to see Shakespeare at the National Theatre and "serious plays" like *The Invention of Love* in the West End, and even the opera *Turandot* at Albert Hall.

Their anxiety about shaping me must have been, in large part, from a desire to both protect me from, and prepare me for, a world of racial injustice, where my true self would never be seen, always invisible—just as Ralph Ellison had made clear. They knew that my being a Black man meant I was entering the game with a major handicap, and so I had to be stronger, smarter, more cultured, always better, in order to be seen. "Whatever a white person does," they would say, "you must do it twice as well to be accepted."

Whites were the ones who decided who went to what schools, and who got what jobs, and who got promoted or not. This is why it mattered how we appeared to the world. And the "world" was white, whether we liked it or not. Even the Gregorian calendar we all follow is set from a Western standard of time. Our inevitable fixed reality is, in fact, merely a white construct. And this is why my parents needed to mold me into that perfect statue, to fit into the construct, or at least to weather it.

On my twelfth birthday, my father's gift to me was a gilded-framed poster of his favorite poem, Rudyard Kipling's "If." The English poet's lofty goals were not merely aspirational, he said, but the rule for us Black men if we were to measure up as *good enough.*

But to take this sad "truth" to heart is damaging to the soul. It is based on lies. No one should have to prove their humanity. I've seen how this undertaking has killed the spirit of many Black middle-class strivers. In all this Whiteness they have only shriveled up, like Langston Hughes's raisin in the sun. In America I've seen it in the kids from Jack and Jill of America, and in the women belonging to The Links, and the men of the Talented Tenth—these elite clubs formed to preserve and nurture the "dignity" of the Black race. And yet, if you are Black and can be saved from the artifice of being an edifying example, you are luckier than some.

My parents in England are no different. They've lived their entire lives literally keeping up with the Joneses, always making sure we had the newest model Jaguar if Marilyn and Robert Jones had one, that I went to the same good schools as their kids. Even the damned Christmas wreath on our front door was not to be outdone by Marilyn's display, with its blinking white lights and golden threads braided among the holly berries. Keeping up with the Joneses was executed with a fervor no white person could even imagine.

But it is not my parents' fault. It is only the result of what happens when one is rendered invisible. A person will go to any lengths to be seen as worthy, no matter the costs.

I have paid the price for this sad situation. I have eaten up and digested those monstrous lies. My therapist says we often regard ourselves not as we really are in the present but as our parents saw us when we were young. We see ourselves through eyes distorted by our parents' own insecurities and flaws. Real freedom is seeing ourselves as we truly are. But just as my parents strived to be validated by "the world," so have I. And I've also never been able to see myself as I really am—just as they haven't been able to see me. I've internalized their distorted vision of me.

But then comes along Idris Elba. Not only did his stardom help the white world to see me—or at least to take a second glance—but it also allowed me to see myself a little more too, to accept my own Blackness a little more. Not nearly enough, you will say, and you're right. But it's a start. So, let's lift a glass and give a toast to the man of the hour: long live Idris Elba!

O ut of the corner of my eye, I see my travel companion shifting. I sense her puzzling over my face. She seems to be wrestling with an idea, her watery brown eyes flitting around as she peers at me over her bifocals. She lays her *Economist* flat on her lap. "So, what about you? Been visiting New York? Are you flying back home now?"

"Just traveling," I say.

"Just traveling, huh?" She seems to have clocked my feigned nonchalance, detected my deeper struggle about my final destination. "That's very mysterious, young man. Yes indeed."

"Yeah." I don't like being so easily read. "Well," I say, with a bit of cheek, "it's no more mysterious than the dead bitch whose funeral you're going to." I smile and raise my eyebrows.

"Oh, she was such an annoying woman," she says, giggling like a naughty child.

She describes how her daughter's dead mother-in-law was a terrible racist and didn't want her son marrying a Black American woman, even though her daughter graduated from Harvard—a fact she is not bragging about, she makes clear to me, since she and her ex-husband, Mr. Garuda, now deceased, had preferred that their daughter go to Howard University instead, just as they had both done. She herself taught anthropology at Spelman College for over thirty years. Historically all-Black colleges are not obsolete, she says, not in an America where white spaces still taint a Black body's sense of humanity. And anyway, she goes on, as far as her daughter's awful mother-in-law is concerned, you'd think that with Prince Harry just marrying Meghan Markle in the "blackest damn wedding England has ever seen," the "English bitch" would at least have had reason for pause—but no, not her!

As she continues to catalog the number of unforgivable slights her poor daughter endured from this insufferable mother-in-law, my mind wanders off a bit. I'm still listening to her, but her voice has a hypnotic quality. As I feel myself somehow transported by her melodious tone, it crosses my mind that she may actually be trying to put me in a trance, like a magician or a hypnotist. But no, that couldn't be possible. And why would she do that? But still, carried on the waves of her smooth voice, I'm slowly slipping into another plane of consciousness.

More and more I'm absorbed by the dreamlike airplane world. The cabin's overhead lights are dimming to create a perfect twilight; the vents blast bracingly cold air; and there is a general muffled sound, all collateral conversations blissfully muted. Long before we have even pulled out of the gate, we are enveloped in a new aura—a world unlike any other.

This too is my Nowhere zone. No matter where we come from, we all follow the same rules here in the airplane world, where none of us are natives. And instead of policemen to serve and protect us, we have flight attendants.

I'm impressed by the attendants as they swish past in their almost-stylish uniforms, efficiently snapping shut overhead compartments, forcing us to comply: seat belts fastened, seat backs upright, trays put up, phones and electronic devices on airplane mode, and handbags stowed securely below the seats in front of us.

As a child I adored what we called "stewardesses." I wanted to be one. What gay boy born before the '90s hasn't fantasized about this vocation? Their glamour has faded nowadays, but as a child I thought they were Amazon goddesses of the sky. Their perfumes as they waft past me lull me into that childlike trance of blissful obedience. Tonight I imagine them as stylish priestesses, making their processions up the church aisle, as we, the congregants, worship respectfully in our pews.

Even airplane air is not the same air we breathe on Earth. I take in a deep breath. The antiseptic odor is only slightly cut by the distant smells of prepared food stored in the galley. I close my eyes and savor the thought that soon we're all going to get the same limited culinary options—chicken, pasta, or beef. Even though I've just consumed an entire pizza in the taxi, I'm thrilled at the thought of getting the little meal. And while I'm also aware of the almost-Soviet-style food service we're getting on board, somehow it still feels like luxury to me.

Of course, there are first and business classes—echelons apart—behind the curtains that will remain closed at all times. While rigorously kept out of sight, we in World Traveller economy class happily accept this inequality. We know we did not pay more than ten times the price for preflight hot towels, fully recumbent seats, cheese plates, and champagne. But why do we accept this so easily, with a kind of old-world fatalism, when back on Earth we balk at these blatant inequalities?

"Why indeed?" I hear my elderly traveling companion say.

"I'm sorry?" I'm confused. I don't know if she's read my mind or if I've been speaking out loud without realizing it.

She leans in, confidentially, and with her deep half whisper she says, "I'll tell you why. We accept it because we know that in here, we are closer to death than ever. We have no control over our lives in this airplane. And it's sobering. We all pray to get out of here alive. Who cares if they have champagne behind the curtain? If the plane plunges into the Atlantic, we will all die together."

I'm perplexed by her uncanny interruption. I feel embarrassed that I must have been gabbing on out loud without even realizing it.

"But this is what I like about flying," she continues with a wicked smile, and for the first time I notice the faint outline of a mustache, little wisps of grey hairs growing over her full lips. "I like that we're forced into a place where we're all the same. We must face the danger of our existences together. We must value each breath of oxygen; respect the given rules; respect each other too; break the same bread together; and, as we land safely, we thank God, or whatever our higher power is, for life. We even applaud together when we land, because we have faced Death—that great equalizer—and we have prevailed. And also, we have felt our human frailty, our need for each other. Up here in the sky, we only have each other. And this is how life is, we realize: every one of us is on the same journey from here to there. And it is a precarious, miraculous crossing for us all."

As I listen to her, I start to feel a little spooked by her voice; not because it's scary per se, but because it's oddly familiar. I wonder if she does voice-overs for TV ads—is that where I've heard her voice? What she says about feeling at one with everyone on board is also making me sad. I can't relate. I feel, instead, as if we're all on our own, strapped into our individual little pods, isolated in our despair. We are even instructed, in the event of an emergency, to think of ourselves first: *Attend to yourself before helping others.* I feel alone. Yet I suppose if I were not busy pretending to be immortal, free from death's grip, then I may actually want to reach out for another. Perhaps the old lady is right, but I turn away from her anyway to look out the little window.

Above the tarmac, the night sky is almost black, a pitch blue. I look at the tiny red and white city lights in the distance, the Earthbound stars twinkling, and the firefly-green dots blinking on the runway. I don't want to look at her anymore. She saddens me. And the more I think about it, I'm believing more and more that her voice was actually putting me into some kind of trance. Look what happened: I ended up talking out loud without even being aware of it. How else could she have answered the questions in my head? I don't feel safe even thinking around her. What if she makes me speak my thoughts again? That could be dangerous. Yes, it's now clear that there is something dodgy about her. She has a steady, cool, detached quality, clinical, like an experienced nurse. Or is it a lifelong criminal? No, I decide. I don't want to talk to her anymore.

I close my eyes to calm myself. I focus on the sound of the plane's engine as it revs up for takeoff. I try to slow my breathing to a dreamy rhythm and to think of tranquil things, like floating on the ocean. I try to concentrate on the big question looming ahead for me: Where will I go to find my wilderness?

"Where indeed?" I hear my traveling companion say.

I look at her to verify she is, indeed, talking to me. This time I'm sure I have not spoken a word out loud. Is she really reading my mind? My heart beats like a drum. "I'm sorry," I say. "I—I don't understand. What did you say?"

She tuns to me earnestly now, knitting her silver eyebrows. "I am not a particularly good person," she says, still in her hypnotic half whisper. "Everyone assumes I'm sweet," she continues. "But I'm not sweet. Must be my big breasts. Gives me a warm, maternal appearance, I suppose. The mammy aura, as you know. But I can tell you the truth: I'm not very warm. I'm not a bad person, exactly, but I don't like people much. Have you ever heard the quote from the poet Edna St. Vincent Millay? 'I love humanity, but I hate people!' That's me. Why is it so hard to love people specifically? Is there a place for us to go where we can live free of guilt for not liking people enough? A place where we are not expected to love or not to love? Where are we to go, those of us who have broken the hearts of others? Or those who have dared to leave behind that which none of us should ever take for granted—the love of another? But shouldn't the perfect love be without any attributes at all, the pure love of love itself? Not the particulars of this person or that? *That* is something I could do, perhaps."

My heart sinks in my chest. Is she some kind of psychic? I realize my sinking feeling is also because we are now climbing a steep angle into the air, leaving New York behind, ascending into the dark. And as we climb, I feel like I'm breaking into a million little bits, strewn from my center, like the tiny white bits blown from the dandelion.

And then the old woman turns to me and whispers into my ear, with her deep, Southern voice, "Look at me," she says. "Tell me: *Who do you really see?*"

I immediately freeze, afraid to face her now. What in the hell is she up to? But then, despite my reluctance, I turn towards the old woman, face-to-face. I notice nothing different, except her gaze seems a bit more intense.

"Be careful when you summon the dead," she whispers into my ears. "They'll come. Yes indeed. No matter the century or the distance. In the wilderness, there is no time, no space, no orientation but One. No duality. Not good, not bad. Not living, not dead.

There is only One." And then she deepens her voice even more. "You have summoned the dead."

"What are you talking about? Who are you really?" I demand.

She smiles wryly, then makes a puckered frown, as if to say, *What does it matter?* before she leans in close again, and with that voice says, "I am the one thus come. Look closely at me and see," she whispers.

In a flash—as if her face is suddenly illuminated by a spasm of lightning—I see my own face staring back at me. A mirror. My heart drops. I turn away as fast as I can.

I must be hallucinating. Could she really be the goddess incarnate? My heart thumps in my ears like the flapping of those giant wings I heard before. Whoever this old woman is, she's scaring the shit out of me. If I'm hallucinating I have to get a grip and make this stop right away.

Before I make the conscious decision, my body is already in motion. It must be the ancient survival instinct. Fight or flight— and my instinct is *flight*. Without a thought I unbuckle myself, jump up with my laptop and backpack in tow, and squeeze past the old lady (or is she the goddess?) without looking back at her. I quickly take the empty aisle seat in the row ahead of us. I buckle myself in again, and finally sigh with relief. I've escaped her.

The blond woman in the window seat next to me is quietly snoring with her mouth hung open, her baby asleep on her lap. I take out Sophia, open her up on the tray table, and try to work on the next chapter of the Mohammed novel. But I can't really work, my mind is in no condition. I cannot stop thinking of seeing my own face reflected like a mirror from the old woman's face, and that she's used the words "I am the one thus come." This old woman must be the goddess. I'd never imagined her like this. Somehow,

I'd pictured her as—well, as sexy. The sultry way she talks and her ability to arouse me. But no, I must be losing it. This must all be a figment of my imagination. The goddess is imagined. I'm just overly exhausted. I need to work, to avoid thinking of the old lady altogether. I count to sixty. I imagine myself floating on a serene sea, the sun on my face. I whisper, pray, to Sophia, "Come on, you can save me, can't you?"

And then, like a miracle, I am rescued by another low whispering in my ear—and this time I know the voice immediately. I sigh with relief. I breathe deeper again, a long exhale: "Listen, my Possibility. Listen to me, I have something to tell you about this present moment. Come here. Come to me."

With a long and deep sigh, I offer my hands up to Sophia, and suddenly, I am with Mohammed again.

MOHAMMED'S STORY

Dreaming of You

At last we are in the present moment. Write as I speak, my poet. As Whitman wrote: "The greatest poet places himself where the future becomes present." "You that shall cross from shore to shore years hence are more to me, and more in my meditations, than you might suppose."

In this present moment, we are also in the future. I am joined with my Possibility. With you. You, who are free to love whomever you please, to travel wherever and whenever you please. Even if you were born in the torrid zone, as I was, you are free to know snow—even to build igloos if you choose. Just imagine! You can live the impossible life.

I write this story because I want you to remember me. I want you to know that it is because of my dream that you live at all. You—my young Black man of the future—you should know, it is I who have dreamed you up, one hundred years before this day. Here in 1919, in my cold cell in Mansourah, in the bewitching hours, I dream of you.

Morgan will come tomorrow, finally. Gamila brought word of his telegram.

Somehow tonight has been worse than ever in here—the floor colder, the stench more nauseating, the threats of rape again, unbearable. It seems that knowing I will soon be free makes it all the more intolerable. But tomorrow Morgan will finally pay the fine. Being British, he'll have the authority to persuade the police to drop the exaggerated charges. And I'll be free again.

But to be honest, my friend, I am not only eager for my freedom from this cell alone. I have a great secret dream awaiting me—a dream I have not shared with anyone, not even with Morgan. I will first test Morgan. And if he is true, then there may be a new life for me. But if Morgan is just another British like all the rest, then I will not have that dream. Don't you worry, my friend, I will make sure to win in the end, no matter what. I have a plan for every eventuality. That's why I need you. But ah, the impossible life . . . this is my dream!

What is that dream? It would be like something one's imagination can never fully capture. It is as if you were to ask a man like me, who has only known the Sahara, to conceive of what it is like to live in an igloo in the Arctic Circle. Impossible! And I realize a person can only actually know snow by touching snow. But can't poets make the fantastical come alive? If Morgan's love is true, even as I die, I will live that impossible dream.

I will know snow. I will live in an igloo.

I will know what it is like to be truly loved.

That is my dream. The impossible life.

According to the live video flight-tracker in front of me, we're now three hours and fifty-nine minutes into the flight, flying past Nova Scotia. The illustrated map looks comforting, like a child's video game, a parallel reality playing out before our very eyes. After working on the novel, I try to sleep to avoid thinking of the old woman. Her changing faces, her talk of the dead—it all spooked the hell out of me. Occasionally I can hear the flight attendants behind me, fussing over her—she must be quite demanding. But I keep out of it. I purposefully keep my eyes closed.

A ping chimes over the airplane's loudspeakers. "Ladies and gentlemen, this is your captain speaking. I'm sorry to inform you—" No one wants to hear these opening words from any pilot. My stomach dips with dread. I brace myself for the news. "Due to a sick passenger," he says, "we will, unfortunately, have to turn the plane around and return to JFK."

There is a collective groan.

The captain says he is sorry for this major inconvenience. He will update us with further details as soon as he has more information.

Whispers are followed by scattered crying and then some demands from angry passengers.

The cabin lights dim. I'm pretending to be asleep, to be sure to avoid the old lady in case she decides to lean forward and pester me or spook me again. Occasionally I peek up to get a flash of flight attendants walking the aisles, smiling reassuringly, offering orange juice and water. Of course they overlook me, the Black man, I think. No smiles and orange juice for me. But then I realize I've been too busy pretending to be asleep. They probably just don't want to disturb me.

The ping comes again. The captain with an update. The situation with the sick passenger is now more urgent. Immediate medical attention is required. We'll need to make an emergency landing at Narsarsuaq International Airport in Greenland. "Sorry for this inconvenience, folks," he says, "but no need to be alarmed. Please buckle your seat belts and put your seats in the upright position. Cabin crew, prepare for cross-check and landing."

Greenland? I didn't even know there was an international airport in Greenland. Is Greenland even habitable? Of course it is. I remember now—I saw a BBC documentary on Greenland. But who lives there? As far as I recall, it's a Danish colony and there are the native Inuit people—people who have shed the name "Eskimo" as Blacks have shed "Negro." Were there igloos too? Yes. Not igloos used as common Inuit homes, as I had once imagined as a child, but igloos made by hunters specifically for overnight trips on the icy tundra. As a boy, I loved the idea of igloos. They seemed safe and protected. But what else is there in Greenland? From what I saw of the documentary, nothing. Just ice and wilderness.

Ah, wilderness!

Although I have avoided looking back at my old traveling companion all this time, I cannot help but lean over and look at her now. I need to confirm she is just an ordinary woman, that my imagination has simply run away with me. And surely she must have something clever to say about this sudden turn of events.

Some wise words about the unpredictability of life, I imagine. But when I turn to see her, she is calmly facing forward, silent, with a strange little smile on her lips, a knowing smirk, it seems.

I look away again, but then I look back at her. I sense something odd, an unnerving stillness. When I look closely now, it seems she's not actually breathing. Her bifocals have dropped on their little gold chain and rest on her large, tiger-print bosom. Her eyes are wide open, but she's not moving at all. She's *dead*! My heart plunges to my gut.

It's all because of her, this landing, isn't it? She's the one taking us to Greenland.

PART 4

The Great Plan

Before the other passengers are allowed to deplane in Narsarsuaq and after the old lady's body is carried away on a stretcher, I'm escorted off for questioning. Deaths, it turns out, are subject to criminal review. The Greenlandic authorities must rule out foul play, and since I was the closest person on the plane to the deceased, I am the prime suspect. Two policemen in their blue uniforms have come to accompany me off the plane. They ask me in English to join them. One of them has a strong Danish lilt.

I can see from their glary eyes that sleep still half possesses them. I imagine about half an hour ago they must have received the emergency phone calls while they were still wrestling with their dreams.

As we walk down the plane's aisle in a single file, one policeman is in front of me, the other behind. Both men are approaching middle age, it seems, older than me, at least. They are tall and well-built. The one behind me looks more Inuit, I think—dark hair, slightly Asian features; the other one, in front of me, has auburn hair and fair skin. They both have thick necks.

At the plane's portal, as we are about to exit, a flight attendant nods and smiles, out of habit, it seems. Her lipstick seems freshly applied, but she has missed one corner. She says, "Thank you. Bye-bye," in a dead-eyed, rote performance.

As we step out onto the stairs, the cold air slices right to my bones. My face burns too. My nose, cheeks, and lips all sting. We walk down the rattling metal stairs. Even in my Timberland boots the frigid tarmac grips at my feet. It is still dark out, but from the moonlight reflected on the white landscape, I can see that Narsar-suaq is in a valley. Under the star-sprayed sky, an aura of pale blue shimmers over the snowcapped hills all around us.

Narsarsuaq Airport is not what I would have imagined of an international airport. It's only a one-story building, mostly glass, framed by wood, with grey aluminum siding and a bright turquoise roof and trim. Definitely smaller than the Home Depot in Brooklyn.

The two policemen usher me through the glass doors in silence. White fluorescent lights blare at us like alarm bells. I shut my eyes and then open them slowly, one after the next. Everything pops out in high definition—too sharp to seem real. We are in a large warehouse-looking space. It seems to be the work of a modernist architect. Probably inspired by Paris's Centre Pompidou, I think. Enormous blue and orange industrial-size air ducts and tubes are suspended from the high, corrugated tin roof and slink across the entire ceiling, like giant caterpillars.

The duty-free shop is slicker than I would have imagined—all glass walls. Hundreds of little boxes of Hugo Boss colognes are on display, beckoning to me as we walk past. Ben gave me a bottle of Hugo for our anniversary one year. I can almost smell the balsam notes stinging inside my nostrils.

I look over at the auburn-haired policeman to my right. The badge on his uniform says *Boss*. Is that his title or his name? It must be a Danish name, I imagine. The lack of shadows in here only adds to the surreal feeling. I feel as if I have X-ray vision. With my new super-vision, I also notice that some of Boss's nose hairs are long and grey. Yes, he's definitely over forty. I also notice he has nicked himself shaving; just under his left nostril is a shiny red bauble of blood. As he marches us ahead, he has a strange, vacant look in his blue eyes.

It occurs to me, out of nowhere, that maybe this Boss hasn't had the life he wanted. I don't know why I think this. Maybe Boss had different dreams but ended up as a policeman in this lonely outpost in Greenland. He sees the futility of his life now; that explains the look, as if he's longing, grasping, for something precious that keeps floating away from him, and the more he reaches for it, the farther his own ripples push it away.

What nonsense, I say to myself, following the solemn officer. I don't know why I'm imagining all of this. I'm seeing too much in this blaring artificial light. And then I think of the Goddess Shakti—did she incarnate as the old lady on the plane? I remember the way I had seen my own reflection in her face, and I wonder if she's done something to me, something to change how I see things.

After the Greenlandic policemen usher me into a little office in the back, they close the blue metal door behind us. The lighting in here is softer; there are lots of shadows, and it's a relief to my eyes. The dark-haired one, who shows me to a seat, is definitely Inuit, I'm convinced. The badge on his uniform says *Tukkuttok*. He stands to the right of the chair he's indicating for me to sit in. He tells me the interview may take about twenty minutes. Tukkuttok's English is more halting than Boss's and I appreciate its succinct functionality. "Just protocol. Few questions. Then you can go. No problem."

I know I didn't do anything wrong, so I'm not worried. But as I take the seat—a metal-framed office chair with cobalt-blue leather upholstery—I suddenly remember my gun, and my stomach sinks. Their X-ray machine must have detected it. I should have declared it with Customs in New York. I don't want them thinking I'm some kind of criminal.

Boss, seated behind a grey metal desk, asks me for my full name. And then, surprisingly, he also asks me for my parents' full names. It's only now, as I utter Delores's and William's full names, that I realize there has been a deeply hidden agenda to my flight: it was to go to London, to see my parents before venturing into the wilderness. I realize this now because when I stare up at Boss as he confirms the spelling of my parents' names, I hear a little voice inside me, my own twelve-year-old voice, and that little boy is calling out for help from his mum and dad.

I'm more frightened than I realized. I try to calm myself with a soothing inner voice: "What do you expect, Kippy? Of course you're scared. You're alone in a strange land, an old woman has just died next to you in the airplane, and you're surely losing your mind with hallucinations." Or else, perhaps I'm not losing my mind but losing my identity. Losing the self that I've constructed.

But this mystical transformation—if that's what it is—is scary as shit. Maybe I should have stayed at home. But where is that? With Ben in Brooklyn? With my parents in Weybridge? I have no idea. All I know is, whether I'm losing my mind or my identity, I feel that something is radically changing. My reality no longer seems predictable.

Soraya and the Stars

Eleven years ago, in the ashram in Maharashtra, I had never felt my reality change so quickly or known such lightness of being. I happily forgot who Kip was before India; and it was freeing to be nobody, as light as nothing, and yet, to feel I had everything. Of course, it wasn't always easy following the rigorous routine of rising at four in the morning for chants and meditation and working *seva* (selfless service) all day as a dish-wallah, washing dirty dishes and pots in the hot open-air kitchen, only stopping for noon prayers. But it was, somehow, completely fulfilling. And in the evenings, my favorite part of the day, I'd attend talks by Guruji, Baba's successor. The talks were followed by more meditation, or chanting, until nine at night. And then the daily schedule was repeated, exactly. It was a demanding yet simple and blissful life.

One evening before Guruji's talk, another devotee, Soraya Agyei, and I were having a long, intimate chat. We were sitting in the courtyard of the main building—a cozy quadrangle where an old banyan tree stood in the center, with all its complicated hanging roots. It was a cool, tropical winter evening; night-blooming jasmine perfumed the air, and the stars were already extravagant in the sky. Soraya and I had just finished our dinner-dishwashing *seva*—we were both dish-wallahs. Soraya was in her mid-forties and originally from Ghana. She sported a neat Afro and a colorful kente cloth top. She was beautiful, with dark satiny skin. She had a cleft lip, but you barely noticed it. She was one of only four other Black people in the ashram, along with me, two African-American women, and Darren, my fellow Caribbean and partner in crime.

That evening, Soraya and I were sitting on a worn stone bench, sipping cups of hot chai, its steam rising aromatic with cardamom. My burgundy wool shawl was wrapped over the shoulders of my white kurta. On the courtyard's ground were porous limestone slabs in a grid, with grass growing between the squares. Occasionally, I'd kick off my sandals and rub my bare feet over the mossy grass or the cool stone.

I ended up telling Soraya about my unfathomable experience of Baba's visitation back in New York, how it had felt so real and caused me to break down crying. Soraya listened to me and laughed. She said it was common to hear of such visitations in the ashram.

Not only are enlightened souls able to appear when and wherever they want, she said, but time and space are less fixed than we imagine. Even modern science has proven this to be true, she said. She herself had studied medicine at Leeds and was an anesthesiologist before she'd given up her householder life and moved into the ashram.

In her work as an anesthesiologist, she said, she had begun to scientifically question the idea of time. Her patients would wake up from surgery astonished that four or five hours had passed, when it seemed to them like only a few moments. It was not until she'd heard Guruji explain the yogic view of that phenomenon that she remembered the old African beliefs of time, and it all began to make sense.

I asked her to explain more. Soraya smiled at me coyly and asked if I truly wanted the explanation. She warned that I would have to be patient because it was complex and would take her a few minutes to lay it out clearly. It required synthetizing both scientific and philosophical ideas, and I couldn't expect it to be simple or quick.

Yes, of course, I said, a little insulted that she might have underestimated me. But then I understood her doubts—I was just twenty-six, practically a boy in her eyes.

Soraya took a deep breath, and then dove in. In yogic philosophy, she explained, "buddhi" is the name for intellectual memory, but it also encompasses memory on the atomic and cellular levels. Our cells, for example, are able to remember, after many years of evolution, how to replicate things like the skin color of our ancestors or how to digest certain foods. It takes memory to function on a physical plane of existence. And it is the memory of our identity—our genes and experiences—that tells us we are separate, unique beings. But, she said, the most supreme kind of intelligence, pure consciousness, *chitta*, is free of the limitations of even that kind of memory.

What anesthesia does on an observable and measurable level, she explained, is to increase the bandwidth of our brain waves' undulations so that memory cannot function in its habitual, limited way: information cannot move forward from one synapse to another, just as a car cannot move forward on a wildly undulating bridge.

As she spoke, I suddenly saw another side of the graceful Soraya—the excited science nerd. I imagined her back at Leeds, crossing the courtyard with her nose in a book, bumping into people as she contemplated theorems; young and eager, giddy to be in a new world of learning.

Normally, she said, we feel pain as a result of memory, not

only by recalling or imagining trauma, but also from memory on a cellular level—the body's memory of what it should and should not be. There is a medical condition called congenital analgesia, she said, that makes a person unable to feel physical pain at all. For some reason, the cells of their bodies have no memory of our evolution. It is no less mysterious than a child with autism flawlessly playing a Bach fugue on the piano after hearing it once. These are two extremes of what memory, or the lack of it, can do. But Soraya's major epiphany, she said, was that, unlike in a dream state from which a person awakens with a sense of time having passed, with anesthesia—which induces a malfunction of our habitual, limited memory—a person awakens having felt no sense of time at all. In fact, a person experiences timelessness.

Time, as the age-old yogic philosophy says, is a construct of memory, born of the arbitrary cycles of the physical world—years, days, hours. In Sanskrit, it is called *Kāla*, which roughly means Time and Space. Space is considered a consequence of Time. But yogic philosophy says *Kāla* is only an illusion due to one's attachment to the fleeting cycles of a material world. But all material things are, by nature, not eternal—even the sun will die one day. So, time itself is not eternal; it is a construct.

This is how Baba appeared to me in my so-called dream, she said. One who has mastered other forms of knowing can jump on and off of time as one pleases; just as someone who has mastered cycling can jump on and off a bicycle while riding it, by holding and letting go of the handlebars. It's not magic, it's mastery.

"It's only the modern Western cultures that have trapped us in our limited memory of who we think we are," she said. "Black or white, alive or dead. And modern man has killed magic. Nowadays we feel we must control everything ourselves. But there used to be mystery and the unknown in the world. Magic has been real for most of the ancient world," she said. "And it is still a way of knowing. We need it."

I kicked off my sandals again and held my feet to the cool stone. I thought about the stories from my many relatives from The Bahamas, not only my grandmother, but also my aunts and uncles, who spoke of spirits and visitations from the dead, often citing these magical stories as readily as they'd discuss local politics or world events. It wasn't only silly superstition, as I'd once thought when I was young. It was an integral part of a deeper reality.

"So is that what happened when Baba visited me across Space and Time?" I asked.

"Exactly." Soraya's eyes closed for a moment. Then she looked at me again, her gaze soft but focused. A true guru, a *sadguru*, she said, can also awaken that state of *chitta* in others, awaken Shakti— the state of forgetting time and space, forgetting the limitations of what you've remembered to be. "This is what happened to you when you saw Baba," she said.

"So if something awakens in us the ability to see beyond the temporal memory, to see the impossible . . . ?" I lifted my head to the stars and smiled with wonder at the idea.

"Yes, then we can see it. We can see what others call magic. But it is not magic. It is just the truth that others do not see—no boundaries of time, no boundaries of space."

"Wow . . ." I opened my eyes wide and let a million stars pulse into me. I thought about what astronomers say, that the stars in the sky no longer actually exist; they are twinkling images from thousands, millions, billions of years ago. I stared up at the sky for a while. The more I thought, the more I realized everything I saw, in fact, could be an illusion. If the stars weren't actually there, nothing

was there—it was all an illusion! Even Soraya was just an accumu-
lation of light and molecules and atoms that could have existed a
million years ago—or maybe even years in the future.

"Why do I feel like I'm tripping, Soraya? I feel like we just took
a hit of peyote and we're riding the wave to . . . I don't know . . . to
Nowhere!"

"Nowhere?" Soraya scrunched up her nose and looked at me
sideways. She smiled as if she were chiding me in the way only an
African woman can. "Where is Nowhere, man?"

"The Nowhere Man?" I smiled. "Right here," I said trium-
phantly, spreading my arms to encompass everything.

We burst out laughing and couldn't stop. We didn't even remember why we were laughing anymore. We merely became the
laughter. Shedding the shells that separated us, Soraya Agyei and
I were gone—our old, familiar, limited selves dissolved. We simply
became two voices laughing in a great big universe, under a vast sky.
And as our laughter merged, we became pure weightlessness. We
became Nothing. And free.

When Boss and Tukkuttok have finished interviewing me, they tell me I'm free to go. There's a daily flight to Reykjavík at eight o'clock in the evening, they say, and I can get connections to England or back to New York from there. I thank them as I'm about to exit their office, but I stop in the doorway. I look out and see the other passengers, now deplaned, meandering about under the fluorescent lights like zombie refugees. I'm reluctant to join them. For some reason I feel apart from my fellow passengers and closer to my Greenlandic interrogators.

My overzealous imagination has convinced me I know Officer Boss and I can't part without some kind of recognition of our intimacy—an acknowledgment that I have "seen" his pain. Even Tukkuttok, who only smiled at me once, just when the interview was over, seems to have communicated some essential connection with his warm, slightly crossed eyes. How is it I feel attached to people I've only known for twenty minutes?

Perhaps it is the information I've shared with them. In this sparsely populated, northernmost land on the planet, these two Greenlandic policemen are the only ones who know me at all. They know Delores's and William's full names and professions. They know that I last spoke with my parents over the telephone two weeks ago and that we got into a row over my needing to borrow more money. They know my parents became cross and said cruel things to me because at thirty-seven, I'm "not grown up yet," "not realistic enough about my pipe dream of becoming a writer," and that I should find a "proper profession." These two strangers also know I'm not married—not officially—but that I am gay, living with a partner in Brooklyn, and that I'm only traveling with a carry-on suitcase because I left in a hurry after a breakup. They also know—and it came up very naturally, a throw-away comment after I had relaxed and realized I wasn't in danger—that I am hoping to find the perfect wilderness somewhere to finish my novel, to find my own voice. In short, they know me as well as almost anyone on the planet.

I linger on the threshold, holding the blue metal door open, and I can feel their eyes on my back. I cannot leave them yet. I turn around, wanting to say something, but I don't know what to say.

"Hey, can I ask you a question?" I say. They nod slowly, in unison. I think of inquiring about the old lady who died—maybe I'll ask if they've contacted her daughter yet. But that's not what I really want to say, and then without thinking, the words seem to tumble out of me: "What will happen if I stay in Greenland?"

They look at me for a while in silence. Then they look at each other and smile at the same time. Unexpectedly, Tukkuttok, the one who speaks less English, answers me. "Well, if you stay here, perhaps you will write about it one day, like the African from Togo. He came here in the seventies. He wrote a book called *An African in Greenland*."

"*Ja, ja*, it's true. And you will also be the second Black to stay in Narsarsuaq this year."

"Really? Who is the other one?" I ask.

"He just arrived two months ago," says Boss. "He's working here at the airport."

"He is now living with my sister and her family," adds Tukkuttok, a proud smile flashing across his face. Tukkuttok looks totally different when he smiles; younger, livelier.

"Another Black man here in Greenland?" I repeat, only to make sure I'm hearing right. The coincidence of another Black man traveling alone and choosing to stay here in this out-of-the-way place on the planet seems uncanny, and then, almost immediately, repugnant. I'd hoped to be alone in the wilderness, not with another Black man. I want to be free of the emotional and political baggage another Black man is sure to bring along. How will I find my own, individual voice with another Black man here?

But since staying here is happening so easily, I'm thinking it all may be predestined. I had imagined they'd require more of me to stay in Greenland, but with a UK passport I'm allowed three months without a visa. Boss and Tukkuttok are happy to facilitate my staying. And it turns out all the baggage must come off the airplane anyway. They are taking everyone else to Iceland on another airline, then switching them to yet another flight to London. Boss and Tukkuttok will also interview the flight attendants, but they say I'm free to go—or to stay if I choose.

Tukkuttok informs me that when he's done with the other interviews, he'll take me to the Blue Ice Café, where I can spend the night until I can arrange for other lodgings. The Narsarsuaq hotel and youth hostel are closed during winter months, he says. He can also introduce me to the other Black man, who can give me some tips for acclimating to Greenland. He tells me the man works as the airport's custodian and baggage handler. "Sometimes he even helps out with Customs, inspecting the baggage," says Tukkuttok.

Baggage. I think of my gun again and my stomach tightens. What will happen if they find the gun in my suitcase? Will they suspect the worst of me? I would hate that, especially now that they've been so welcoming and kind. My heart hammers near my throat, and I make the snap decision: with a quavering voice, I hear myself confess that I have a revolver in my suitcase. Immediately I regret the decision. But now that I've opened my big mouth, I have to explain. I describe the gun's details. I dig out the legal registration from my backpack. My hands are trembling as I unfold the documents.

Boss and Tukkuttok look at each other, puzzled. Then they break out into laughter, real belly laughs. "A Glock 22!" exclaims Boss. "What good will that do you up here? If you want a real gun, you need a rifle. You better go down to the gun store later, it's just about five hundred meters past the Blue Ice Café. My brother works there, Storm. Tell Storm that Magnus sent you. He'll get you a proper gun for Greenland."

"A proper gun? You mean I could just go in and buy a gun—just like that?"

"Sure," says Boss. "Everyone here has a gun. Even my ten-year-old daughter. You'll need it for shooting musk ox, or cáribou, or seals. Reindeer won't be good for hunting until August. But if you stay around until then, me and Tukkuttok could take you up north to the big ice. Almost as far as the American military base in Thule."

"Best hunting is up there. Polar bears too," says Tukkuttok.

I can't believe this is happening. They've welcomed me to stay in Greenland, no problem. They know I have a gun, no problem. I could even hunt reindeer with them if I stayed until August!

But I can't seem to get over the idea of this other Black man being here. I'm thinking of how to let Tukkuttok know I'd rather not be introduced to him. The wilderness is calling me, I can feel it, and I need to go alone without any distractions.

"This man," I say, trying to sound indifferent. "Is he from the military base up north?"

"Ah, no. This guy is not American," says Boss. Then he closes his eyes momentarily, as if to gather his thoughts, or his pluck, maybe. "But I must tell you, when I first saw you, I thought maybe you were related to this young man. He told us he had a twin brother. Are you his twin?" He laughs, but he also seems to be asking in earnest.

"Twin? No, no," I say, and then I hear myself speaking my thoughts out loud: "Why on earth would a single young Black man come to live in Greenland?"

Boss and Tukkuttok look at each other and then nod with a mysterious air.

"Okay, okay," says Boss, motioning me back into the office and shutting the door behind me. He seems to have a renewed sense of professional seriousness. He sits on his metal desk and folds his arms across his chest, one foot planted on the floor, the other foot dangling with its shoelace undone. "Since you are going to be staying here in our town, you may as well know the deal. This Black man came here on a secret mission."

"A secret mission?" For some reason my heart skips a beat. I'm thrilled by the idea, but totally confused. And I'm also not sure why Officer Boss would tell me, a complete stranger, this secret information. Is he toying with me? Is it a trap? The kind of trick detectives play to knock a suspect off-kilter?

Boss clamps his lips closed, furrows his brows, and exhales through his nose in a single heavy huff. "This young Black man is very ill with some kind of disease. He collapsed at work two weeks ago. Hit his head on the floor by the Customs desk. Blood all over the tiles."

"We had to rush him to the nurses' station in town," adds Tukkuttok.

"*Ja,*" says Boss. "Nurse Holte says he has a rare and fatal disease only Black people get."

Sickle cell anemia, I thought.

"Nurse Holte is Danish, she worked in Africa for many years, eh," adds Tukkuttok, nodding at the gravity of the matter. "She knows Black people diseases."

"*Ja, ja,*" says Boss. "She says he confessed to coming here for his last wish. A secret mission: to live with Inuit people, and to build his own igloo before dying."

I get a shiver. I immediately think of Mohammed El Adl and his wish to build his own igloo, to know snow, to prove his fitness for survival. "Dying? An igloo?" I repeat.

"Yes," says Tukkuttok. "Nurse Holte says the young man got the idea from that book by the African who came here years ago. Now he's come to fulfill his last wish."

"But Nurse Holte is worried this man may also be a suicide risk," says Boss. "She had to inform us. Sad. Suicide is our biggest problem here, especially in winter."

"Polar hysteria, it's called. All this darkness, people go mad," says Tukkuttok.

"But," says Boss, standing again, "now everyone in town knows about the Black man's *secret.*" He looks askance at Tukkuttok, who looks down guiltily. "Anyway, the poor man doesn't yet realize there are no secrets here in Greenland."

I'm still trying to imagine what kind of dying Black man comes to Greenland to build an igloo. "And you say he's not from the American base?" I confirm.

"*Nej,*" says Boss. "He's from North Africa. His name is Mohammed."

As I wait for Tukkuttok to take me to the Blue Ice Café, sitting on a bench in the airport, I laugh to myself with excitement, but also with a mounting sense of trepidation. Tukkuttok said he'll introduce me to this Mohammed in an hour, before we leave for the café. It's unreal. Soon I'll meet with a young man from North Africa. Is he from Egypt, this man named Mohammed?

As I sit here waiting, trying to avoid random conversations with the itinerant zombies, I look around to see if I can spot this young Mohammed anywhere in the airport. There are only a few other Black passengers from my flight, not so many that I couldn't spot another Black man, especially one who supposedly looks just like me. But I don't see this Mohammed anywhere.

Finally, I decide to put in my earphones and pull out Sophia to begin work on the novel. I've got at least an hour before Tukkuttok will come to fetch me. But I procrastinate. I pull my iPhone from my jeans pocket and Google information on Greenland. I read all I can find on Wikipedia. Right away, I see that Narsarsuaq, where we have landed, is a word in the Eskimo-Aleut language, and it means "the Great Plan."

My heart stops. So, there has been some great plan for me to come here all along! I remember my grandmother confiding to me with her singsong Caribbean cadence, "The Lord works in mysterious ways, dearie." This place is where both the Goddess Shakti and Mohammed have brought me. This is where I'll find my wilderness, and my true voice. It has all been predestined. After all, this place is the Great Plan.

And then, with a calming air, as if to settle me into my own body again, I hear Mohammed El Adl whisper, "Now, my friend. Now we can be free!"

MOHAMMED'S STORY

Never Mind

Finally free from that wretched cell! For my homecoming, my closest friends—Farid, Salim, Yusef, and Yusef's uncle, Professor Ganda—all gathered at our house on El-Abbasi Street. Gamila prepared my favorite dessert, *mahallabiya*, a rice pudding topped with crushed pistachios. It was meant to be a party. But when Morgan and I arrived—three hours late, since negotiating my release proved trickier than anticipated—Gamila flew into a rage, screaming at me as she ran down the hallway, pulling her white scarf over her head, refusing to present herself to Morgan. She locked herself in the closet, shouting that I knew better: an unmarried man was not allowed to visit the house with a woman present—especially not a British. She was dishonored, she said.

I reminded her of the significant amount of money Morgan had given us and said that without Morgan I might still be in jail. And besides, Morgan had also brought her a late wedding gift—a little mahogany jewelry box, with the design of a crane of inlaid pearls. She cracked the door and reached out to caress the pearls on the box, finally softened, and came out. She then served us all the *mahallabiya* and hot, mint tea, making sure to cover her face with her scarf all along.

After dessert, all the men were sitting around on cushions, smoking from the hookah. There was laughter as Professor Ganda, the only other one who spoke English, showed Morgan how to smoke it, resulting in Morgan's garroting coughs. But all seemed well until Salim asked Professor Ganda to ask Morgan if he had read of the news in *Al-Ahram*, or perhaps in the new English newspaper, *Egyptian Mail*.

Morgan asked what news, and Professor Ganda shook his head woefully and said the sad news was about Saad Zaghlul, the leader of Wafd, our national resistance party. They are saying the British high commissioner has exiled him to Malta, he said. After Saad Zaghlul demanded Egyptian independence at the Paris Peace Conference, the British have finally exiled him!

This can't be true! I said. They cannot do that! The British are monsters!

Dr. Ganda nodded solemnly.

Morgan looked sheepish and shaken. Then, with all eyes on him, he said, I cannot support my country in this. I would change the situation if I could, he said, but I am only an English writer. What can I do?

Professor Ganda said that Shakespeare and Milton and even Dickens were also English writers and they had made a great impact. Perhaps Morgan should write books that forced the British to truly see themselves, Ganda said, and to think of how they used their power in the world.

Morgan looked stunned; his head made little shakes from side to side. He said he agreed, but he stuttered as he spoke. Perhaps it was true, he said. Perhaps he *could* write more important books if he tried—that is, he added, if he had the faculties to do so.

Morgan was silent after that, and from time to time, when I'd catch his gaze, he'd force a sad smile and look down. All the others shot Morgan daggers with their eyes, as if to call him a shaitan—a devil. Morgan soon said he was tired and needed rest. He looked back at me as he left the room. I don't think I'd ever seen a more pathetic look on anyone.

But all along, I cannot lie, I too was questioning Morgan's true motives. Was he also a white devil? There was no doubt he wanted me, but was I simply an exotic conquest for him—just as Egypt itself was a conquest for the British Empire?

After the guests left and Gamila put our little Morgan to bed, she came to our bedroom, where I was reading. We had arranged for Morgan to sleep with me and for her to sleep with the baby. There were no other bedrooms. Gamila asked where Morgan was. I told her he'd gone to fetch water from the pump in the alleyway. He wanted to wash before bed, and I was too weak to carry water buckets. Gamila nodded. I saw the fear in her eyes, the fear of my proximity to death and of the shadow it cast upon her. I'd tried to suppress my coughing as much as I could, but when I couldn't, I'd seen the looks on everyone's face—on that of Salim and Dr. Ganda, Morgan and Gamila—all giving each other silent glances. All afraid to say what we all know: I am dying.

Gamila now looked as if she was pitying me as I lay on the bed in my white djellaba. She said, You don't look well, Mohammed. Like a pile of bones in a white sack.

I looked up from my *Leaves of Grass* and nodded. Her black, droopy eyes were softening, almost with tears, it seemed. I saw her bite at her bottom lip intensely, close her eyes before she opened them again to show two black pupils alit, like coals on fire.

I suppose you are so ill you have lost your mind, she said, steadily and with a controlled voice.

I could hear the rumble of the volcano about to erupt. And then she let it go.

I cannot imagine why else, in the name of Allah, you would ruin us with this English shaitan! she said. Why did you marry me, if you were just going to destroy me? I should have died with Ahmed! That would have been better. At least then Allah would have been able to accept me in the afterlife. But now—there is no heaven for me! Perhaps because you went to that Christian missionary school, you have no respect for our religion, for our customs? Is that it? But couldn't you consider me and our son, at least? Ruining him with that stupid name. Ruining us all, for all the world to see! And I know what you *do* with that man. *I know*. You let him treat you like a little boy. *His* little boy. But you are a man now, Mohammed. You have a wife and a son! That man has no right to tickle and caress you, and—and all the rest! Why do you let him dominate you? Don't you care how it makes me seem? You make me nothing! I am only the wife of a sick little bitch! Whoever heard of a bitch with a wife? It's unthinkable! *That's* what you make of me! Nothing at all! Why did you marry me?

I wished I could have dismissed her words, but she was right. Everyone can see that Morgan treats me like a wife. It is not just his affection—after all, we in Egypt are accustomed to being affectionate with our friends—but it is the *way* he looks at me, the *way* he reaches out to hold my hand. There is an expectation that I am his and I comply.

I wish I could explain to Gamila that I have not chosen for my heart to fall under such a command. I also wish I could explain that I have married her out of duty to my family, and to her family. I did not have any other choice. And, as a Muslim, I must have children. It is expected, required. And also, as expected, I have promised to provide a house, food, and clothing for her and our child. I have even promised not to beat her, as many men do when their wives shout at them. But I cannot explain what has happened with me and Morgan. There are no such words in our language. The missionaries call it "sin"—of that I am certain. On one side of me there is Morgan, who does not understand my marriage to Gamila, and on the other side Gamila, who also does not understand my connection to Morgan. And I feel, perhaps, it is a great sin to make Gamila suffer so. Should I finally abandon Morgan? I cannot do the right thing no matter what. Gamila is right: I have brought a curse upon us. I am a monster.

Yes, I finally said to her, it is a terrible fate to have a bitch like me as a husband. But I only wanted to help. Ahmed died and I did what I was asked to do. But I am sick and dying now, and how else am I to get the money for my family? Morgan has money.

I put it in those terms, terms she might understand, terms she might, unhappily, accept. But I did not mention the crisis of my heart.

Gamila stood there saying nothing, sighing heavily, her thin lips pursed. Then she widened her black eyes—once sleepy, now fiery—and, as she left, she hissed at me like a cat, as if casting a fatal spell.

Before Morgan returned with water, my coughing fit started and the convulsions grew more violent. Morgan rushed in and held me tightly. My body rattled. I was a slave to the coughing. The fit lasted an hour, maybe—it seemed an eternity. As Morgan held me, the smells of the lanolin and lavender of his moustache wax were a comfort. In the short pauses when my coughing would cease, I watched how the flickering candle made trembling silhouettes of us on the wall. Sometimes we were a still mountain range or sleeping water buffalo. Then I'd erupt into coughing, and the mountain would quake, and the buffalo buck.

After some time of Morgan holding me, one arm around my waist, he reached over with his other hand for my copy of *Leaves of Grass*. He read aloud to me. He started with my favorite, the ferryboat poem:

> *And you that shall cross from shore to shore years hence, are more*
> *to me, and more in my meditations, than you might suppose.*

Morgan read until my body was spent from coughing, until I collapsed and the angry mountain stood still; and I fell into a deep sleep, already dreaming of you.

There is something about yesterday I almost forgot to say. Before he went to fetch water, Morgan came to the bed where I was reading. He showed me his black notebook. He flipped it open to a page he'd titled "The India Story." He said he'd started a novel a year ago, set in India, but it had proven too difficult. He'd felt stuck, he said, depressed by the thought of completing it. But after Professor Ganda's admonishment, he now felt forced to look at the story again. It told the truth about the British. Perhaps, he said, it was his duty to write the thing that frightened him most—the thing that broke his heart in two. The novel was about muddles that occur when British try to connect with their subjects.

But why does writing that frighten you so? I asked Morgan.

He shook his head and said, Never mind. And then he looked at me, as if in a panic, and said, We can make it work, can't we, Mohammed? Can't we?

When I saw Morgan was so irresolute about his love for me, I was shaken. And it occurred to me he could only be frightened by one thing: he saw no possible happy end for a relationship like ours. I knew then that conjuring you may be my only chance to live the impossible life. In my bones, I knew I would need you more than ever. Whitman's words were also swimming around in my mind, and I too was meditating on a young man one hundred years hence—a man who might suffer like me and love like me.

My plan to put Morgan to the final test is yet to come. I am waiting for the right moment. But I must speak the truth to you, my Possibility: I'm only delaying because I fear Morgan will fail my test. And then my heart will break.

I glance down from my laptop to see a pair of dark ruddy-brown feet in sandals. Dried ashy skin in russet leather thongs. Two shiny straps across the top, with toes exposed. Immediately I know who it is. I'm not sure why, but I'm afraid to look up. I examine the cuffs of his uniform trousers: pleated navy blue, a polyester blend, it seems, silky as his skin. His long slender toes descend perfectly, like well-worn steps. His toenails are more yellowish than white but clean and thick and well manicured. Only one big toenail has a purplish mark, like a bruise. I know it's odd, but the word "confident" springs to mind. Suddenly these confident toes curl upwards for a split second, and then their owner addresses me:

"You are the American from the Brooklyn?" The Arabic accent is thick and seems harsh to my ears.

I muster the nerve and look up at him quickly, like ripping a plaster off a wound. There he is: Mohammed. He doesn't look at all like me. How could they have said we look like twins? His skin is darker than mine; his hair, wavier. He is taller, thinner, and younger too—in his late twenties, perhaps. Something about his clean-shaven face seems Picassoesque, slightly askew: a hooked nose curves in one direction, the mouth angling in another. As he smiles I notice his teeth are coffee-stained and crooked. Yet there is something lovely about him too. He has a sense of poise and seren-ity in the length of his neck, the slackness of his jaw. I think of the famous statue of Nike in the Louvre, the body maimed, headless, and yet these flaws only accentuate her essential beauty. It is only when I look directly into his eyes—a dazzling, fiery black—that I have to look away. I try to control a reflexive gasp. My stomach muscles tense. I saw myself in those eyes. Now I understand what the policemen meant about us looking like twins. I've never looked into the eyes of another and seen myself so clearly. It feels danger-ous, like gazing directly at the sun.

"American from Brooklyn?" he asks again.

I avoid the blinding sun and focus on his thick burgundy lips—lips expecting my reply with impatient little movements. "No," I say. "Not American exactly, but—"

"Is not your bag?" With his right hand he is holding the raised extendable handle of my red carry-on suitcase. He jangles the handle. "This? Not yours?"

"It's mine. Only I'm not—"

"You are man to stay in the Greenland?"

"Yes, that's me."

"From the Brooklyn?"

"Not originally, but yes. Yes." I shake my head firmly to clarify the confusion. "Yes, it's my bag."

"I find gun case inside bag," he says. "Officer Boss says no problem."

"Yes," I say. "They tell me everyone here has a gun."

"Hmmm." I sense Mohammed rolling his eyes. I look up and notice his raised eyebrows—heavy but shapely, like well-placed brushstrokes. "Yes," he says. "Everyone has a gun, but not me. Me—they won't let!"

"Really? Why not?"

"Why not?" He raises those dark eyebrows again and looks at me as if I've asked the most inane question. "Suicide risk, they say!"

I feel his stare penetrate. He seems to be observing to see how I will react to his mention of suicide. I try to keep a deadpan look, but it's awkward now that I know more about him than he suspects. I wonder if my face is revealing sympathy for this young dying man—sympathy he would not expect from me. I look down at his confident feet.

Finally, to my surprise, he bursts out laughing. "Suicide risk! Can you believe how *nice* are the people here? They want protect me from myself!"

"Yes." I try to smile with him, but his forthright, practically brazen, manner is throwing me off. Why is he telling me about being a suicide risk and then laughing? Me, a complete stranger. Is he trying to intimidate? Or ridicule me somehow? I play it neutral, polite. "They all seem to be very kind here," I say.

"Yes, very kind," he says. "But they have no idea! If after everything I have experienced I have not already committed suicide, why would I do it now? Greenland is paradise for me! I have no need for suicide now. Only time I think to kill myself is when I eat Greenlandic food!" He screws up his face comically and with palms raised beside his ears, he twists his wrists several times. "*Wafaqani Allah!* God help me!" he proclaims up to the ceiling. "I tell you, you will have to prepare yourself for eating a lot of *mattak*—raw whale fat. And reindeer fat soaked in coffee. And too much alcohol—akvavit and *immiaq*, Greenlandic beer. Everything with alcohol here. And more *mattak*! Only when I eat here do I think most fondly of home, of Morocco." He closes his eyes dreamily for a moment. "My mother's chicken tagine, her warm *mesemen* flatbread, her seafood *bastilla*!"

"Morocco? You're not from Egypt?"

"Egypt? No way!" he says, wide-eyed. "And I am not Arab either.

Arabs treat me like a dog. Egyptians too! All Blacks they treat like dogs. They know I have Sudanese blood and so they abuse me."

"Sudanese?" Didn't Mohammed El Adl suspect he had Sudanese blood?

"But I am from Agadir, Morocco," Mohammed says emphatically. "My father's ancestors were brought to Morocco many years ago in the trans-Saharan slave trade. But once you are Black in Arab country, no matter where—you are simply *kahlouche*, a Blackie. *You know what I mean, brother. Les Damnés de la Terre.*"

"*The Wretched of the Earth*. Frantz Fanon." I smile and look up to a flash of his blinding suns before I look away again.

"*Mais oui!* You too have read Fanon in French?"

"I read him in English, in university. Back in London."

"There is always something lost in translation, no? This is what my English professor at university always says. Have you also read French book by Tété-Michel Kpomassie from Togo? About his quest to Greenland? *L'Africain du Groenland*. I read it as a child in Morocco. Only because of him I am here!"

"Really? The book inspired you that much?" I am beginning to warm up to Mohammed. He has a buoyant and charming way about him—even his harsh accent seems to be getting softer, easier on my ears. "The book must have made quite an impression."

"More than that!" says Mohammed. He releases the handle of my suitcase again, apparently to have the full range of hand gestures. He leans in closer to my face and I smell the lingering scent of mint toothpaste mixed with coffee. He pulls his fingers and thumb together in each hand and moves them up and down at chest level. "That book saved my life! I realized that there were people on this earth who allowed children to find their own path. In Greenland it is forbidden to force children into a rigid mold. I read about the Greenlandic custom for each child to be free without any expectations from parents. In my family, it was only my father's way, the traditional Islamic way. I dreamed of being free of all that—an impossible life! And here I am in Greenland!" He raises his palms skyward. "*Alhamdulillah!* Thank God!" I sense from the crack in his voice he is deeply moved.

I also have an odd sense that something, almost like a voltaic current, is emanating from him. It must be my imagination. But then a tingling, like an electric shock, zips throughout my body. Instantly I'm hard. What's happening? Thank God my laptop is covering my crotch. I try to pray the erection away. I make myself picture kittens and nuns. When I open my eyes, Mohammed's right hand is extended towards me.

"My name is Mohammed El Majhad," he says.

I stand to shake his hand, trying to cover my erection with my left hand, but his eyes dart down for a second and I think he notices. I introduce myself. He asks me to repeat my name and then he laughs.

"Kipling! *Kipling!*"

I ask what he finds so amusing and he asks me if I know of the English poem "Fuzzy-Wuzzy" by Rudyard Kipling. I've never heard of it, I say.

"It is a poem about my father's ancestors. The Beja warriors from Sudan. The warriors who fought off the British colonials in 1884. Mr. Rudyard Kipling showed the world my people as true warriors."

We stand face-to-face now. I realize Mohammed is not as tall as I thought. We are roughly the same height, eye to eye. It must be the way he holds himself—he has the air of a taller person. He seems to be searching for my gaze but I look down. In the armpits of his white work shirt with its epaulettes, I see damp semicircles. I get a whiff of his powerful musky pong. Then I dare to meet his eyes, dare to get burned.

But as I meet his gaze, he slowly moves his eyes about my face as if he's deciphering a formula written somewhere beneath my skin. "Yes," he says. "You can be very useful to me, Mr. Kipling. I will see you later at the Blue Ice Café, no? *Then* we shall see."

Only because I am looking directly into his eyes now do I detect a subtle shift in his gaze—something fleeting. A menacing coldness? It's like an eclipse quickly blocking out the sunlight. A chill runs down my spine.

I make myself focus on Mohammed's dark eyes again, but now they are dazzling as before. He smiles and nods once, military style. Standing upright as a soldier, he turns. I am left there with my little red suitcase, watching him walk away.

I know it's his job to have inspected my baggage, but somehow it feels like an intrusion. I imagine his probing brown fingers rummaging through my private things; unfolding and rearranging my clothes; brushing along my black cashmere jumper; stroking my white Calvin Klein briefs; opening the gun case and fingering my pistol. It feels as if this Mohammed has already touched all of me.

———————

When Tukkuttok said he'd take me to the Blue Ice Café, I thought he meant he'd drive me in his police car, but we're walking there now in at least a foot of snow, in the dark, with my backpack and my carry-on suitcase. Tukkuttok says the sun won't be up until 9:00 a.m. He walks ahead, lighting the way with a large yellow battery torch. "It's only about six hundred meters away," he says, "just over there, towards Hospital Valley and Flower Valley."

My suitcase is getting heavier with each step. The wheels are useless here; I can't drag it in this snow. After about three hundred meters, my fingers are cramped and frozen, my toes gripped like eagle claws in my boots. I can barely walk anymore. I pant, unable to get sufficient breath, blowing clouds into the air, but my lungs only seem to be constricting more. I ask Tukkuttok if we can rest for a moment. He says okay. But he seems impatient and bored by the idea.

After planting my suitcase upright in the snow, I sit on it, winded and shivering. I pull my blue hoodie up from under my down jacket, shielding my face from the stinging snow that's blowing up from the ground as if we are in a sandstorm.

"Flower Valley?" I ask Tukkuttok, trying to engage him. I can't imagine anything ever growing in this vast icy wasteland. "Are there ever flowers in Flower Valley?"

"Of course," says Tukkuttok. "That is why they call it Flower Valley."

I wonder if he's being sarcastic, but his words seem devoid of any attitude; he's simply stating the facts. He rests the yellow torch on the hard snow, digging it in a bit, so it shines up, and as he steps away, I can see him now. His dark eyes seem motionless, mysterious. He stands, hands clasped behind him, like a statue in his navy uniform. He's apparently unfazed by the cold. He is also rather handsome, I realize. His stature and features remind me of Marlon Brando's—Tukkuttok has that same strong jaw, thick neck, and lifted eyebrows; he even has Brando's pouty lips.

"Well," I say, not giving up on engaging him, "you never know about the names of things. They say Greenland was named to fool people into thinking it was green here, to lure settlers. I thought maybe Flower Valley—"

"No," he says. "Lots of flowers in spring and summer. White and purple flowers. And yellow ones too. Lots." He looks away at the horizon, at a pale-yellow glow beginning to peek over the white hills. "Anyway, Greenland's real name is Kalaallit Nunaat; it means 'Land of the Kalaallit,' the original Inuit."

"Yes, I know." I'm excited to share my knowledge, to impress Tukkuttok. "I also learned that the name of this town, Narsarsuaq, means 'the Great Plan.' And, I know it sounds crazy, but I think it's a message to me. To go into this wilderness, where I'll have the space to find my true voice, to write my own truth. This is my great plan."

Tukkuttok gives me an enigmatic smile. "Come on. Let's go. You look cold. It's warmer in the café. It's just over there." His chin points the way. "Not far."

As we trudge through the knee-high snow, I fire away questions about Narsarsuaq, with my puffs of icy dragon breath. Tukkuttok answers me in a deep monotone: he tells me the population here is about 150; most work for the airport or hotel. The big hospital closed way before he was born, after World War II. There is no jail because there is no crime. The only crime is kids getting drunk and stealing boats for joyrides in the summer, or making too much noise after-hours, or some domestic disputes. And then the winter suicides. Otherwise, his job is easy, he says; lots of time to read up on things over the internet.

He likes American wrestling from the 1990s WWF, he adds. He knows everything about Dwayne Johnson, the Rock. But he doesn't like that he's become a movie star. Movie stars are problematic, he says. He tells me about how Brigitte Bardot is the perfect example of the Movie Star Problem. She caused great unemployment in Greenland, making many people abandon their villages and move to Nuuk. She made a big fuss—an international campaign—against baby seal fur, and so the entire industry died. Now whole villages are ghost towns, and all the villagers are still without work.

"I do not want to offend you," Tukkuttok adds, "but Europeans have destroyed this land. They brought their democracy to improve our standard of living, and made all villagers leave their land to move to big towns for proper running water, and sewage, and schools. And now so many are not happy. Even Europeans here are not happy. Look at my partner, Boss—even he's not so good. Always arguing with his wife. His children are not even talking to him ever since he moved them down here from Paamiut. No one is happy with these new ways." I realize that I had mistaken his monotone accent for a lack of proficiency, but his English is much better than I'd thought. "You have to live in the wilderness to remember the true gods," he says. "Like the goddess Sedna of the sea. Or to see the ancestors dancing in the Northern Lights. We were people who saw things with the help of our old shaman seers, the Angakkuq. We saw the invisible things—ancestors and gods. We lived better in nature. But the whole world is crazy now. Western civilization is destroying everything. Even our ice is on fire!"

As I struggle with my suitcase—the snow is now packing into my boots, soaking my socks, gnawing at my ankles—Tukkuttok explains that the glaciers here are melting at a rapid speed. All of the climate scientists have confirmed this. As the glaciers melt, the global sea levels rise. The frigid water from Greenland flows down into torrid regions and then the hot water flows up to polar regions and changes the weather on the entire planet. He says last August more ice melted in Antarctica than ever before: 220 gigatons. Five years ago, it was 43. And now, because the ice here is melting, the gases once buried underneath it—carbon and methane—are being released into the atmosphere. "In some areas of Greenland, if you poke a hole in the snow and light a match, fire will leap up like a torch. I've seen it myself," he says. "The last time in history that this much carbon was released into the air there were mass extinctions. Soon there will be no more of our icy wilderness left, perhaps no more people. We humans need nature to survive."

We have finally reached the Blue Ice Café. It is lit up by several spotlights attached from the roof, illuminating both the surrounding area and the café itself. It's a single-story, oxblood clapboard building with white trim. As we stop, Tukkuttok rests his hand on my left shoulder. "I'm sorry to tell you, Kipling," he says, "but you're wrong about something. This is *not* the great plan."

I'm taken aback by his conviction about my destiny. "Why do you say that?"

"Narsarsuaq, in English, means 'the Great *Plain*.' We are on a great *plain*."

"A *plain*?" I think he's confused. His English is much better than I initially thought, but it's not perfect. "No, no, no. You don't understand," I say. "It says so in Wikipedia. I read it. In the Inuit language, Narsarsuaq means 'the Great Plan.'"

Tukkuttok's stoic face reveals that winning smile again. "I know, I saw it in Wikipedia. too." He tries to suppress his laughter, but can't, and makes a mock apology with a clownish frown. "It's a mistake in English! It's—how do you say?—it's a typo!"

"*A typo?*" I feel like an idiot. I've constructed an entire life-defining narrative, all based on a typo in Wikipedia? "I see," I say, humiliated.

"Sometimes the internet is useful," says Tukkuttok. "Sometimes not useful."

Useful. As soon as he utters that word, I think of Mohammed El Majhad. Back at the airport, he had used that word referring to me. What did he mean, "useful"? In a flash I see Mohammed's blinding black eyes; I smell the pong of his underarm as if he were before me again. I remember the length of his neck, with a single vein running along the side, thick and throbbing. Why had I hardly noticed that vein at the time, but I see it clearly now? My heart starts to race.

I smile at Tukkuttok, my lips half frozen. I feel something stirring in my chest—a warm confidence. I'm possessed, perhaps, by the spirit of Mohammed. Or is it both Mohammeds? I feel my neck start to lengthen too. And I recall Forster noting how charming it was of his Mohammed to invent his own names for things. He called his house the "Home of Misery" and the Municipal Gardens the "Chatby Gardens" because they were near the Chatby tram stop.

"Well," I say to Tukkuttok, as I imagine how both Mohammeds might retort, "some say there are no such things as mistakes. So Wikipedia has decided my destiny. For me, Narsarsuaq shall always be the Great Plan!"

PART 5

The Snow Men

Tukkuttok closes the café door behind us and the howling wind is silenced. At once I'm aware of my own heartbeat thumping in my eardrums, my staccato breathing, and the rapid-fire chattering of my teeth.

"Here we are," says Tukkuttok, patting me on the back. "The Blue Ice Café." He paces in front of me looking around as if somehow he's also seeing it for the first time. "You can stay here until you find a permanent place. Don't worry, it won't take long. The North African, Mohammed, had over twenty invitations from our townspeople. He finally chose my sister's home. She told him if he stayed with her she'd get *me* to teach him how to build an igloo. It's true. Anyway, when Aguta gets here she'll have food for you. She's the one who runs this café. Cozy, eh?"

"Yes," I say, putting my bags down. "Very cozy."

I give the café a quick perusal, trying to imagine where I could possibly sleep in here—and on what? It seems smaller than it appeared from the outside. There are about eight or ten shiny aluminum café tables that seat two comfortably, but with four chairs crowded around each. The chairs are the folding patio kind with pinewood slats and green metal frames. The clapboard walls are white with accent walls in pale blue at either end. At the far end of the room, there's a service counter where the food and coffee are sold. To the left of the counter is an alcove, a separate little chamber with a free-standing poster board announcing VISITOR INFORMATION CENTRE, and below that, added in handwritten blue Magic Marker, "Glacier Hiking Equipment. Rent It Here!"

The air smells faintly of cedar, burnt coffee, and a familiar odor I can't quite place. Then I realize the scent reminds me of sex for some reason, and I feel embarrassed, as if somehow Tukkuttok can tell what's on my mind. To make up for it I make a show of nodding approvingly, piously, as I look around the place.

"Well okay," says Tukkuttok, removing his thermal gloves one after the other and shoving them into the pockets of his uniform trousers. "Make yourself at home, Kipling." He rubs his bare palms together in an unhurried manner. There is something very manly about his gesture. "Before I leave I can show you how to make the coffee."

As he makes his way over to the counter he stops for a moment and peers into a narrow glass curio standing just inside the alcove. He shakes his head. I follow him a few paces behind. Inside the case on its three glass shelves are objects that appear to be native totems carved from bone, gruesome fanged figures. On the top shelf at about eye level is a sign reading DO NOT TOUCH THE TUPILAQ. ASK FOR HELP.

I ask Tukkuttok about the strange figures.

He continues to shake his head. "These things should not be for sale." He bites at his bottom lip for a moment. "Fakes! For tourists!"

He tells me the *tupilaq* are totems originally made by the ancient Greenlandic shamans. The Angakkuq would carve the totems on behalf of people who wanted to seek revenge on someone who had harmed them. They would take weeks to make them in a secret ritual that included rubbing their genitals over them and then summoning the ancestors for support. "The ancestors have a lot of power in our Inuit culture," he says. "They also say the ancestors used to be responsible for many suicides here."

"Why would the ancestors want suicides?" I ask.

"Well." Tukkuttok lets out a deep sigh and raises his Brando-like eyebrows knowingly, as if to say, Now this is very complex stuff we're getting into. "Nowadays there are all kinds of reasons for suicides in Greenland. Ever since colonization—and especially with the end of the seal business—more young people kill themselves. They feel they've lost their culture or have no way to make money. But in olden days, it was common for a widow or widower to disappear in winter, go away from everyone, build an igloo out by the great fjords, and then starve themselves to death, or shoot themselves, in order to be reunited with the dead husband or wife. Suicide was an accepted tradition here. And sometimes when a young person died—for instance, a woman in childbirth, or a young husband—a hunter who'd gotten mauled by *krêmit*, wild huskies—they would say such a person becomes a demon-ancestor in the great beyond, unsettled and unfulfilled until they reunite with the lover they left behind. And so they possess their lover on the earthly realm, induce them to madness, and force them to commit suicide so they can be reunited. But that was rare." Tukkuttok shakes his head and seems to be considering something he may or may not say. "Well . . . I can't say what's true, but many people here believe such things. And now Danish law says we policemen must prevent suicides. So . . ." Tukkuttok slowly rubs his palms together again.

"I see," I respond. Now I think I understand Tukkuttok's fixation on the issue: it is not suicide per se, but rather the fact that he is in conflict with himself. "The old Greenlandic laws, or the new Danish laws, huh? It must be hard to know what's right these days," I say.

Tukkuttok is looking down now and blinking a lot. "Yes," he says. Then with a sudden, wide-open innocence he looks up at me. "What do you think is right, Kipling?"

I don't know what to say. I don't want to offend Tukkuttok, but I understand why Danish laws need to prevent suicides. I wonder if there isn't some higher law to consider. An eternal law that says all souls, dead or alive, must fulfill their destiny for love, maybe so?

"Maybe so," Tukkuttok says, as if he's read my mind. "But to sell these imitation *tupilaq* for tourists is not right. It could be dangerous to play with the ancestors."

Now I'm feeling guilty for my casual curiosity about these totems, as if I were yet another obnoxious tourist.

"So"—Tukkuttok shakes his head as if to free himself of an invisible grip—"what about your coffee, Kipling?"

"Yes, yes, please," I say. "I'd love coffee. Please!" I'm embarrassed by the way I blurt it out, but Tukkuttok making coffee would keep him around a little longer.

"Or," he says, looking down at his watch, "you can make the coffee yourself, if I show you how, eh? I should get back to help Boss at the airport." He points out the tins of coffee and the coffee machine, then walks back to the café's main door. He stops for a second and looks up, as if he's forgotten something. "Oh, Kipling . . ."

"Yes." I follow him. I don't want Tukkuttok to leave me yet. "What is it?"

"One more thing . . . " Tukkuttok takes off his thick blue policeman's jacket to reveal a hooded, ash-brown, fur parka beneath it. Then he takes off the parka and hands it to me. "For you. You'll need it when you go to the wilderness. My anorak. Greenlandic. Caribou fur. Very warm. Your city jacket is no good for here." I'm speechless and shake my head, but he insists. "My gift. Take it. And these . . . " He pulls his thermal gloves from his pockets. "You'll need these too."

"No, I can't . . . " But I accept them anyway. I'm stunned at his generosity. My eyes suddenly well up as if I might cry from Tukkuttok's kind gestures. But I get self-conscious and clear my throat, and say "cool" in my most nonchalant and macho voice.

Tukkuttok nods without smiling. "Okay. Goodbye then." But as he steps out of the door, he sticks his head back inside again. "So, Kipling . . . " He looks at me for a moment in silence. He maintains eye contact but his face doesn't move at all. I can't imagine what he's thinking. And then he nods once and says, "Welcome to Greenland."

I stand by the café's front window and look out over the snowy landscape. The sun is pale but rising quickly. In just moments, I watch the sky grow lighter—powder blue, lavender, orange, all shades rising up and spreading wide across the atmosphere like watercolors on Japanese rice paper. We are indeed on a great plain—not plan! Miles of snow with little slopes, but mostly flat. To the left, I spot Tukkuttok in the distance, trekking back to the airport like a little black beetle trudging in the snow. In the other direction, miles away to the right, are specks of what must be houses, a colorful cluster of red, blue, and green dots in the haze. And directly in front of me, about six hundred meters away, is a great fjord, as wide as an ocean. It's barely distinguishable from the sky—just a pale gray-green swath in the distance. The movement of giant turquoise icebergs is the only indication that there's a body of water there. They are the size of Gothic cathedrals, slowly floating by on the gray-green horizon. I can't believe I'm actually in Greenland.

After taking in the spectacular landscape I make my way to the café counter and busy myself making coffee. It is not as simple as Tukkuttok made it seem. There's a sleek, minimalist Scandinavian coffee machine. So minimal, in fact, that I can't find any buttons. It takes me five minutes to figure out how to turn the damn thing on. It takes even longer to understand how to add the water, the filter, and then the coffee.

Finally successful and cradling a white cup of steaming coffee in my hands, I return to the front window for the view again. I could take in this panorama forever. Above the vast stretch of snowy stillness, the somnolent movement of the icebergs on the fjord is hypnotizing. It lulls me into a meditative state. My breathing slows down and the air I take in sinks like an anchor, deep in my belly. I have a sensation I've had before in rare meditations, when I feel the boundaries of who I am dissolving. From dense flesh, to a paper-thin shroud of skin, to nothing at all. I am no longer "me" anymore.

I think about my favorite poem, Wallace Stevens's "The Snow Man." This must be what it feels like to become Nothing. I am like the mysterious subject in Stevens's poem—who's not an actual snowman, but the allusion to a man who has attained such a clear consciousness, "a mind of winter," that when he beholds the world he sees not misery but "nothing that is not there, and the nothing that is." I feel indistinguishable from what is around me, inseparable from everything beyond.

Then I hear his voice: *Come. Come with me to the wilderness.*

Mohammed?

Yes, it's him. I can even feel the warmth of him. He is close by. Where? I look in front of me and see dark eyes gazing directly at me. And then it occurs to me: these are the same dazzling black eyes of Mohammed from the airport. Is the Mohammed from Morocco actually the reincarnation of my Mohammed? Has my Mohammed come to me from across a century, in the body of the young man from Morocco? I remember my talk with Soraya at the ashram years ago—her scientific explanations for the nonexistence of Time and Space, for the illusory distinctions between the dead and the living. Could this be Mohammed El Adl coming to me here?

Immediately I dismiss the idea. But I am in Greenland, and what would Tukkuttok say? "Maybe so?" What would the traditional people of Greenland say? "The ancestors of old come back for us"—isn't that what they say? The souls who have died young do not rest until their destiny is fulfilled, until their love is complete.

Is that really you, my Mohammed?

I lean forward and I can feel his breath, hot on my face, on my lips. I meet his gaze. It no longer blinds me like the sun. Now I see two dark pools, like midnight ponds, inviting me to dive in. I'm staring at his deep inkwell eyes and they mesmerize; I could drown in them. He is going to kiss me, I'm sure. His parted lips are trembling, almost touching my nose. Here it comes. Yes, I want him to kiss me, I realize. I want him completely, so badly. *I want you, Mohammed!* I lean further forward. I dare to get closer.

Thud. My face knocks against the windowpane. My forehead smarts from the cold glass. I gasp. Confused. Horrified now. No, it can't be. I shake my head to unsee my own reflection floating there in the glass, ghostly, above the snow. But I can't unsee myself. I turn away from the window. What is happening to me? I close my eyes but I still hear him whispering, *Come. Come with me to the wilderness.*

We are interrupted, my ghost and I, when the café door swings wide open. Cold air rushes in like a pack of the wild huskies, fangs first. A woman appears. She quickly slams the door shut with her left foot. Wearing black rubber snow boots and dressed in black overalls with a white cable-knit sweater underneath, she stands at the entrance, stock-still. She doesn't take off her red-plaid, white fur–lined trapper hat. Her straight black bangs fall flat on her forehead, as if on a painted Chinese doll. Her dark eyes take me in with an unmoving stare. "Hey," she says, without a smile, then she says nothing else.

She is not old—barely forty, I'd guess—but she moves with matronly assurance, like a woman who has hauled many children on her hips or beaten the dust out of countless old rugs.

She tromps towards the counter with a large blue Ikea shopping bag in her arms; several baguettes are sticking out. She unpacks the bag. She puts the bread and a heap of croissants, about twenty, on the counter, and then a roll of paper towels, two big plastic jugs of milk, and several cans of items I don't recognize. Next to the breads she places a large jar of lingonberry jam, a brick of butter, and a jar of Nutella. Then she walks over to the sideboard, where there are souvenirs, maps of Narsarsuaq, and brochures for Blue Ice Expeditions on display. She opens the cabinet beneath it, and on top of the sideboard she places a stack of T-shirts with words on them:

I DON'T NEED THERAPY, I JUST NEED TO GO TO GREENLAND. Then she returns to the service counter.

She practically ignores me as she goes about her business. It's as if she's seen me every day for the last ten years, as if we're old co-workers meeting on the factory floor, with nothing left to say to each other. It is only when she stops and stares at me again, her hands leaning on the counter, that I dare to approach her.

"Mohammed's friend," she says.

I'm totally confused by her statement. "*Mohammed?*" I say.

"Mohammed told me you'd be here." Without a smile, she introduces herself. "I'm Aguta. Some people call me Madame Dupont." Her accent doesn't sound French.

Her wide face is unmoved, her high cheekbones like tawny porcelain. Her eyes meet me directly, unflinchingly. There is something in her eyes that immediately reminds me of Concha. The confident gaze? The arch of the eyebrows? The more I stare at her, the more uncanny the resemblance seems. She could be Concha's sister. Immediately I feel at ease with her. Perhaps it is a false sense of familiarity, but nonetheless I'm comforted.

"I'm Kip," I say, soon realizing that no matter how much I smile, she will not smile back. "And you are . . . Madame *Dupont*, you said?" I've already forgotten her first name.

"Yes. Dupont. Charles Dupont is my husband. He's from France. Isère. I'm not from France. I'm from Nuuk. Call me Aguta, it's easier." Her English seems good but she almost speaks without any variation in cadence, as if she's learned English from Siri or Google Translate.

Standing behind the counter, she places four long baguettes on a wooden chopping block. She turns around to grab a bread knife from a magnetic strip on the wall behind her—a strip on which several knives hang, all pointing up, with their black handles arranged from short to long. She begins slicing the golden, crusty baguettes into sandwich-size pieces. Brittle crumbs fly up but she looks unbothered. It all seems effortless. She only appears to apply any force at all when it comes to cutting through the tough crust at the bottom, for which she makes a quick exhale and a snap of her wrist with each slice—cracking through the hard part and punctuating the act with a satisfied twitch of her bottom lip.

After cutting up two baguettes, she looks over to me with her daring stare. "Only reason I'm here today," she says, "is because the policemen told me New York people had deplaned. A dead woman. *Humph.* Odd. Anyway, now it looks like the plane for Iceland's delayed. Those New York passengers may need some coffee and tea and pastries. Officer Boss said we can't have the Americans getting upset. He begged me to help out, prepare some food. My husband's in Nuuk today. So just me here. I told the officers I'd do what I could. We don't want the Americans rioting because there's no coffee and croissants."

I swear, the way she refers to "the Americans" is exactly the way Concha would; perhaps Aguta is a bit more subtle than Concha, but it's with the same saucy, wry attitude. And when I think of the last time I saw Concha, I get a sinking feeling in my gut, a pang of guilt.

I stand there watching Aguta slice up the baguettes. I'm left alone with my guilty pangs. What have I done to hurt Concha so? Was I really so cruel and selfish? Should I have reached out to her? Is it too late? Although Aguta seems perfectly comfortable in the long silence, I feel awkward. I need to quiet my guilty pangs.

I ask Aguta if I can help put groceries away. She declines my assistance and goes about doing it herself. I can't tell if she's annoyed with me or just a woman of few words. Perhaps she's bothered by the arrival of the Americans, me included, with all their inevitable demands. I'm realizing that perhaps not everyone in Greenland will be as welcoming as the two policemen. Although I'll only be here for a week to finish the novel, I don't want to be seen as a bothersome tourist. In *The Sheltering Sky*, Paul Bowles writes about the distinction between a traveler and a tourist. I don't want to seem as if I'm consuming or exploiting the native people as a tourist would. I want Aguta to know I'm here for something real, to know this world and the people, and to allow them to change me.

Trying to sound as sincere as I can, I approach the counter, cradling my now tepid coffee. "So," I say. "What's it like for you, Aguta, dealing with the tourists?"

She stops in the middle of unscrewing the white top off the Nutella jar and looks at me blankly. "That is a very complicated question, eh?" she finally says. She puts down the jar and sighs heavily. She wipes her hands on a white cloth, seeming to examine the red lingonberry stain she's just made on it, now working it in more with her thumb until it's faded and pinkish. Finally she looks at me, more earnestly than before, as if she's finally decided to speak frankly.

"I'll tell you," she says. "The foreign men sometimes actually look afraid of me." She smiles mischievously. I notice a small black mole just above her top lip, on her right side. "But also, they are fascinated. I think they come here thinking, you know . . . 'Oh, an Inuit women: sweet and docile.' But then they meet me. I meet their gaze in a way they don't expect. I don't back down. I think it scares them. But then I see a strange desire light up in their eyes. This is why they have come to Greenland, you see: for something to frighten them. The desire to cross into the danger zone, eh?

"But with the women, it's different. I have the most interesting conversations with the women. They are usually visiting from Europe or Canada or America. They are white women, for the most part. They don't know me at all, of course, but they stand here, right there where you're standing, and they have their coffees and muffins and croissants, and they confess things you wouldn't believe.

"After university in Nuuk, I studied journalism in Montreal, and I think that's where I must have developed my skills to get people to talk, eh? The women tell me everything: all about their extramarital affairs, or affairs they never had the courage to have. How they feel trapped in relationships they don't know how to leave. How they wish they had the courage to pursue their desires. Many of them have come to Greenland because they believe it will give them courage. Greenland, for them, is a place of possibility. A clean slate, another chance. It will be the great adventure that will bring them back to life. They confess all this to me, as if I were a woman they already know.

"They are rich women, mostly, who have made the most of themselves. They have achieved their optimal bodies with their Pilates and the sharpest minds money can buy at the best universities. They've got the best skin care products to preserve their youth. The ones who are single are 'good catches,' desirable commodities on OkCupid and Elite Singles. But they're still lonely, they say, still unable to feel alive with their desires. They can tell me all this because they think they know who I am. I am like, you know, like a psychoanalyst for them—a blank slate. For them, Greenland is a blank slate.

"And it's odd because obviously I am not who they think I am. I'm a Greenlandic woman. I am Kalaallit—an Inuit woman. My history moves through me; my ancestors sing through my voice. I am not a blank slate or a blank voice. I am everything my ancestors have made me to be. And I think these foreign women are silly and vain. Deluded. Dead inside. They have no sense of who they really are, no ancestors guiding them. But it is interesting that all these dead lovers come to me, eh? I suppose it is my destiny. My name is Aguta. In our language it means 'Gatherer of the Dead.'"

I'm sitting at a table by the window, watching the morning sun ascend over the fjord. The diffuse white light brings out a bright turquoise in the icebergs. I've been studying pamphlets and maps of Narsarsuaq. I've decided to trek alone into the wilderness here. Aguta has given me the Wi-Fi password and some tips for my trek, and then prepared a fresh cup of Greenlandic Coffee for me. When she offered it, I didn't realize it was alcoholic. Black coffee with whisky, Kahlúa, Grand Marnier, and topped off with "two big icebergs," as she says—two dollops of whipped cream. Greenlandic Coffee has me tipsy already and it's not even noon yet! But I've got Sophia open and ready. If I can concentrate, I'll work on the novel. Despite all the strangeness around me, the novel is still advancing, thank God. Fiction consoles me. It's the one reality I can depend on. But I only have a week left to find my true voice, otherwise my work will be too late for the publishing legend. And only one chapter left to write.

Just as I click open the Word document, there is a rap on the door. A second later, Mohammed enters, a burst of wind rushing in with him. Even though he's wearing a fur anorak—brown, dusted with snow, its shaggy hood pulled over his head—I recognize him immediately. He's also carrying a black rectangular thermal bag over his shoulder. It's the insulated kind used for transporting food. Mohammed lets the bag fall from his shoulder and it flops to the floor noiselessly, collapsing. Before stepping further inside, Mohammed stomps snow from his high furry snow boots. He bends over, facing the wall as he pulls his boots off, then his socks too. He stuffs each sock into its respective boot. When he stands upright again, he yanks two flat brown objects from his coat pockets and flings them to the floor. The leather sandals land soles down, with a single slap. Mohammed slips his bare feet into them quickly, easily, and then he turns to face us.

"Aguta!" he calls out across the café, flipping his hood back. "Good morning, my darling! How is the most beautiful woman in all of Greenland?" He flashes a big, crooked-tooth smile.

To my surprise, Aguta actually smiles back. "Oh, Mohammed. You think your flattery will work with me?"

"Why not, *habibti*?" He laughs. "It is only the truth!"

I'm further surprised to see Aguta blush like a schoolgirl or a flirt. "You are impossible!" She wags her index finger at him. "A little devil—you know that?"

"Don't forget to save one of your baguettes for me, my darling." Mohammed turns to face me. "Mr. Kipling, you must know something: this woman makes the very best baguettes in the world! She knows the way to a man's heart!" He winks at me.

"Oh, stop it!" Aguta swipes her hand in the air and beams. "Anyway, what's the news about the passengers from New York?"

"They have sent me for *des pâtisseries* and for the sandwiches. They say Blue Ice Café is too far for the Americans to walk in this snow."

"Of course, of course," says Aguta, revealing none of her previous bias about the "delusional" tourists. She only seems to be basking in the warmth of Mohammed's attention. She begins to hum dreamily to herself.

As Aguta hums and prepares the croissants and sandwiches for Mohammed to transport, busying herself behind the counter with cellophane wrap and with this container and that, Mohammed approaches my table. He stops about a foot away. Looking down at my laptop, I hear him breathing through his nostrils, slow and steady. He stares at me as if, perhaps, I were not aware of his presence. It reminds me of the way a person might examine a bird in a cage, assuming a kind of observer's proprietorship. I'm not sure if it's a hostile move or a friendly one.

"Mr. Kipling," he says with a half smile. "What are you writing there?"

"Oh." I wave one hand in vague circles. "You know, nothing really." I'm lying, pretending only now to become aware of him. I really don't want to talk about my novel. It's feels like exposing a child prematurely to the harsh elements. "It's just my work."

"Ahh." He lifts his chin and jabs it forward, towards my table. "I see you got the Greenlandic Coffee. I told you: too much alcohol here in Greenland! Are you drunk yet? Seeing double?"

"Seeing double?"

He laughs, lots of brownish teeth. "Let me see if you're drunk," he says. "Let me see your eyes."

I laugh with him. So quickly after seeming threatening, he disarms me with his smile, his charm, his electricity. "No, no. I'm not drunk," I say. "Look! No double vision!" I open my eyes wide to prove it, but as I meet Mohammed's gaze directly, I see two sets of eyes: Mohammed's and the same black eyes I saw on my ghost floating in the window, the midnight ponds.

I quickly refocus to see Mohammed staring at me. He keeps looking. And then I can't look anymore. I don't know why, but it feels too dangerous. I look away, down at Sophia.

"Okay, Mr. Kipling," says Mohammed. "I will come and see you later. Then we can talk, no? Then we shall see. Okay?"

I nod, but I have no idea what he's talking about.

"Frantz Fanon," he says, winking at me knowingly. In his blue uniform trousers, he then seems to subtly scratch at his crotch, or to grab it, or something—a gesture I've seen from many men in the Caribbean, and in Morocco too. An innocuous macho habit? A covert signal?

"*Les Damnés de la Terre.*" He winks at me again.

The Wretched of the Earth. The English translation, not the literal translation of the French, which would be *The Damned of the Earth.* I nod but look down at my computer, avoiding his face and his crotch. What is he up to? I often get confused with North African men. Their social cues are different from what I know. Puzzling, especially to a Western gay man. I remember noticing that difference on my trips to Marrakesh, at the hammams. Some of the men there seemed to give me such longing stares, tender and affectionate, and then suddenly they'd curse all faggots to hell! I have to be careful.

"I'll see you later," I say to Mohammed, tapping at my keyboard. "Gotta get back to my work." I click open the web browser, pretending to busy myself, but Mohammed remains there observing me. I don't look up at him, but I can still smell him. His pungent underarms are stronger than before, both sharp and sour, musky and chocolatey—they stink, in fact. But in a way I can't resist returning to. The whiff reminds me of men I have loved urgently, in a hurry. Is that the same odor I detected when I first arrived at the café? Was it the scent of Mohammed in here, all along? I try to refocus on my work, but I cannot stop inhaling him.

I probably shouldn't have had that Greenlandic Coffee. Ben says I'm not a fun drunk. Alcohol makes me sullen and overly emotional, he says. But so far I'm only feeling light and tipsy. Now that Mohammed has gone, Aguta arrives at my table offering yet a second Greenlandic Coffee. I make a goofy smile, cross-eyed at the two creamy "icebergs" floating on top. "No, thank you, I really shouldn't," I say. But I finally surrender to her warm elixir with a bashful "Okay, okay. If you insist."

She takes a seat at the little aluminum table, sitting across from me, sipping her own steaming cup of Greenlandic brew. Being so close to her I feel shy, exposed. She seems to see through me.

"You must be writing something very important there, eh." She makes a curt little nod towards my laptop. Her black bangs don't move at all.

"Yeah. I'm just trying to write an email. To a dear friend."

Aguta nods once. I'm usually good at reading facial expressions, but I can't tell what she's thinking. She looks as if, perhaps, she's waiting for me to say more.

"I'm writing because I need to apologize to a friend," I explain. "Only I'm not exactly sure what I did wrong. She's my best friend, really, and I—"

"Your girlfriend?"

I'm surprised Aguta doesn't realize I'm gay. My gayness seems so obvious to me. But I remember how often this has happened in my life, and how awkward it always is. To come out or not to come out—that is the question! And my shameful confession is, I feel some delight at being perceived as straight. It's a perverse pleasure because, at the same time, I also resent heteronormative assumptions. And to complicate matters, there is also the covert expectation that as a Black man I should fulfill the stereotype: to be the macho sexual animal. The big-dicked Mandingo. And the sick part is, deep down, part of me wants to meet that expectation. I want to be seen as strong and virile. I even feel that other Black people expect the same of me. They too are disappointed if I seem less than the macho, chest-thumping, sexual beast with the anatomy to prove it.

Struggling with these thoughts, I'm deciding how to respond to Aguta's question about my "girlfriend." "No," I finally say. "We're just friends. She's not my girlfriend." But I don't disavow the idea that I may be straight. In my mind, I can still be that Mandingo for Aguta.

"Hmmm," she says, licking at her iceberg dollops. Her gesture seems purposefully sensual. She lolls her red tongue over the whipped cream as she meets my eyes with her gaze. "You know, I think Mohammed likes you."

"Mohammed?" My heart races. "What do you mean?"

"I saw him talking to you. Be careful. You know, he's a gay."

"He is?" My heart is now pounding and I'm feeling a shortness of breath.

"Don't worry." Aguta smiles wryly. "He's not the type to force himself on you. He's very forward but not rude. Still, gay people can get confused sometimes. Especially around attractive men. You just need to be firm and up-front with him."

"Okay." I nod. Did Aguta just refer to me as attractive? Before my mind starts spinning too much—wondering if she's attracted to me, or if she knows I'm gay and is toying with me—Aguta, luckily, changes the subject.

"So," she says, "about preparing for your expedition . . . " She pauses to sip at her steaming coffee. "I can tell you exactly what you need to rent from us." She begins to list the necessary gear for my weeklong trek—the time I'll need to find my wilderness and finish the novel: a dome tent, a sleeping bag, an inflatable mattress, a Trangia stove with several butane and propane gas cartridges, a set of hiking poles, as well as a variety of glacier trekking equipment—an ice ax, crampons, a harness, and a helmet. As she rattles off the list, I feel a mounting panic that I've bitten off more than I can chew. What am I doing? Aguta must detect some change in my expression, because she stops talking and looks concerned.

I remember what Aguta told me earlier, about all the "dead" women, the tourists who make their confessions to her, and I feel somehow she is talking about me too. I feel ashamed that even though I'm a Black man, I oddly fit into her category of lost Western white women, rapt in a romantic fantasy of Greenlandic wilderness.

"Kipling," she says, her hands cradling her coffee cup. "Why exactly do you want to make this trek alone to the wilderness, eh?"

Why exactly am I doing this? Half woozy with the booze now, I hear myself prattle on, barely intelligibly, about the need to write a novel that is authentically *me*, to speak in a voice of my very own. I tell her I've reached the final chapter now and I need to be sure I've found the right voice.

"But if you're at the final chapter, you've already written most of the novel, eh? What voice have you been using all along?"

I'm struck dumb. My brain seems to freeze. I don't know what to say. I hadn't thought about that, but it seems obvious now that she's saying it. *What voice have I been using all along?* The question seems to crack through some kind of illusory screen upon which I have been projecting everything. I've lost my perspective on reality. *What voice have I been using all along?* I don't know. Who is this thinking and talking right now? Me? Who is that? I don't know. It's as if the ground beneath me is quickly vanishing. I have the odd feeling that I'm suspended in the air, about to plunge into an abyss. I grip the café table to keep myself from actually falling. "I don't know," I say. "I—"

Aguta leans forward and rests her forearms on the table, clasping her hands. She looks at me straight on. Her face seems stoic, but her eyes are alive. There is something magnetic about them. And then I remember Concha's face and I look at Aguta again. It is as if her dark eyes have earth-moving powers; they seem to wrench up something deep in me—a profound and tremendous fear. I feel myself begin to shake, my hands trembling. I have not even realized the depths of this fear until this very second. What exactly am I fearing? What is so terrifying? I don't understand, but then I see it: I am terrified of falling into the abyss. Terrified to fall and be left there alone, unseen, unheard, to be nothing. I clutch at the table even more—I cannot let myself fall.

It isn't until I see Aguta looking at me with widened eyes that I look down to see my hands now clutching tightly onto hers. How did that happen?

Reflexively I smile, shocked. Independent of my own will, my smile seems to automatically remember its ability to charm, and it grows in confidence. It's like the smile I saw on Mohammed, isn't it? Has he possessed me somehow? But no. I too have employed this smile before to save myself, haven't I? I don't want to fall into nothingness, and the woman with the daring gaze can save me. She desires me, doesn't she? Yes. Her eyes keep on me steadily—and that is the proof: I am seen, I am wanted. And then it occurs to me, I can keep myself safe from falling if I secure my grip on her. I can be the virile Black man she wants me to be. I can be Mohammed—dangerous, defiant, sexy, and Black. I feel Mohammed rising in me, a heat and stiffening in my pants. And, yes, she wants me, doesn't she? Again, I notice that exotic black mole above her lip. I lean over the café table, extend my neck towards her, smell her apple-scented cheeks, and kiss Aguta on her pert red lips.

"What are you doing?" She jumps up, flinging my hands away.

I'm jolted backwards by her force. I don't understand what's happening. My head is spinning. Immediately I feel tears pounding behind my eyes. I smile, but that charming smile doesn't stick. It can't save me now. I keep shaking my head. "I'm sorry. It must be the alcohol. I—" I truly don't understand what's happening. I can't contain the oncoming tsunami. I'm losing control of my body. I feel I might vomit. And then from nowhere a guttural sob erupts from me: "I'm so sorry—" I hear myself begin to weep.

I don't know what Aguta is doing now, I only see a blur of her standing there through my tears. I try to wipe the tears away but they keep coming.

"I am a liar!" I keep repeating as I sob. "A liar! A liar!" I cannot say anything else. It's all I can think. "I'm a liar. I'm so sorry!" But I don't even know who I'm apologizing to—Aguta, Concha, Ben, myself? More than anything, I keep imagining Concha's eyes glaring at me. "You were right, Concha," I cry out. "I led you on!"

Even as I'm crying, in all my confusion, the facts somehow

come quickly into focus—unbidden but sharp, crystal clear. It is as if they've only been waiting to be unveiled. Now I see everything: Yes, I knew how Concha felt about me since we first met, from the time we went to the Museo de Bellas Artes in Seville. It was the way she looked at me as we stood before Valdés Leal's "Temptation of San Jerónimo." And even much later, when she was ending her marriage with Trent, I knew her desire for me was still there. And I kept giving her reasons to hold on for me because I was a coward. I used her because I was afraid of falling. As long as she wanted me, I was safe, I thought. And I was desperate to protect myself from plunging into the abyss.

"I'm so sorry." I look up at Aguta standing there, seemingly unmoved. My tsunami has passed now, but I'm feeling mortified by my brazen actions and my emotional outburst. "I really didn't mean to grab your hands like that," I say. "Or to kiss you. I was just— just—trying not to fall."

After a few seconds of silence she only says "I see," but I'm relieved to hear anything from her—at least it stops me from blabbering on. "So," she adds. "It's not for your book that you need to go to the wilderness after all, eh?"

"What do you mean?" I say. And then I find myself resenting her—the cool, aloof way she seems to be looking down at me. How dare she tell me what I need! A hot rage rushes to my face, my eyes burning. How dare she! After I've just apologized, and made a fool of myself, crying like a baby in front of her, she (she who has plied me with alcohol, she who has licked her lips suggestively at me) now stands there aloof, telling me what I need to do?

"Of course! I know what I need!" I say, feeling muscles clenching in my jaw. "I know why I came to the wilderness. I know it's not just about my writing. You think I don't know I'm a liar? I know it's my truth that I'm here for! I've known that all along!"

Aguta says nothing. Then she sighs heavily. "Men," she says, shaking her head. Reaching over, with one index finger, she hooks up both coffee cup handles. With the cloth in her other hand, she wipes up the coffee I've spilled. She looks at me in silence for a few seconds. "I'll leave the sleeping bag and other hiking gear by the counter," she says. "Tonight you can sleep here. Tomorrow it's up to you."

Now that Aguta has finally gone and I'm alone in here, the only way to calm my nerves is to write. Quickly, maybe even rashly, I compose an email to Concha—begging her to forgive me. Asking her to meet with me when this adventure is over, to make amends. I hope we can repair and rebuild the strong walls of our friendom. I push "send" before I give myself time to chicken out. But now I'm left with myself again. And the silence. I realize I'm still feeling unsettled after what's happened with Aguta. But at last I hear his voice whispering to me. Yes. He's coming to my rescue again—my Mohammed.

The Englishman's Virtue

Yesterday afternoon, after the forty-minute train ride from Cairo's Bab el-Louk station, riding across the Sahara, passing the great pyramids of Giza, we finally arrived here in Helwan and settled at the English Winter Hotel and Pension. It is a modest, pinkish, two-story place with balconies off each room. Morgan says this pension has surely seen better days. But the views from the balconies are spectacular: the Nile, with clusters of palms along its riverbanks, and beyond that, the desert, shimmering like an infinite golden sea.

This trip is Morgan's idea. He hopes Helwan's springs can cure my consumption. I am not so naive. Clinging to hope is a torturous thing. Hope won't change the fact that one day soon I'll die from this disease.

Morgan paid for the train fares all the way from Mansourah. He has also paid for the hotel accommodations and my spa treatments. So far the trip has cost him over forty-five pounds sterling! But money is the easiest thing to give if you have it. It is a different matter to give something of your heart, something that hurts or frightens you. The cost of love is not so easy. Forty-five pounds is simpler.

Yesterday evening, when I came back from the special baths, Morgan and I had English tea on our hotel room balcony. A dark-skinned Egyptian boy delivered it, placing the tray on the white wrought-iron table between our wicker chairs. The boy had large lips, like mine, and a chipped front tooth. He kept peering over at me; not paying attention to his task, he knocked over the sugar bowl, dropping the spoons, staring at me as if he were seeing something utterly alien—another Egyptian just like himself!

On the tray, along with the tea, were English sandwiches, crustless little triangles of bread. Cucumber. Bone marrow. Awful. The tea was black and thick and acidy. Not like mint tea. I put six lumps of sugar in mine. Sipped it again, but it was still bitter.

After a long exhale, Morgan said, What a view! Ah, Egypt!

The entire view was framed by the arched white trellis of the balcony, covered with its coral-red bougainvillea, forming a kind of proscenium just like the one on the stage of my missionary school auditorium. It was as if we were looking at a painting. The sun was almost setting, and the sky was streaked with pinks and oranges. The palm trees by the Nile were silhouetted and motionless against the great wilderness of the Sahara.

Now is the perfect moment for the final test, I said to myself.

Morgan, I said, smiling to encourage him. Tell me the story again, of Edward Carpenter and George Merrill, the two men living alone in the wilderness, of their spiritual magic.

Morgan lowered his chin, looking at me across the little table, his cup and saucer in his lap. His hair fell over his eyes and he pushed it back with a limp fist. He said, I thought you said it was nonsense, Mohammed.

I repeated what I had always said: a marriage like that, between two men, made no sense to an Egyptian. But since I had agreed with Morgan that beauty and nonsense had much in common, it was, in the end, a beautiful story. I especially agreed with Carpenter's views that civilization was the result of a human illness, that it ran contrary to man's truest nature.

Morgan looked at me as if I'd said something hurtful, then looked away, across the Nile. I could see tears forming in his eyes. Then he said, I hope you get well before I leave, Mohammed. It's now only a month before I must return to England. Now that the war is over my job has ended at the Red Cross.

I know, I said. I will miss you, Morgan.

Morgan kept looking at the horizon, and then slowly, as if fighting a headache, he squinted more and more. He bit at his bottom lip, then suddenly, sobs came sputtering out with his words. Oh, Mohammed! I don't know how I'm going to live without you. I don't know how! I have never loved like this. Not ever. My heart is breaking! I cannot part from you! Perhaps I should stay in Egypt.

I told Morgan he would not be happy here forever, and that deep down he knew it.

But at least I will be with you, he said. That's all that matters, isn't it?

I was calmer than Morgan. I had thought of all of this, for many months, in jail. I had already cried. I knew the chance of the impossible life was slim, but soon I would find out how slim. I said, Morgan, I have a great idea.

Morgan dried his tears with a handkerchief and held his face in the palms of his hands. He asked me what my great idea was.

I began by making hints. I said, Yesterday, at the souk in Cairo, you bought little clay pipes. Gifts for your English friends, for your dearest friend Florence's children. And you said you also wanted to keep one for yourself, as a souvenir, to always remind you of Egypt.

Morgan's eyes ticked back and forth; he seemed to be trying to predict what I might say.

Well, I said, I have a very simple idea that could solve everything. Why not take back more, costlier souvenirs? How about real live Egyptians?

Morgan looked suddenly relieved and laughed, as if I'd made a great joke. He said, Oh, Mohammed! What a silly boy you are!

But I'm serious, Morgan, I said. Why not take us back to England with you?

Morgan's incredulous grin quickly faded, like something etched on the sand as the waves surge up to erase all traces of it. Then his words came slowly, almost as if he were muttering them to himself in a dream: You? Come to England?

I laughed and reached over and jostled his shoulders. Yes! I said. And we could bring Gamila and little Morgan, of course; but they would stay apart. And we could live together. Just you and me. In our own cottage, far away from civilization, in the wilderness. Just as you wish! Doesn't that solve everything, Morgan? Take us back to England with you.

Morgan dropped his hands to his lap and then stared down, as if expecting his fingers to do something.

What's the matter, Morgan? I asked. Have you not thought of this before? So often you have said how you envy Carpenter and Merrill and how what matters most is for us to be together—

But you don't understand how England is, Mohammed. Morgan spoke gently, as if he were still talking to himself.

I reminded him that he always said we must *love and connect* and always be true to our human nature.

But he replied that England has always been disinclined to accept human nature. He said it gruffly, seeming irritated, as if I were a stupid schoolboy.

My heart began to thump. I was not angry, I was afraid. Afraid of hearing the truth. I had known there was a chance Morgan would fail this test but I had not anticipated how much I would fear this moment. I was not ready to hear Morgan say the words. Oh, what a fool I have been!

But Morgan had once looked at me as no one ever had, on that first night in the tram. And he had cared for me, helped me in ways my parents and friends never could. And through him, there is still a chance of regaining my innocence . . . isn't there?

How could it all be so easily given up? Is it to be a short goodbye before he'll set sail for England and be gone forever? I wondered. What has this all been about? Why have you let yourself fall in this trap, Mohammed? An ache began to tug at my heart. But my head still resisted, saying, No, no, no. Not yet! Morgan is not like the others. He can't leave me so easily.

Morgan, I said quickly. Just think for a moment. We could have what we've always wanted. A new life. A new kind of marriage, as you say!

Morgan looked over at me, guiltily and supplicating too, as if now *he* were the naughty child caught in a lie. The way he spoke was so pathetic. Oh, Mohammed, they wouldn't know what to make of an Egyptian and his wife living with me. Or of your little Morgan, with *my* name. The English can be so very— and Mother. Oh Lord! She would—and even my friends, they wouldn't understand at all. Virginia and Leonard think you're some kind of raja, for some reason, and—and for me to drop out of society altogether, to live in the absolute wilderness—I live in

Weybridge—and I am not—there is my writing, you see—and people depend upon me. I have a reputation. It's all so terribly complicated, Mohammed. I wish it were as simple as you say, but it's not. Not simple at all. You know I would wish for nothing more, but it is all so complicated.

I exhaled and closed my eyes to tell myself, It's all right. You will be all right, Mohammed. At least you have loved. At least you have dared. But I felt as if I were sinking in a dark whirlpool, ever plunging into blackness, with my heart and guts suspended somewhere way up above me, and my body rapidly plummeting.

Oh, Mohammed! Morgan began to sob again. Oh, this is wretched! Please, Mohammed, please understand!

I turned away from Morgan and looked at the sun setting over the desert—a ball of fire swallowed by the scorched earth. I said there was no need for him to cry like an old woman.

Why are you so cold with me, Mohammed?

How would you like me to be, Morgan? I asked

He implored, Don't you have any feelings, Mohammed? Everything with you is so easy.

I didn't say anything. I do not think a heart being torn apart inside your chest is easy at all. I do not think offering to sacrifice your home and your native language and to live in a strange land, among people who will never accept or understand you, is an easy suggestion. I do not think loving a man who is a fatal coward is easy. But I didn't say anything. I let Morgan feel in the right. He needed that, didn't he?

He finally said, Mohammed, let's be honest. I have exaggerated our love. Lied, really. To convince others, or even to convince myself, perhaps. But I have seen how indifferent you are to my love. You have allowed me to love you, Mohammed, and I have pretended that you loved me too, but I don't need you to pretend anymore! It hurts too much. I must face the facts, mustn't I?

Face the facts? I repeated. I reminded Morgan of what he had often said about the matter: how impossible it was to face the facts when they're like the walls of a room. You face one wall and you must turn your back to the other three.

So, what am I to believe, Mohammed? he said. You have so often scoffed at my ideals, calling me foolishly romantic. I know you have been kind, and pitied me, but—

I had to stop him there. If you think I have only pitied you, I said, you have been blind. Do you remember when you read to me from your friend Dickinson's book? You quoted him, saying the English colonist couldn't possibly govern the colonies in the cruel manner he does if he allowed himself to open his eyes and actually *see* the natives. And, if he did open his eyes, then doubt would enter in. But that is the virtue of the Englishman—he never doubts. Never really sees. He must always be in the right.

But Mohammed, I don't think it's fair to say that of me. I have only loved you!

Yes, Morgan, you are right, I said.

The evening was as still as death. Not a breath, not a breeze, not a sound from below reached us up on the balcony. The wicker chair finally creaked as Morgan slumped. He sighed heavily. Oh dear! What muddles we make!

Yes, I said, what muddles.

Morgan sighed again. He wiped tears from his cheeks with his palms, and said, What a beautiful view!

Yes, I said. You always find rooms with the best views, Morgan. Always looking on.

Morgan turned to me, injured, it seemed, and asked what I meant.

I got up. I couldn't even stand him looking at me. I couldn't stand feeling unseen while his clear eyes still perused me. I didn't trust that gaze anymore.

I realized something for the first time: it was I who had seen myself when I thought he had seen me. What muddles we make, indeed! There was a great irony. I had needed Morgan in order to see myself. But that doesn't mean he truly saw me, I realized. It was a trick of sorts. I only imagined when he looked at me that I myself seemed to be good. I saw myself through his eyes, and yet they were not his eyes at all—they were my eyes; I had only placed them in him. And yet, the goodness I saw in myself was true. I was capable of giving love, being loved—that was real. Is all of life only a trick, an illusion like this? Are we all walking through a hall of mirrors, reacting to our own reflections as if they were our enemies, our teachers, our lovers? Could we all be living in our own fictions?

Morgan repeated his question: Mohammed, what do you mean about me always looking on?

I leaned over the rail of the balcony and addressed Morgan, even as I still looked away from him. Is having a room with a view the same as really seeing? I said. Doesn't a view depend upon how things are framed? If we look beyond the frame, over this rail, to the left, for instance, we can see the dirty flat rooftops with the white paint peeling and the washing rags hung out to dry. And below, the squalor of the beggars in the streets; old men and women with diseases and missing limbs; and the sewer pipes over there to the right, by that old horse's trough, leaking and making a puddle of shit and piss. Egypt is all of it. *I* am all of it, Morgan.

But what do you really see from your view? If we get rid of your frame, and thrust you into the scene, out there into the desert, where there is no frame, is your view as pretty, after all? Or do you prefer to stay here and fall in love with your frame and your beautiful view?

I realize now that if I am to live the impossible life, it will have to be with you, my Possibility. Morgan cannot be counted on. That is clear.

When he finally fell asleep after our talk, after he failed my final test, I lit a candle and took Whitman's *Leaves of Grass* with me to the balcony. I sat alone, facing the endless wilderness, under the stars, and I read the Brooklyn ferry poem again and dreamed of you—my young Black man of the future.

And just as Whitman speaks to me, I say to you:

Closer yet I approach you,
What thought you have of me now, I had as much of you—
I laid in my stores in advance,
I consider'd long and seriously of you before you were born.
Who was to know what should come home to me?

Mohammed is here again. He returned to the café about half an hour ago. It was still light out then, but the winter sun sets early here. It's only four o'clock and it might as well be midnight. In the darkness, Mohammed and I are alone, sitting on the floor by the counter, reclined at either end of my sleeping bag, which is rolled out on top of the inflated mattress. The dark blue nylon sack is puffy and the air mattress is bouncy. It feels as if we're floating on a raft, gently being pitched this way and that, in a vast ocean. Mohammed insists we drink our mint tea and talk like this, shoeless and sitting on the floor, semi-recumbent, "just like back at home," he says.

"But where is home?" I ask. Being a Nowherian, I'm always curious how others cope with living in exile, with being suspended in a place where home is always yearned for, but never reached.

"Morocco is home. This I told you already, Kipling." His voice is softer than earlier. It's as if he's trying not to disturb the darkness.

"But then why did you leave?"

He laughs. "Oh, come on. Really? Don't be so boring!"

As my eyes adjust to the dim light I can see him better when he faces me; when the pale moonlight, shining through the windows, catches his face, making his dark skin appear indigo and glistening.

Mohammed raises his heavy eyebrows and tilts his forehead towards me. "You tell me why I left Morocco!" he challenges me. "I bet you know exactly why!"

"Me? How would I know?"

"Oh, come on!" When he smiles in this darkness his teeth seem whiter. Then he takes a long sip of his mint tea, slurping it, but keeps his eyes on me. "Anyway, it wasn't safe at home. What do you expect—that I stay and let them abuse me? No. Not Mohammed. Mohammed El Majhad protects himself!"

"So you're here to protect yourself?"

"Yes, of course. Isn't that all that matters—that we protect ourselves? Who else will protect us?" From sitting cross-legged, Mohammed then stretches his legs out in front of him and rests back on his elbows.

I'm leaning back too, feeling more relaxed around him now. Although I've been somewhat intimidated, I'm realizing I may have the upper hand: I know more about him than he knows about me. I know his secrets. That gives me power. But as we chat, I'm mostly distracted thinking how long it will take before either one of us comes out as gay to the other. I'm wondering if this leisurely conversation is only a long seduction. Is it Mohammed's reconnaissance mission to discover whether I'm gay or not? Is that what he meant before when he said "We shall see"?

Looking down, I examine his feet again, those confident toes. I notice that one big toe (the one I'd seen before that had the purple bruise) is now illuminated in the moonlight, and it has a white cotton pad with surgical tape wrapped around it. "What happened to your toe?" I ask.

"My toe?" He shakes his head. "Nothing. I fell."

"You fell?" I'm assuming it must have been from the incident Boss and Tukkuttok told me about at the airport—Mohammed's collapse. I almost leave the subject alone, but I'm still woozy from those two Greenlandic Coffees, and my impulses grab the reins and propel me beyond propriety. "So why did you fall?" I ask, sitting up, challenging him more than I intend to, but refusing to back down now that I'm feeling a sense of power.

"What do you mean, why?" He seems genuinely confused by my question.

"Why does a strong young man suddenly collapse?"

Mohammed looks at me and narrows his eyes. He frowns for a second or two, then clamps his jaw as if biting down on something hard and looks away. He finally turns back slowly. "So." He nods knowingly. "They told you. About my illness."

"Yeah, they told me," I admit. "I didn't realize you knew that *they* knew."

"Of course. There are no secrets here in Greenland." Then he leans in abruptly. "But please, Kipling. Never speak of this again. Promise me that."

"I promise," I say. I feel guilty now, foolish; toying with him about something so serious and personal. Mohammed is a sick man, dying of sickle cell anemia, I'm sure (What else could it be? What else is a fatal "Black people's disease"?), and here I am, playing coy. It's wrong of me to flaunt my knowledge of his secret. Obnoxious. I'm just grasping for power, aren't I? And let's be honest: I only have the courage to confront him at all because of the alcohol—otherwise I'd have to face the terror I feel when looking into his eyes. I shouldn't be such a coward. I need to level the playing field immediately. It's the only decent thing to do.

"Mohammed," I say, "I have to tell you something: I'm gay too."

"Gay?" He sits upright now, looking at me askance. "I never said I was gay."

"Oh." I am struck dumb for a moment, totally confused. "But I was told—"

"And how can *you* be gay?" He speaks so forcefully spit lands on my face, cold and wet on my cheek, just below my right eye. "We are Black men," he says. "Gay is not an option for us. 'Gay' is when you have the power to choose your identity. The luxury. We are Black, we cannot be gay!"

"I don't—" My head is spinning, trying to grasp his argument. "Maybe in Morocco it's different," I say. "But in the UK and in America, I—"

"Oh yes, of course! God bless America! And God save your gracious queen!" His voice is raised and harsh again, his hands emphatic in their gestures. "I don't understand how you Black people in the West still believe God is on your side!"

"Who said anything about God?"

"You talk about freedom to choose your identity, no? But I am no fool, Kipling. I see the Black man has no freedom in America or the UK. How can you say you are gay when you have no freedom? Whites can be happy and gay—but not us. They all use God to control us, to deny our humanity!"

"But isn't God also Love?" I ask, hearing my voice come out feebly in comparison to Mohammed's strident tone.

"Love? Oh, Allah loves you, they say! But you must do *only* what He wants. Otherwise He *hates* you! What kind of love is that? It was the supposed 'good, faithful worshippers of Allah' who took me as a boy of eight, in the abandoned house down the street from our family home, and fucked me on a dirt floor, there in the rubble. Fucked me until I bled.

"I had a twin brother, Mustafa. He was rough and more boyish than I was. I was soft and girlish, so I was chosen. Mustafa even helped the bad men to rape me. He'd pull me from my hiding places—from underneath the orange seller's cart on our street corner, or from the rooftop where I'd crouch behind the bedsheets hanging out to dry. Mustafa, my twin brother, helped these men rape me because it saved *him* from being the one.

"And later, these same devout men laughed and spat on me when the boys from my lycée called me a little Black *cheth* and *harām*—a pervert, a sinner. And when my God-fearing father discovered what these other God-fearing men had done to me, he beat *me*. He said if I ever let a man fuck me again he would kill me." Mohammed now nods repeatedly as he seems to observe my reactions to his words. "Yes, Kipling. Hard to believe, isn't it? But it's true. He said he'd *kill me*. And eventually that is what happened. My father tried to kill me! Only *I* have the right to take my life, and no one else!

"Do you really want to hear my story, Kipling? It is a long and miserable story. Are you sure you want to hear it?" He raises his eyebrows, challenging me, and I nod in silence. I can tell he wants to tell me, that this is important to him.

Mohammed very matter-of-factly now tells me of how one afternoon after school, Mustafa discovered him being raped again in the narrow alleyway behind their house by a neighborhood boy of nineteen. The older bully held Mohammed down, bent over a wooden crate. Mustafa informed their father, who then swore in the name of Allah that he would kill Mohammed that day. His father borrowed a gun from a man he knew from the mosque and he got a machete ready too, just in case.

Mohammed's mother, frantic, ran to meet Mohammed as he was leaving school, the Lycée Al Qalam. She ran all the way in her long brown skirt, despite being overweight and with one bad hip. Breathless, she warned her son not to go home, that his father would kill him. As Mohammed shuffled away, then ran, he looked back one final time to see his mother weeping, her desperate hands gripping at her yellow headscarf.

He survived on the streets for a while, he says. He got paid by married men who wanted a Black dick for a night—and later, by gay tourists. With a Black man they always wanted dick, he said. The Mandingo fantasy. Eventually he made enough money to rent a room of his own in a *riad*. The *riad* owner was paid, so he asked no questions. Mohammed lived and studied on his own until he was old enough to get his high school diploma and take the college entrance exams, which he passed. He went to Agadir's Université Ibn Zohr for a year before he met an architect from Holland named Mogens.

My heart stops when he says the name. A chill runs through me. "Morgan?" I ask to clarify. Was he trying to pronounce the name Morgan with an Arabic accent? Could it be?

"No, no," says Mohammed. "His name is *Mogens*. Everyone asks about his name, he says. It's Danish but he's not Danish. Mogens Ziegler is from Munich. He only moved to Amsterdam."

For a moment I'm distracted by the coincidence of the name being so close to Morgan's. But Mohammed continues: Mogens was a thirty-six-year-old white man with short blond hair and a devilish smile. He fell in love with Mohammed. He said he could help Mohammed get to Amsterdam. Mogens had money, he was from a wealthy family, and he also had connections with the Dutch embassy in Rabat.

"It's funny." Mohammed smiles with his teeth showing. "We met at Jour et Nuit, 'Day and Night,' a seaside café with the tables that had white umbrellas. I saw Mogens looking at me. He was handsome, I thought. He approached me, but I was with my university friends. I had been picked up by many tourists before, but I wasn't thinking of sex. Just hanging with friends. And Mogens pulled me aside and said, 'How much?' He assumed I was for sale. I almost gave him a price, but something about him was different. Although he approached me like that, when we talked I didn't feel he just wanted a big Black dick, you know. He seemed to really look at me. He asked me to go to the cinema with him. I said yes. I wanted to see *Batman v Superman* at the Cinema Rialto. And that's how we started.

"For a year, he kept coming back from Amsterdam to visit me in Morocco. And I kept feeling he cared—more than anyone else had ever cared for me. He knew I loved glass snow globes—I collect them—and every time he'd visit he'd bring me one from a place he'd traveled. A snow globe from Paris, New York, Berlin. Then one day it happened: my student visa was approved. Mogens must have paid someone, I'm sure, and I was off to Amsterdam. Free at last!

"But I was wrong about Mogens. He was moody, and then cruel if I didn't give him sex when he wanted it—which was all the time, sometimes many times a day. And then he'd say, 'Oh, I do all this for you, and you can't even give me a good fuck? Maybe you don't like living in this nice house in the Jordaan, after all?' Threats. And when my visa was about to expire, he promised we'd marry. That was the plan all along. He even gave me this—a gold engagement ring—as a promise.

"But then he started saying he wasn't sure we were 'compatible.' How could he take me to parties with his colleagues when I didn't show interest in culture? He knew I was obsessed with reading about the Arctic, but he had mistaken that for a true intellect, he said. He now realized we had nothing in common besides sex. I had no intellect, no culture, he said. But is that a good reason not to marry someone? And I had no choice. If we didn't marry, I'd have to go back to Morocco. 'That wouldn't be so bad, Mo-mo, would it?' he said. He used to call me Mo-mo, which I hated. 'Back to Morocco?' I said. 'Yes,' he said. 'I could still come and visit you, just like before.' Visit me? I thought: In my grave?

"That night I got a call from my mother. She only calls with bad news. The first time was when my grandmother died, a year before that. This time it was Mustafa, my twin. He had died that afternoon. A sudden collapse. A blood vessel broke in his brain. We have the same illness, my brother and I. The same ticking bomb inside us. The next morning I packed up my things, took Mogens's credit card, and left. I don't have time to wait for my freedom. This is my only chance. Before the student visa expired, I had to make it to Denmark, where I could get a visa for Greenland.

"And, Kipling, I got lucky for once in my life! In Copenhagen, the officer who interviewed me at SIRI—the international integration and recruitment office—was gay and obviously wanted me. He did not take his big eyes off my crotch. And so I also made it clear to him: I'd do whatever he wanted for a night, or a week, or even a month—as long as I got a renewed visa to study and work in Denmark and Greenland. It was an odd kind of luck. I was Black—it was just this man's thing: master and slave sex. Degrading. But that's how I got here. And now, here in Greenland, I can go out on the snow, in my own igloo, and get away from them all." Mohammed lifts his chin to point out the window. "No white people out there. And no God either. A perfect ending."

Mohammed and I are in the darkness; we haven't turned on the lights. We seem to prefer it this way—our silhouettes bobbing and merging on the bluish moonlit café walls. I don't know if it's because of all the disclosures he's made, but our potential for sex seems to have fizzled. All that talk of death and God—not exactly great foreplay. Mohammed puts on his anorak and his high furry boots and is ready to go. I stand by the café tables to say good-bye, but he hesitates at the door.

"Kipling." He looks up at me now. Even though we're only a foot apart, with all the shadows, I can barely see his eyes. "I have something to ask you."

I brace myself. Mohammed says he's heard from Aguta I plan to go out to the glaciers on my own, to trek into the wilderness. He asks if he can go with me. He says he's already cleared it with his boss at the airport, and they can manage three days without him if he wants to take the time off. "Kipling, can we go together?"

I get a sinking feeling in my stomach. This is exactly what I dreaded from the moment I was first told about Mohammed's existence. I feared another Black man would be an impediment to my being alone in the wilderness. I feel my lips twist into an odd, almost mangled smile. "Mohammed," I say. "It's just that, for me, this trek is—"

"You don't know what it would mean to me," he says slowly, almost whispered. "It would be a dream. To be with you—another

Black man—out there where no white man will reach us. Where we can finally be who we really are." Mohammed steps in closer. I feel his breath on my face. I smell the remnants of mint tea and something yeasty. "I won't be around for long, Kipling. Not long at all. If we don't go together," he says, "who will witness us become free? Without each other, we still won't be seen."

Mohammed is starting to make sense. After my revelation with Aguta, there is no doubt I need to find my truth—I can't go on being a liar—but if I go alone, he's right: no one will see who I become. And from the Still Face Experiment, I know the importance of being seen. Is Mohammed right about us needing a witness? What should I do?

Right now, feeling his breath on me, I only want to lean in and kiss him. I'm overcome with desire for Mohammed—or is it to *become* Mohammed, to become fearless?

"Kipling," he whispers into my ear. But why is he whispering? There is no reason to whisper unless he is communicating something sacred, or forbidden, like the name of God. "Come to me." He breathes on my neck, moist and hot, just behind my ear.

In the darkness, I sense Mohammed's hands reaching out. Instinctively I reach out too. When my hands find his—soft and warm, but thick and rugged too, like the rope tied to a boat's anchor—I grab both his hands and hold on. I feel a jolt of something in my chest. I can't define it. I only know immediately I want to cry.

"Come with me to the wilderness, my friend. Come."

The café door slams open. Suddenly a blast of cold air rushes in, razor sharp, cutting at my eyes, making instant tears. A spotlight blinds us.

"Hello?" I call out, startled. "Who is it?"

The café lights are switched on and Tukkuttok is there. With one hand on the switch, he's standing in the doorway under the fluorescent glare, his yellow battery torch keeping us in the spotlight. "Kipling. Mohammed. What are you doing in the dark?"

"Hey, Tukkuttok!" Mohammed shields his eyes from the brash light. "*Polarpungan*," he says. I've never heard him speak the native language before. "I've just come for a short visit," he translates to English for me. "But I am just saying good night to Mr. Kipling now." Mohammed pulls his furry anorak's hood over his head. "And I was telling him that since you taught me how to build an igloo, perhaps I can go with him on his trek to the glacier. We could stay in a real igloo. Much warmer than a tent."

"Yes." Tukkuttok nods, stoic as usual. "Much warmer." He looks back and forth from me to Mohammed. I see him trying to figure something out. I don't know if he caught Mohammed and me poised to kiss, but he seems to pick up on something. "Mohammed is a very good student—he's becoming a real Inuit! He can build a proper igloo now. And my sister says he's even learning our language so well he's flirting with all my nieces." Tukkuttok's eyes smile even though his face doesn't.

"That's not so, Tukkuttok!" says Mohammed. "*They* are the ones always calling me *kussannâ*!" Mohammed turns to me. "That means handsome in Eskimo."

"Never mind," adds Tukkuttok. "My sister's making dinner for you now. They tell me you love Naja's cooking. Especially the *mattak*."

"*Mattak!*" Mohammed winks knowingly at me. "Wonderful food!"

I now notice Tukkuttok is carrying something in his free hand. At first, I think it's a dead animal. A rabbit? I can't make it out.

"Kipling. For you," he says, extending a pair of long, floppy brown leather boots with dark fur in them. "Greenlandic mukluks," he says. "Reindeer skin. Your city boots won't do out there."

"For me?" I feel embarrassed, undeserving of Tukkuttok's generosity. He extends the boots and not to be rude, I take them. Immediately, I remember my knee-high, brown UGGs from primary school, for which my fellow students ridiculed me. I bite my bottom lip to keep myself from crying. Why is he so nice to me?

"You'll need these boots tomorrow. And take this too." Tukkuttok pulls out something from his trouser pocket but he doesn't let go of it immediately. He looks me in the eye. "This is my compass," he says. "Police standard. It even has the Danish police motto on the back." Tukkuttok translates it carefully for me. "*Insight, vision, and foresight*. All you need to make your way."

He reminds me that the trail to the Narsarsuaq Glacier will be covered over with snow this time of year, so I need to rely on the compass. If we go straight up from the Qooroq Glacier, the fjord is due east of that, directly uphill. We won't miss it.

I tell Tukkuttok I can't thank him enough. First, his fur anorak and thermal gloves, and now the mukluk boots and compass. Such kindness. But he doesn't smile back at me. He reminds me I need to get going as soon as the sun rises, to give myself enough daylight for the trek. The sun will set just before three-thirty tomorrow afternoon, he says.

"Yes," says Mohammed, smiling now. "So we must leave at nine o'clock sharp, then. I'll be here first thing in morning, Mr. Kipling." He winks at me again. My heart races.

Tukkuttok gives me a stern look and then addresses Mohammed. "Come, Mohammed, my friend. *Igloo-mût!*"

"Yes," says Mohammed. "*Igloo-mût*, let's go home!"

Tukkuttok motions for Mohammed to lead the way out, and then closes the door behind them both.

From the café window, I watch the two black silhouettes walk away, out into the dark blue night, finally disappearing under countless stars.

I wake up screaming, gasping for air. I'm shaking all over. I'm hot. I wipe sweat from my forehead, and my hands are cold and wet. I can't figure out where I am. Not in Brooklyn? Not in Weybridge? My heart is thumping. I frantically try to free my arms from the sleeping bag and the cold zipper scratches my forearm. I see moonlight pulsing in through the windows, and bluish-white snow for miles out there. Now I remember: I'm in Greenland. I force myself to take a deep breath. Returning my arms to the warmth of the sleeping bag, I clutch Tukkuttok's soft mukluks. I've been holding these furry boots close to my chest, like a child with a teddy bear.

But why is my heart still thumping so? Oh yes! The dream. An awful dream. But what was it again? Something terrifying. I shut my eyes to remember, to reconstruct, to make sense of the dream— but also, mostly, to put it to rest.

How did it begin exactly? I was running. Yes . . . I remember.

I am running to catch a ship for a journey. It's nighttime, and I am late. The ship is already pulling out of the pier. But somehow, miraculously, I'm able to grab onto the anchor's rope as it's being pulled up. Even in the dream, I realize how odd it is that the anchor is in the stern or that a ship this big even uses rope for the anchor at all. As I climb up the rope, I swing precariously above the black roiling sea, waves leaping up at me. At any moment I could slip into the dark waters and drown.

Then I am finally able to pull myself up on deck. But I realize I'm not supposed to be on this ship after all. Just then, I sense something behind me, like a shadow. I turn and see a huge, terrifying man approaching me—or maybe some kind of beast. He is either dressed in all black or covered in black fur, I can't tell which. He's also holding a pistol and pointing it right at me. I scream but no sound comes out.

Somehow, I now find myself belowdecks, in a maze of long, narrow corridors. I run from one level down to another, getting deeper into the ship's bowels. I finally come to a cabin door and I open it. Concha is there, in an all-white room. She is surrounded by hundreds of infants; some are even floating like little cherubs. "Can I hide in here?" I ask her, but she laughs and shuts the door in my face. Then farther down the corridor I find another door. I open it and find Ben with Mohammed from Morocco having sex on the floor—Mohammed fucking Ben, both of them wearing nothing but sandals. Ben shouts at me, "Go away!"

I'm angry and jealous, but I can't stop; I have to keep running.

Finally, at the end of the corridor, I see another young Black man running towards me. It looks like Mohammed from Morocco. Is he in danger? Does he want me now? But I realize I'm actually running towards a mirror—it's *me* running there, not Mohammed. And behind the reflection of me, the dark beast-man is approaching fast. He's making a loud, ugly noise, like a growl. My heart races. I turn around and he is immediately right on me. He growls and pulls off his black furry hood and it's Mohammed El Majhad. He smiles with his twisted, sinister mouth. "No more God!" he says. Then he aims the pistol and shoots me in the chest. I scream. Veins bulging in my neck, at my temples, and even in my eyes. A great scream.

And then I wake up.

I don't know what this dream means but it must be a sign. I should stay away from Mohammed. There's something sinister about him. My first instinct was right: I need to be alone in the wilderness. But am I crazy to be swayed by a silly nightmare? After all, it would be warmer to stay in an igloo with Mohammed, wouldn't it? And the truth is, just thinking of how close we came to kissing tonight, I'm getting hard again. No. I can't let lust sway me either. I'll go alone tomorrow. No Mohammed. Just me and my wilderness.

I've got my glacier trekking gear waiting for me by the café door, all packed and ready in the enormous black backpack. I've rented everything, including the pack, from Aguta. But I'm not sure how to use half of the things she's suggested. The tent I can figure out, but I'm intimidated by the Trangia stove with its propane cartridges. Just in case, I've packed food that doesn't require cooking: canned sardines, Carr's crackers, Nutella, and chips (to my delight, Aguta has a massive supply of Doritos). The ice ax, crampons for my boots, and helmet are in the side compartments for easy access. The hiking poles I'll carry. And, of course, I have several bottles of water. But I can also boil virgin snow, if necessary—there's an endless supply of that up here. Yes, I'm ready.

I secure the cumbersome black backpack on my shoulders. Aguta pointed out it's "one of the very best," with a hundred-liter capacity but still lighter than most. It's a new model by The North Face named Prophet, which I find strangely reassuring. As I pull at the toggles on the straps, adjusting for a snug fit, I'm feeling more convinced this is the right decision—to leave much earlier than planned, and without Mohammed. It's still dark out this morning, but with my battery torch to light my way, and with Tukkuttok's compass, I should be fine. I just have to remember the route: out the café door, take a right, then pass through Hospital Valley, then head exactly east-northeast. That will lead me to the plateau between the

Narsarsuaq Glacier and the Qooroq Glacier, those great mountains of ice and snow. My wilderness.

All right, Kip, this is it. With the black Prophet on my back, I'm on my way.

On the snowy plain, the stars flash in the night sky like sequins on a silky black dress. The full moon lends a sharpness to everything. Every undulation in the snow is clearly defined, like ripples on a shiny white sea. Thanks to Tukkuttok's fur anorak and boots, I'm cozy. But I can tell I'm going to have a problem with the wind. Every now and then a brutal gust slashes at my face, cuts at my lips, and burns my nose; even my teeth hurt. But when the wind dies down again, I'm okay. Apart from my face, I'm warm. In an hour or so, when the sun comes up, it will get even warmer. In the meantime, I find singing helps me. It keeps my tropical, Negroid lips from freezing.

For no particular reason, I begin humming a song from a Stephen Sondheim musical. It's an ironically rousing little ditty, "Every Day a Little Death." I don't remember all the lyrics—they are too clever, and too many of them. But I fake them—it doesn't matter. Singing keeps me warm.

Suddenly the wind whips up again, piercing and violent. Even with the torch's light it's impossible to see more than three feet ahead of me. The air is thick with whirling snow, and the only thing I hear is a steady, deafening whirr. In effect, I'm momentarily blind and deaf. I have to rely on my other senses. The smell of snow is stronger when it's whipped up like this—salty and mineral. And through the soles of my furry leather boots, I can feel the different textures of the ground beneath me: hard snow, powdery, crunchy, slippery. They say the Inuit have over fifty words for snow. I'm beginning to understand why. And there is another sense I'm aware of too—a kind of sixth sense. I'm detecting something near me. A life force is pulsing. I feel it.

"Kipling."

I gasp. Breath seems to freeze in my lungs. Who is it?

Out of the white blur, Mohammed is suddenly standing in front of me. He's staring at me, with his furry anorak hood pulled over his head. The moon shines blue on his dark face, dazzles white in his eyes. The wind finally dies down, and the chaotic blur settles around us. I see him more clearly now.

"Where are you going, Kipling?" I see his dark pupils calculating—he seems to be realizing the truth. He makes an odd, forced smile. "Why so early?" There is something stern and chastising in his tone. I don't know what to say. There is no explanation other than the truth—that I've decided to go without him. "I brought lunch for us," Mohammed adds. "Naja, Tukkuttok's sister, made us a thermos with coffee and reindeer fat, and sardines in a can. And I have bread from Aguta, and—" He cuts himself off. "You were leaving without me?"

I nod but I can't bring myself to say it out loud.

"I see," he says after a few moments. "Then go, if you want. Go!"

"I'm sorry, Mohammed, it's just that—"

"Goodbye. I won't follow you. I will leave you alone. Forever." He turns away.

I don't know what to do. I don't want to hurt his feelings. The poor young man is dying and I'm denying him a final wish. Why am I suddenly afraid of him? He isn't actually a beast-man. It was only a dream, after all. My own dark shadow, conjured up from my unconscious. How could I hold that against Mohammed? But yet, even just now when he smiled at me, I caught a glimpse of something sinister—a twitch in his lips, a coldness in his dark stare. No. I must follow my intuition and go alone—and quickly too, before I change my mind. I decide to say nothing and walk away. I leave Mohammed standing there in the moonlight.

After a few minutes, I hear his boots and hiking poles stabbing at the ground. *Crunch, crunch, crunch.* As he approaches, I look to my left to see the arms of his dark furry anorak pumping the air, his hiking poles flashing like batons.

"You said you wouldn't follow me." I'm annoyed at him for ignoring my wishes.

"I heard you singing. Why are you singing, Kipling?"

"Why am I singing? What do you mean, why? I'm just singing." I turn to him, not hiding my annoyance now. "You said you'd leave me alone. Forever."

"I lied. Lies are sometimes necessary!" he says, raising his voice against a new upsurge of wind.

Lies are sometimes necessary? My heart jolts. I stop dead in my tracks. These are the exact words Mohammed El Adl used! A tingle rushes to my head.

"Why have you dropped your hiking poles?" Mohammed says, shining his torch on my poles splayed on the snow as if tossed aside, crisscrossed and rattling in the wind. Somehow my empty hands are now up around my spinning head.

The coincidences are too uncanny. There is only one possibility that makes any sense: I must actually be in the presence of Forster's Mohammed. The reincarnation, the visitation, of Mohammed— that's who this is. After all, there are no boundaries of Space or Time, are there? Mohammed—or his ghost or spirit—is haunting me. He won't let me go. The ghost has communicated to me with the exact words of Mohammed El Adl! As clear as day.

"Of course lies are sometimes necessary," Mohammed continues. "If I don't say this lie just now, you would not stop to consider how selfish you are to leave me behind. It was necessary to lie." He looks at me and smiles crookedly. "Let's go! I forgive you. So, Kipling, have you packed everything we need? Do you have your little gun?"

"My gun? Why?"

"Protection, Kipling." He furrows his brows insistently. "Protection."

I'm not sure I want Mohammed knowing I have my gun on me. I definitely don't want him having access to it. I think of telling him I've left it back at the café in my suitcase, but I'm trying not to be a liar. The truth is, I was a little afraid of being alone in the wilderness without it. And yet, some lies are indeed necessary.

"Tukkuttok says there are no bears or wild foxes out by the glacier," I say.

"What does he know?" Mohammed looks as if he's about to spit—and then he does. He spits in the snow. "*Nothing!*" Managing both of his hiking poles and the torch in one hand, he reaches out for me with his free hand. He squeezes my hand through our gloves. "Self-protection is everything, Kipling."

I give in to his pressure. "Don't worry, Mohammed. The gun's in my backpack."

"Good. Good," he says, still clamping down on my hand, but too tightly now.

I shine my torch directly at Mohammed's face. This time, I mean to ward him off by the blinding light, but I catch something frightening. Something I saw before when I first met him at the airport: a cold darkness like an eclipse flashes across his eyes. Who is this Mohammed, really? A ghost or a man?

Song and Sympathy

Why sing? Mohammed's question to me. But also a question I've contemplated many times before. Years ago, when I left Columbia after Mr. Asshole pointed out my fatal flaw—that I had no voice of my own—I took the critique literally and found a professional vocal coach to learn to sing. He was a tall, rotund man who had trained at Juilliard and gave lessons out of his cramped apartment in a six-floor walk-up in Hell's Kitchen. He was a jolly, Santa Claus type who would stroke his white Persian cat as I sang my scales for him. My reason for taking voice lessons followed a certain Zen idea that how a person does *anything* is how they do *everything*. So, I thought if I could find my real singing voice, I would also find my real writing voice.

The lessons lasted for a month before it was clear to me that I did, in fact, have my own unique singing voice, only it wasn't a particularly good one. Flat more than not. Yet one important idea stuck with me from the jolly instructor: "Leave the whys to the philosophers. The artist just sings, no questions asked," he said. "The more you think, the worse it will be. The voice has to come from the body and soul, not the mind!"

After that, every time I found myself singing randomly—while washing the dishes or waiting on the subway platform—I'd think,

Don't ask why you're singing, Kip, just sing! But, ironically, that reminder was like saying, "Don't think about pink elephants." You can't *not* do it! All I could think was *why* am I singing?

When I ask myself that question, even now, I think of the title of Maya Angelou's autobiography, *I Know Why the Caged Bird Sings*. Why would any of us sing, imprisoned as we all are in the endless cycles of suffering? Angelou's title is lifted from the poem "Sympathy" by Paul Laurence Dunbar, one of the first great Black poets in America. I know the poem's last stanza by heart. I've often recited it for Ben, the way my mother used to recite Milton to me at bedtime, like a lullaby:

> *I know why the caged bird sings, ah me,*
> *When his wing is bruised and his bosom sore,*
> *When he beats his bars and he would be free;*
> *It is not a carol of joy or glee,*
> *But a prayer that he sends from his heart's deep core,*
> *But a plea, that upward to Heaven he flings—*
> *I know why the caged bird sings!*

So there is the answer from the poet Dunbar: singing is a prayer flung up to heaven from the heart's deep core!

As I was doing research for my novel, I often thought about Paul Laurence Dunbar. Like Mohammed, Dunbar died an early death of consumption—only about fifteen years before Mohammed himself succumbed to the same illness. And Dunbar also died alone, without his lover.

Dunbar was taken over by depression and occasional mania. It was all too much for him, being a Black man yet never allowed to fly as freely as his wings would permit, and then having his life cut short at the height of his artistic abilities. His depression led to abusing alcohol and beating his wife. In the end, she could no longer support his rageful abuse. She had to abandon him when he was sick and dying.

But why did Dunbar, a previously loving and sensitive man, become so intolerable and abusive to his wife? I imagine he must have grown tired of singing in nice pat structures, with perfectly metered rhymes; that he finally had to let out a visceral, deafening scream—a horrible bloodcurdling sound. And I guess no one could bear that kind of fury. No one could take the unshackled roar of a Black man. He was like the caged bird in his poem "Sympathy," with the splat of blood and the crack of exposed sinews in wings beaten against the cage, time after time, year after year. His wife just couldn't bear the torture and abuse. Who could have sympathy for that?

Forster, too, abandoned Mohammed when he was sick, didn't he? The circumstances were completely different; but in both cases, in the end, sympathy and love were not enough to keep the ravages of Whiteness from leaving the Black man shunned— always the outlaw.

I realize now that part of my drive to tell the stories of these ill, abandoned Black men is that I'm thinking of Ben and me, too. No, I'm not dying of a physical malady, nor am I abusive, but I'm also plagued by an illness, a deadly virus—the parasite of Whiteness. I can't seem to shake it. And yes, it's also killing me. At the very least it has killed my marriage. Ben can't bear the sound of my angry wings beating against the cage either.

Who could?

And yet, Oh, Ben . . . how can it all end like this? How can there be real, lasting sympathy?

Standing side by side, Mohammed and I stare up at the steep slope. It's a climb of about three hundred meters of snow and ice, practically all vertical. We're heading to the plateau between the Narsarsuaq and Qooroq glaciers, our final destination.

It's taken us three hours to get here. After Hospital and then Flower Valleys, we headed east-northeast towards the great glaciers. Losing all sense of time, we plodded ahead into the infinite whiteness. A white-tailed sea eagle hovered with its wide black wings, way up in the cerulean sky. How limited we must seem to the birds, I thought, trapped in our plodding ways, unable to soar. We passed by gullies to our left, trenches in the snow, running for miles. In the summer, streams flow through them, but now they are frozen. This landscape, in all its stillness, seems pensive, with infinite space and time to ponder.

It feels as if Mohammed and I are the only two human beings in the entire world. Just us two Black men alone in the snow. I remember those racist children's books about golliwoggs by Florence Upton. Golliwoggs were the author's name for Little Black Sambo–like rag doll characters, with pitch-black skin and giant red lips. One of her books, *The Golliwogg's Polar Adventures*, had two Black Sambos roaming around the Arctic. Graham Greene mentions this odd book in his novel *The End of the Affair*. I'm not sure what point Greene was making with that reference. Perhaps it's only the juxtaposition of polar opposites: Black men and white snow. Greene created a world so particular in its ideas of goodness and evil, so fraught with danger and political and racial tensions, that literary critics have given his entire oeuvre a name—they call it "Greeneland." So here we are, Mohammed and I, like two golli-woggs in Greeneland.

Standing at the base of the steep slope, looking up, I feel slightly nauseated at the prospect of the climb. We are both winded and panting. My nose feels raw and is running like a faucet. My eyelids are stuck open. I can barely blink. I notice Mohammed's lips shivering; they are cracked and almost white.

"We can rest here," he says, leaning on his hiking poles, breathing heavily. "But only to eat lunch." He pulls off his large green backpack, plunking it on the snow.

I'm relieved to have a pause before we hike up to the plateau. We each sit on our respective backpacks to catch our breath. I try to get comfortable, but I feel the Glock poking up through the black Prophet, burrowing into my left buttock like a fist. I shift my position, punching at the spot where the gun has jabbed me.

From his anorak, Mohammed reveals a white plastic bag from which he pulls two cans of sardines and a baguette. He rips the bread, handing me half. From the thermos he pours steaming coffee into two thermal cups. He shares the food and we eat in silence.

This landscape is truly breathtaking. It's as if the entire world were at rest, pausing between breaths. Nature itself seems in a state of meditation. The two high glaciers on either side of us are so enormous they frighten me. I feel inconsequential, like a speck, almost nothing at all. The insignificance of a single human life is sobering.

The longer I stare at the glaciers, the more I also begin to see all the different shades of white. There is actually as much blueness as there is whiteness, I realize. Multiple shades of blue—from pale aquamarine where the sun hits most brightly to a deep navy in the long, vertical cervices and shadows of the glaciers. The fjord to the right is covered with a sheet of clearer, yellowish whiteness, on which the large icebergs—my steel-blue cathedrals—slowly float by.

What expansiveness! I exhale. This world seems a giant blank canvas, unmarked by human history and civilization, with enough space to create a vision of one's own.

Once in a while—and now is the second time since we've been sitting here—something very dramatic occurs. A huge chunk of a glacier as tall and colossal as the Wall in *Game of Thrones* comes crashing down with a mighty rumbling. It resounds like thunder, with the fury of all the gods in heaven. It echoes into the distance for a full minute, maybe more. Yesterday, Aguta warned me about this. She explained that this natural explosion is called "calving." The great Mother Glacier is giving birth to a new calf—another, little iceberg—and the entire landscape quakes with the noise of the new life.

After the wall of snow explodes, a vast white cloud rises and spreads in the air for miles. Then the cloud finally disintegrates into tiny white atoms falling to the fjord.

"Isn't it spectacular?" I say, looking over to Mohammed, to share the moment.

"Yes." Mohammed also looks out at the distant fjord, making his crooked smile. "When the snow cloud falls it looks like—how do you say—like white fireworks. But I've seen all this before. Tukkuttok brought me out here last month to teach me how to build an igloo."

When the cacophonous calving is over, the infinite silence returns and the land is a blank canvas again. "As a child I always dreamed of being here," says Mohammed. "It is all just as I imagined it. My Possibility."

My Possibility. Mohammed El Adl's words again! I cannot ignore that I am with a ghost—or whoever he is. I should address him directly now. I should ask this ghost what he wants of me. But how? Yet now is the time; we are finally here, alone in the wilderness. And my mind seems as sharp as the arctic air.

"Mohammed," I say. "Do you know why I came out here?"

"Perhaps not." Mohammed wipes crumbs from his mouth with the cuff of his anorak. "Why did you come here, Kipling?"

"Because I needed space to find my own voice," I say. And then immediately, I feel self-conscious and look down at my furry boots. "I can imagine how silly that sounds to you. But it's true. I'm a writer, and I'm writing a novel—"

"A novel?"

"Yes. It's about you and—" The words come out before I know it.

"About me?" Mohammed laughs loudly, showing his irregular, brownish teeth. "Impossible!" He shakes his head and collects our empty sardine cans, stuffing them back into the plastic bag. "Crazy! You can't write about me if you don't know me!"

"Perhaps," I say. "But what if I told you that I think you are someone else. Someone who lived long ago. Do you think it's possible that you are both yourself and not yourself? What do you think?"

"I think you are crazy, Kipling." He stuffs the plastic bag back in the pocket of his anorak, laughing and shaking his head. "Mad!"

"But what if I knew secret things about you, and I could tell you things to prove it?"

"Kipling, are you a witch?"

"No. I just mean—what if I knew that Morgan had really

loved you. Is that what you want to know from me? Is that why you're following me?"

"Morgan? No!" Mohammed jumps to his feet. He screws up his face, quickly annoyed. "His name is Mogens. *Mogens!* And I don't want to talk about him!" Mohammed flings his gloves to the snow, then claps his bare hands together twice, like a lion tamer. "Okay. Enough crazy talk! Get up! We've got to climb!"

"But if it's not about Morgan, then why are you following me out here?"

Mohammed raises his snowy eyebrows haughtily. "I told you, Kipling. Now it's only us, we can be alone in our igloo. With all the quiet we need. Do you understand?" He steps closer and reaches his bare hands to my freezing face. His palms are warm against my cheeks. "No more talk about the rest of them," he says. "Just us."

Looking him in the eyes, I want to kiss him more than ever, to fulfill what we came so close to fulfilling last night. To feel the warmth of his touch all over my body.

"Yes," I say. "No more of their noise. Only us."

Immediately I hear a strange, small sound, as if it's emanating from deep inside my body. A faint tune is emerging. Is it the sound from my heart's deep core? I stop and listen. It starts again, muffled, but it's clearly a musical melody. It reminds me of bells—no, perhaps a faraway, wooden xylophone. Wait . . .

"What is that noise?" Mohammed puts on his gloves again, preparing to go.

"Jesus! It's my iPhone!" By the time I get the thermal gloves off and fish the phone from the inside pocket of my anorak, the marimba xylophone ditty has stopped. I wonder if it was Tukkuttok calling. Yesterday we exchanged mobile phone numbers in case I should have an emergency out here. But it's not Tukkuttok's number. The area code is 212. New York City. I'm amazed I get reception out in the wilderness. I often have trouble getting a good signal in my basement in Fort Greene. But out here in the farthest-flung arctic region, I've got five full bars of reception! As I'm putting my phone back in my pocket, the marimba starts again. Immediately I answer.

"Kipling?" I don't recognize the man's voice. "Kipling, is that you?"

I say hello. The man on the other end mutters to himself, something about not being able to hear me. I say hello again, and again. The man sighs heavily and grunts before blurting out, "What the hell? Fuck!" And then he hangs up.

Now I've lost all reception—my five bars have gone down to none. I try to call back, but no matter where I hold the phone there's no signal. I don't know why I suddenly care who's calling. For two weeks I've been locked away, disconnected on purpose. I'm still on my mission to find my truth out here. Perhaps it's better I wasn't able to answer the call. Fate. The gods or goddesses reminding me that I should not be connecting with civilization. Now is the time for the wilderness. For Mohammed and me.

"This is the spot!" Mohammed stabs his single hiking pole into the ice. This act reminds me of Neil Armstrong planting the flag on the moon. I didn't expect this moment to feel so momentous, but Mohammed's gesture has really moved me. I'm on the verge of tears and I don't know why. Here we are, almost doubled over and out of breath, our muscles sore, but we're victorious. We've scaled the steep slope and have reached the plateau between the Narsarsuaq and Qooroq Glaciers with a great, placid fjord below us. The wide open wilderness is all ours. Above us, a sea eagle hovers, black wings spread wide, as it lets out a mournful cry. Is it the same bird that has followed us here? I think of how the Great Goddess would ride on a giant sea eagle, and of how she led me here to this wilderness.

"Okay," says Mohammed, still trying to catch his breath. "If we hurry we can finish the igloo before sunset."

He instructs me, following all that Tukkuttok has taught him. We begin with a hiking pole dug in place in the snow. We tie a rope to the pole and attach a spike on the end of the rope, to etch out a circle—just as I'd done in geometry class with a compass, its point in the center. Then we dig out the circular ditch with our snow axes. The hardest part is chipping out and then chiseling the rectangular snow bricks from the hard, compacted snow below the surface. This is mostly my job. When I hand the bricks to Mohammed, he has a careful system, with the pole and rope and a chisel, to make sure the bricks are carefully staggered and cut at a precise angle, to form the igloo's walls upward in a spiraled elevation, making a perfect dome with a big hole at the top.

Working on the igloo, I'm not cold anymore. From time to time, I have to mop sweat from dripping into my eyes. As we work, I try to chat, but Mohammed's responses are curt: "You talk too much." "Hand me the next block of snow."

"Yes, sir!" I salute sarcastically.

"This is not humorous, Kipling! Soon the sun will set on us. Hurry up!"

"But we have hours of sunlight left, Mohammed."

"Next block!" Mohammed barks, then he clamps down his jaw, almost baring his teeth.

He is feverish in his need to build this igloo.

Three hours of nonstop work and we've nearly finished the igloo, just one last brick to put in place on the top of our snow dome. Because we began by digging our initial circle two feet down in the snow, we're now able to stand up inside our little igloo, with almost a foot above our heads. It's surprisingly cozy in here, warm enough that we've both shed our anoraks and gloves. I'm only in my black cashmere jumper, and Mohammed's in a Nehruish white muslin shirt with long sleeves. There's also much more light in here than I'd imagined. Apart from the open hole at the top of the dome, sunlight is also filtered through the snow bricks, permeating the igloo walls with a diffuse bluish-white light. Mohammed finally smiles as I hand him the last brick. I stand behind him proudly while he chisels it into place.

Just when he's making sure the fit is snug, the marimba xylophone sounds.

This time I'm ready—my iPhone is resting on my backpack, next to me on the igloo floor. Ben's name pulses on the screen. I snap it up. My heart pounds. I shouldn't answer the call. I'm not sure I'd even know what to say. I see he's calling on FaceTime. I'm startled, confused. What should I do? Without thinking—just to stop the damn xylophone music—I answer the call.

"Kip? Are you there?"

"Ben?"

"Finally! Finally!" He sounds out of breath, frantic. "Wilson and I have been trying to reach you all morning. Where the hell are you, for Christ's sake? I can't see you—ah, now I see you!"

The video finally comes into focus. And there he is: Ben, standing in our kitchen in Fort Greene. Morning light from the front windows streaks across his face, making him squint. He's wearing his red plaid flannel shirt—the one I gave him for Christmas last year—with the top few buttons undone. I have forgotten how handsome he is, how clear and loving his hazel eyes are as he stares at me through the phone screen.

"Kip?" he says, the empathy lines in his forehead furrowed. "It's so white behind you."

I move the camera closer to my face so my igloo background doesn't show.

Behind Ben, I see our glossy white kitchen cabinets and all the familiar items on the countertop: our stainless steel toaster, the Vitamix blender, the wooden mortar and pestle, and the blue and white ceramic jug Concha brought me from her *abuela*'s *cortijo* in Málaga. My heart immediately aches, as if it's been stabbed.

"Kip, are you listening? This is very, very important." Ben's eyes are wide open, insistent. Then breathlessly, he tells me the news:

my agent, Wilson, has been trying to reach me. He's in a panic. An editor from Paramount House, who had previously passed on my historical Forster novel, has now changed her mind, and wants to acquire it after all. She said that E. M. Forster is making a major comeback since the acclaimed West End and Broadway hit *The Inheritance*, and the new PBS miniseries of *Howards End*. Now is the time for my novel, she said. The editor also showed the novel to their publicity director, who says if they get my book out before next November, I'd be a perfect candidate for the Lambda Literary Award and—who knows?—maybe even one of the big national awards. But they'd have to get things moving as soon as possible. They're also interested in seeing the new novel. So I need to sign the contract ASAP.

"Kip . . . Kip . . . are you there?" Ben groans and shakes his head. "Shit. I lost you! I can't see you now."

"I'm here, Ben, I still see you." Yes, I think. I am here—and yet, I'm not here. I think of how Guruji defined the truth: *neti neti*—neither this nor that. I'm neither here nor there. All I know is that I'm stunned. Am I dreaming all this? Of course it's a dream! That's the only logical explanation for Mohammed's ghost being here, and for the old lady on the airplane, and Aguta having Concha's eyes, and the igloo. And now this incredible news from my agent.

"Kip . . . can you hear me?"

All right, if it's a dream, I'll play my part. "Yes, I'm here, Ben."

"Good. I was afraid we'd lost the connection. Your video keeps coming and going. You okay? You must be in shock, I guess. Anyway—Kip! Wherever you are, get your ass to your agent's office and sign the contract before they change their minds!"

"Okay," I say, going along with this crazy dream. "Okay. I'll fly back ASAP!"

"Fly? Where are you?"

"If I told you, you wouldn't believe me."

"Well, call your agent now! Isn't this just incredible? Your dream!"

I'm still not sure how to take this news—it's too unreal. I want to believe that it's not just a dream. This is what I've wanted forever. To be a published writer. But I don't feel the joy I expected to feel. What about my Mohammed novel being seen by the publishing legend? I don't want to give up on her, but I guess she'll have to wait. I feel guilty for not being happier, as if I'm betraying my old self somehow. But in spite of my trying to feel happy, there is a growing sense of resentment, disappointment, even. I have come all the way to the wilderness to find my voice, to become the writer I dream to be, and before I'm barely here, I find that all of this is unnecessary. This isn't how it was supposed to be. And, yet, what did Aguta say? It's not for the book alone that I need the wilderness, right? I still need to find my true voice, don't I?

"Kip? Kip? You okay? You look strange." I realize Ben can see me again. I try not to look so stunned. "Kip." Ben presses his lips together hard, deepens those vertical ridges between his eyebrows. "I'm sorry about before." Ben puckers his lips and kisses the screen. "I really do love you, Kip."

"Me too," I say reflexively, not sure what I even mean anymore.

"But Jesus—what a mess you left in the basement! Broken wood everywhere! Looks like you went ballistic getting out of there!"

"Yeah, I'm sorry about that." I must have been in an altered state. I have no idea.

"But never mind. Listen, Kip, I have something else really important to say, and—"

The screen goes blank. "Ben, are you there?" The call has dropped. Now there are no signal bars at all. I try to call back and can't get a signal. In spite of the fact that we've lost the connection, I feel compelled to say it again, anyway: "Ben," I say. "Ben, are you still there?"

M ohammed's expression is fierce, his lips set in a sneer. "So you are leaving now?"

"I guess so," I say, dazed, still trying to absorb the news from Ben. I sit, plunking myself down on the black Prophet. The gun jabs up at my buttocks through the backpack again. I avoid Mohammed's eyes, somehow feeling guilty now. "I've got to get back to Brooklyn right away," I say to him. "Everything's changed. My book's getting published."

"But, Kipling, our igloo—we just—" He sounds hurt for a moment, but then cutting: "You can't leave now." I look up to see him staring down at me. The coldness of his gaze gives me a shiver. Does he want to hurt me? Here I am, alone in the wilderness, in an igloo with a man I hardly know. What was I thinking? What if he's a criminal? A killer? I clutch my phone tightly in my fist—if I have to call for help I have Tukkuttok's number saved. Mohammed lowers himself to sit beside me on my backpack; his thigh presses against mine. "Kipling, stay at least for tonight. We have to witness our world together. Isn't this what you've wanted too?" He rests his bare hand on my knee. I flinch reflexively but he only tightens the grip, keeping his icy stare on me. "Why must you rush away? Why is it so important to be published?"

I'm almost forgetting why myself. Mohammed seems to desire me, or to possess me, I can't tell which. And I don't fully understand it, but I want him too.

"I don't know what to do," I say. "I promised I'd go back right away. I could still make the eight p.m. flight to Reykjavík, and then to New York. Part of me wishes I could stay out here forever, with you, and yet I have people back in New York who'd never understand if I weren't going back. And I know it's probably hard to understand, but as racist and homophobic and fucked up as that crazy world is, there are things I've gotten accustomed to. There is art! Books and films. Shakespeare, Tolstoy, Toni Morrison, even Forster. I don't know if I could—"

"Books! Films! I've heard these words before. Words of the Imperialists!"

"But I'm not like Morgan!"

"His name is *Mogens*." Mohammed stands, raising his hands high in the air. "But you are just like him—always needing to be in the right. Needing so many requirements to love someone! Books! Films! Art!" Mohammed now pulls off his white Nehru shirt—it is practically drenched with perspiration—and he turns to dig out a dry shirt from his backpack. The new shirt seems almost identical to the last. With his glistening brown back to me, I gasp when I see the welts slashed across his spine—five or six keloid scars, diagonally across his entire back. I wonder how and why he was cut or beaten like that . . . and then I remember Mohammed El Adl had scars on his back too. The souvenirs of his encounter with the drunken Imperial officer.

Still bare chested, Mohammed turns and takes a step closer to me, his dry shirt in one hand. He leans in and presses his free palm on my chest, against my heart. Suddenly the ground begins to rock; it rumbles as if a great edifice—the Taj Mahal or the Empire State Building—is collapsing and crumbling into rubble. Mohammed seems shocked and looks down. A thin line appears in our igloo floor. Then the crack widens and zips across the snowy foundation—a jagged fracture splitting the ground between us.

"It's happening again," I say, realizing the source of the rumbling quake. "It's another glacier breaking out there."

Mohammed looks at me with a flash of urgency. "Kipling, what did you mean when you said perhaps I am both myself, and not myself? You said you knew secrets about me. What can you possibly know?"

I don't know when would be a better time to finally address this ghost head-on. We're alone out here and he is asking for help, I know it. But I'm feeling nervous about delivering the news. I take a deep breath, and then another. "All right, Mohammed. I'll tell you. It's about you and Morgan."

"No. I told you, I don't want to talk about Mogens. He used me. He betrayed me!"

"But isn't that why you're here at all—to resolve things with him?"

"Enough about him!" He raises one hand as if he might hit me. "This is *our* space!" Slowly he lowers his hand, and narrowing his eyes he cocks his head suspiciously. "Kipling, I don't understand you. I only want you to stay for one night. That's all."

I nod. I wish I could give him what he wants. But since he's asked me, I need to tell him the truth. "Mohammed, in King's College's archives, when I was doing research on my historical novel, among Morgan's possessions I found the gold ring you left him."

"My ring?" Mohammed holds up his ring finger. His hand shakes. "You don't understand. I only wear this ring to remember how easily Mogens betrayed me. How quickly he gave up on his promise. He swore to be mine forever. This ring is to remind me of what a liar he was! They are all liars! You cannot trust them."

Mohammed's eyes seem bloodshot and are blinking rapidly. "You must only protect yourself!"

"But Mohammed," I explain, "Morgan wore that ring for the rest of his life. To remember you. Once a day, in private, he'd put on your ring. For fifty years. Every day. For a short while he had another lover, a policeman named Bob Buckingham. But until Morgan died he loved you the most. You were the one he missed every day. You were his one chance for the impossible life. And he ruined himself when he left you. And he knew it. He never got over it."

Mohammed stops and stares at me in silence. His lips are quivering, and he has a strange look on his face, as if he's just seen a ghost. "You're not making sense, Kipling." There are thick, heavy tears forming at the rims of his eyes. "You're frightening me. I—I don't understand what you're saying."

"Morgan only wrote one novel after he left you, Mohammed," I continue. "The India novel he was inspired to finish when Professor Ganda challenged him at your house. Do you remember that day? It was a novel about the impossibility of the British to connect with their colonized people. About how racism kills the chance for real love. After that, Morgan never wrote another novel. He lost all hope of writing with his true voice—with the voice of a man who had lost the one thing that mattered most in his life. A man who had walked away from a love he would never find again. Morgan had not been able to make it work with you, Mohammed, but in the end, your love was the only true thing he had. Even after your death your love sustained him. And your ring was the most important thing he ever owned. No—it wasn't a pure or simple love, Mohammed. But you were loved. You were really loved."

Mohammed is trembling all over now. It's not from the cold—

we're protected from the elements in our igloo. With teary eyes he stares at the floor, at the rupture in our icy foundation. His shoulders drop, and his arms droop to his sides as if he's suddenly been doused with buckets of warm water. A great release. I hear a quiet mewling, like that of a baby calf. But the mewling grows to a moan emanating from Mohammed's body. And eventually he lets out a massive cry.

"*Ahhhhhhhhhh!*" The echo of his cry bounces off the walls of the igloo, comes at me from all directions at once. It is all that can be heard.

I step closer, over the crack in the snow. I put my hand on his shoulders. He squeezes his eyes shut and flops his head all the way down, as if his neck can no longer support the weight. Silently, his body heaves, and then he begins to sob. I embrace him tightly, rubbing his shoulders, then his back. With my fingertips I feel the keloid scars running the length of his spine, like a mountain range along the topography of his body.

Still embracing, I lean back to see his face. Beautiful. He has grown stubble now; really more like peach fuzz, over his cheeks, above his top lip. All of the hardness seems to have melted from his face—nothing is taut or held anymore. His cheeks, his eyelids, his forehead are relaxed. He looks like an angel. His thick lips are parted. The lips I've been yearning to kiss. I lean forward, only slightly. I smell the sweat of Mohammed's underarms again, and the fishy breath from the canned sardines we've eaten.

"Stay," he whispers warmly to me. "*Stay with me.*"

I want to resist his pull, to stop looking at him. I glance at his sad brown eyes and then glance away. But when I realize his gaze is steadily fixed on me, I find the courage to look back. We finally stare into each other's eyes. I see the little black flecks in his irises, like rays around a dark sun—a sun that, despite its darkness, somehow shines bright. There is a light emanating from Mohammed's eyes. I can feel the heat from its rays. I even see the light waves moving through the air, waves that I didn't think were possible to see with the naked eye. They undulate, traveling to meet my own eyes. It takes me several seconds to realize what is happening—there is an electrical current running through my body, from him, and from me.

And now, somehow, I can also see behind his dark pupils. I can see something else that was also previously invisible to my normal vision: a reflection of myself in his eyes. And the more I look, the more I become clearer. Me looking back at myself through Mohammed's eyes, like a mirror. And as I look into that mirror, I can now see an entire universe unfolding. My own reflected eye—the shiny brown sphere—is like a planet floating in its own dark galaxy. But there are stars too, moving lights flickering around it, illuminating everything. And now I see everything there is to possibly see. The entire universe. And everything in the universe is looking back at me, seeing me. All the world is here in Mohammed's eyes!

And when he moves in to kiss me, I am already on fire. My body is pulsing; all my necessary parts are already gorged with blood, all of me is ready, heart drumming, breath electric. I feel his hot breath whisper in my ear, "And if the body were not the soul, what is the soul?" Whitman's words in the voice of Mohammed El Adl. I feel Mohammed's words brushing the skin of my neck. "What is the count of the scores or hundreds of years between us? Whatever it is, it avails not—distance avails not." And our clothes, like tissue shackles, are shed in seconds. Warm lips meet the other warm lips, but the source of the fire is in our eyes. Eyes lit up with seeing, being seen. Flame meets flame. And together, we sacrifice ourselves to the fire.

I am almost fully dressed again, putting on my second fur boot. Mohammed is still naked, his glistening brown body lying on top of the blue sleeping bag, stretched out on the igloo floor. He has rolled up his white muslin shirt under his head as a pillow, but now he lifts his head, pulls out the shirt, and playfully drapes it over his face like a shroud. I tell him it looks spooky, and he laughs. Even with no clothes he doesn't seem cold at all. It's hard to believe we're enclosed in nothing but ice and snow. I don't know why I've jumped up to dress so quickly, until Mohammed asks me. Then I realize I'm feeling guilty. Have I betrayed Ben? But isn't Ben the one who wants to divorce me? Why should I feel guilty?

Just as I'm thinking of Ben, the iPhone's melody cuts through the silence: it's Ben calling on FaceTime again. I decide not to pick up. I don't know what to say. Besides feeling guilty, I'm also still angry at him. But immediately he calls again.

"Shit, shit!" I stomp my feet like a child. I don't want to have a conversation with Ben while Mohammed's lying here naked. I pull on my anorak and crawl outside through the igloo's access trench, the narrow little tunnel.

Once outside the igloo, standing on the plateau, I see there's still enough sunlight to take in the entire landscape—the fjord, and the enormous glaciers, and the endless miles of snow—all shimmering under a twilight yellow sky streaked with lilac.

"Kip! Kip!" Ben sounds frantic again. "I've been trying to call you back! We got cut off. Where are you? I can't see anything!"

"I'm at the North Pole," I say, turning off my camera.

"Okay, smart-ass. Very funny."

"I can't get my camera to work, Ben," I lie. I don't want him to see where I am. This landscape is meant for me and Mohammed alone.

"Kip, I want you to listen to me." Ben is still in our kitchen, another button is undone on his red plaid shirt, and I can see the freckles on his chest. He's also now sitting on the floor, his back leaning against the cabinets. I've never seen Ben sit on our kitchen floor. It's not a very drastic thing to do, but it's highly unusual. He's not himself. Something is up. "Kip," he says, "can you still see me?"

"Yeah, Ben, I'm here. I see you. What is it?"

"Kip, I've realized something important while you're away." Since he can't see me on the screen, Ben's looking up, not at the phone, and the low angle catches the dark circles under his eyes. He looks as if he's not slept or has been crying. "Kip, I know I said I was done with us, but that was because it was too painful. All the ways you've been affected by being Black, all the ways you've felt unseen by the world." He pauses for a second and pulls at his bottom lip pensively, anxiously. "And Kip. I felt like there was nothing I could do to help you, and I was only making it worse. It was too painful for me to bear, day after day. And then I realized, 'Hey, that's not fair!' Kip, I finally got it!" Ben now looks directly into the camera, right at me, it seems, with his watery hazel eyes. "You don't have a choice about living with that pain, Kip. It's just there. Always. It's in this world. I didn't want to deal with it any longer, but you don't have a choice, do you? Not if you want to keep on living."

Ben's voice feels as if it's getting closer. I sense he is nearer, pulsing.

"Kip, I've thought about a lot of things," he continues. "I thought about you writing your novel about E. M. Forster, about how Forster also couldn't deal with the repercussions of staying with a Black man. It was too hard for him too. And I felt like an asshole." Ben's voice becomes more insistent, his face more animated. "This is just life, isn't it? Life is struggle. It's not supposed to be easy or comfortable, is it? And I got scared of the sacrifice. But there is no love without sacrifice. That's the nature of things. 'Samsara,' you said it's called in Sanskrit, right? The wheel of suffering. We can't protect ourselves from it. We have to find a way to make sense of it, to find joy in the midst of all this shit. Right? And I got lazy too. But as Bette Davis would say, samsara is not for sissies! No. It's for fierce warrior queers like us!" Ben says, laughing at himself, but I see that he's also crying; a single tear is running down one cheek.

"I'm sorry, Kip. Please come back." Ben looks for a long time into the camera, as if he's trying to conjure my face before him. "Oh!" His eyes suddenly open extra wide. "I almost forgot to tell you! I found my wedding ring! It was in my damned pants pocket. The logical place! Oh, Kip, let's break down this crazy barrier we've made. Come back."

I'll have to say yes, of course. My book and Ben are waiting. But I can't bring myself to say anything. And when I finally look down at the phone, I realize the signal's dropped again. I'm shaking, trying to understand it all. Have I come all this way only to go back to where I started, with no clue of the point of it all? I can't make sense of it. I look out over the great expanse, and I feel small, like nothing. And then . . .

BANG!

The silence is broken.

The gunshot echoes, and echoes, across the vast white wilderness.

I know I should be feeling something, but I feel only a strange sort of numbness. I'm not really in my body, it seems. I'm not cold or hot. I'm nothing. I'm frozen, a snow man.

I finally sit, sink, on top of a little mound of snow, with my elbows up on my knees, looking out. The silence after the echoing gunshot is the same as after the colossal calving of the glaciers— infinite and indifferent. I watch a spot of blood spread to the outside of the igloo, like red ink gradually appearing on white paper. Mohammed's blood. I know he's dead. Mohammed wouldn't miss. It was only one shot; intentional, methodically planned, I'm sure. I must have been part of his great plan. He needed my gun, but he also needed to be seen by me, another Black man. He needed us to share one moment of true freedom. His final moment. But it doesn't seem real.

No, this can't be happening. If this were really happening, I would feel something, wouldn't I? I would be hurting. I would be panicked. It must be a dream. But slowly, after about fifteen minutes, I sense the beating of my heart again; I feel air fill my lungs too. Then I feel punched in the gut, a deep spasm. I double over from the pain. I can hardly bear the aching in my stomach muscles. My heart is now plummeting into the abyss, and I can't stop it. I reach out but there is nothing to hold on to. I grasp at nothing.

Why did he have to kill himself? He could have lived many years more, perhaps, couldn't he? And he was a good person, so full of life. He just wanted to love. Life is unfair. Why, why? I keep repeating the pointless question. With both hands I'm holding my head so it will stop spinning. He just wanted to love, didn't he?

I was numb and now I'm feeling too much. It's as if electricity is zapping throughout my body. My arms and legs and guts contract in spasms. It's Mohammed's life force. Somehow he's still with me. I can feel him. I can practically hear his voice: "In choosing Morgan's love, I must also choose death."

But that's Mohammed El Adl who just said that. Not the dead young man in the igloo. I've confused them. My Mohammed is not dead—he's still here, still speaking to me. I don't understand what's happening. But I know he's not dead. I feel my Mohammed in me.

I feel his pulse and all his pain and anger and fear. I feel his joy and yearning for life, his love—all pulsing from him through me. And before I know it, somehow I am on my feet—my body surrendering to all that pulsing. I face the infinite wilderness, and from nowhere I let go of something in me that has been clenched forever—an effort to be good enough, to be acceptable. I let out a giant sound, a deafening cry. It is a noise I have never made before. My entire body is screaming. Every sinew and muscle of my body is vibrating, electrified with my noise: my heart, my hands, my throat, my lips—all fully engaged. And even in the strain of my cry, there is a strange joy, a pleasure in my body's capacity, in its resilience.

Oh, Mohammed! I see it! I understand now! Noise is all that matters! All this time, I've been trying so hard to make my voice perfect. To craft how I sound, to be acceptable. I only have to make my own noise. It's like that glacier crashing and banging out there. I don't have to make it sound good, or pretty, or even unique. I just have to let it out! And I can make my noise in response to them all, can't I? To Shakespeare, Tolstoy, Toni Morrison, and Forster! My own noise responding to the entire fucked-up world! And there is some kind of harmony that can come from all our different noises too—not necessarily something pleasant, but an honest noise. I don't want to be locked away and protected from it all anymore. I need to make noise with everything around me!

I feel a shiver run up my spine. My chest burns deep inside, around my heart. I can feel a pulsing and a kind of confidence growing there. "Mohammed?" I say. "*Mohammed?* Are you really here?"

I'm rocked with another jolt of electricity. And before I know it I am crying out Mohammed's name. My entire body is screaming his name, but it's as if I am singing the song of myself—my sinews, muscles, heart, loins, and lungs; my hands, vocal cords, eyes, and tongue, and lips—straining and pulsating. And the wilderness returns my voice to me. It echoes over the fjord and glaciers, all the way across the tundra and back.

And then, the land itself responds with a great noise of its own: another calving. My voice roars and the roaring world bellows back. A birth is happening. The glacier's birthing makes a thunderous roar. Ice cracks like whips of lightning. And after the crash, a cloud of snow lifts and spreads across the sky.

High up over the scene, the lone dark sea eagle soars. I hear its rasping, plaintive cry. It echoes—waves of sound undulating forever into the arctic vastness. Watching the bird, I am filled with the overwhelming sense of rising up. It is as if I too am taking flight and ascending into the white cloud; as if I am crying up to the heavens. And when the cloud of whiteness dissipates, all the snowy particles cascade to the fjord, languidly, like fading white fireworks. As the great bird climbs against the lilac sky, its grating call echoes across the land. And I hear my own voice, joining the bird's magnificent cry. The endless sound of Possibility.

ACKNOWLEDGMENTS

In my research on E. M. Forster and Mohammed El Adl, I have relied heavily on Forster's own writing, including his diaries and letters. For extensive access to Forster's archives and permission to quote short passages, I am extremely grateful to The Provost and Scholars of King's College, Cambridge, and The Society of Authors as the E. M. Forster Estate.

Of the many books and articles consulted for writing this novel, I would especially like to acknowledge P. N. Furbank's *E. M. Forster: A Life*, Wendy Moffat's *A Great Unrecorded History: A New Life of E. M. Forster*, and Michael Haag's *Alexandria: City of Memory*. Readers familiar with these historical works will see that in shaping this work of fiction I have taken many liberties regarding inventing characters, ignoring others, and rearranging the timeline of historical events. For information about Greenlandic customs and language, I am indebted to *An African in Greenland* by Tété-Michel Kpomassie, translated from the French by James Kirkup.

This novel would not have been possible without the support from so many people. As the well-known African proverb goes, "It takes a village to raise a child." This child of mine is indebted to the following villagers:

My family: I have to thank my parents (Tim and Donna), grandparents, brother (Kevin), and many cousins, aunts, uncles, and caregivers (Tessie Bodie and Ethelyn Longley). You were my first and most generous audience. You received my plays and stories with curiosity and enthusiasm. You always encouraged my wild imagination and never once discouraged me from being an artist. To my sister (Tatiana): you're the best fan a brother could ask for, and I couldn't be more in awe of you.

My mentors: C. William Bennett, John Stix, and John Monroe. Your faith in my talent came just when I needed it. Your steady and deft guidance allowed me to develop the audacity to write. I have taken you in so deeply that I don't know where you are not. You are always with me. Thank you.

My inspirations: Jaime Manrique, you show me what a great writer looks like in the flesh. Your bravery, honesty, exquisite skill, and powerful heart are everything I hope to embody as a writer. Thank you for doing the near impossible: being both an idol and a friend.

Sidney Poitier, you belong to the world and the world is better for it. But, to my great good fortune, you also are part of my Bahamian family. For as long as I can remember, you have been my beacon—a perfect example of the man and artist I hope to be. Your phone calls, notes of encouragement, wisdom, and compassion (even in the moments as Dad lay dying) all mean so much to me—more than you'll ever know. I am eternally grateful.

And Jonathan Galassi, thank you for planting the seed that grew to become this novel. Your generosity with both your time and encouragement means the world to me.

My cheerleaders/life buoys (in alphabetical order): Harry Birckmayer, Darién J. Davis, Tony Frankenberg, Idris Mignott, Luis Nuñez, John Welch, and Robert "Chip" Williams. What can I say? At one time or another, you have all saved me from the brink of despair, lifted and carried me when I faltered, and cheered me on to run faster when I was weary. The joy and utter foolishness we all share in kinship makes me giddy sometimes, and I wouldn't have been able to write this book without you all. You have believed in me when I didn't see why or how it made sense. John, you especially have done the most heavy lifting, of course—additionally reading several drafts and offering the smartest critiques. My heart grows bigger each day because of you. John Wilkinson, you kept me thinking positive when I really needed it. How can I thank you all enough?

My lifelines: James Grissom, thank you for your generosity. For me, you have embodied the spirit of our mutual goddess/teacher, Marian Seldes. I can't thank you enough for your support and all the connections you have made for me. Without you, my friend, this book may never have happened.

Morgan Stebbins, Jungian and all-round human being extraordinaire, when I was stuck in my writing of this novel you urged me to go to the wilderness—and then the entire novel made sense. I began to write more daringly. Without you I wouldn't have had the courage to be the writer or person I am today.

Harris Nasution, your generosity blows me away. You allowed me to write when I didn't see how I'd ever have the time or space to do so. Thank you, sir. You are the best!

Juan Lázaro Behín, *el respeto por mí como escritor y su cariño y apoyo durante tantos años, incluso cuando parecía imposible, nunca se olvidará. Como me dijiste, El que persigue, consigue. ¡Gracias por todo!*

Joseph Rosenthal, you are never far away.

My expert advisors: Sebastian Naidoo, you easily fit into all of the above (and below) categories. You have corrected and guided me on all things British, and the readers should know if I got anything wrong, it is due to my own streak of British stubbornness. You have also been an invaluable reader, slogging through several drafts and always offering the most delicate but incisive comments. You have saved me from literary (and personal) disaster so many times with very simple yet ingenious solutions. To have a friend as gifted as you is a dream come true.

Yahia Zaidi, you gave me so much of your time and knowledge. I am grateful for your information about gay asylum seekers from Africa and the Middle East. I am in awe of your work in Belgium with this population. You are helping to make our fellow invisible gay brothers and sisters visible. I am greatly indebted to you.

My writing team: Without the intelligence, talent, diligence, and dedication of the following writers and literary professionals, this novel would not be what it is today. They have all read several drafts of the manuscript and given the kind of detailed, thoughtful feedback that any writer would die for.

Tauno Bilsted, my cigar-puffing buddy, thank you for your love, support, challenging questions, and insights—you helped me sharpen the focus and voice of this novel.

Kathleen Flynn, what can I say? No one has ever read my work with such care. You have an unparalleled eye for detail, and you offered such great knowledge of storytelling. I don't know how this novel could have been birthed without you. You are the book doula I never knew I needed!

Scott Sager. Oh, Scott, what haven't we discussed over the years? You have been my wise literary sounding board since we were eighteen years old, over bottomless cups of coffee at Sam's to blintzes at Teresa's! You are a writer of great skill and subtlety, and a friend like none other. You always seem to get where I'm coming from, and your critiques (ever diplomatic) always feel supportive. Thanks from the bottom of my heart.

David Samuel Levinson, writer par excellence, your stamp of approval boosted my confidence when I needed it most. I can't thank you enough.

Zach Gajewksi, your talent and skills not only saved me from exposing embarrassing mistakes, but your astute observations and subtle shifts with my prose, here and there, may have saved this novel in more ways than you realize. I am truly indebted.

Tom Miller, you are the one who made this book possible. You saw the first draft of the manuscript and knew you could work your magic. Besides being an impeccable editor (what a blessing for me), you proved yourself to be a miracle worker of an agent. My friend and champion, you understood at once what I was going for and helped me get there. You are the very best—a rare breed indeed!

And last, but absolutely not least, my publisher and editor, Tara Parsons. Needless to say, I would not be writing these words of gratitude if you, Tara, had not taken a chance on an unknown writer and believed in this novel. I never dared to dream I'd find an editor with all of your amazing qualities: razor-sharp intelligence, boundless enthusiasm, and an ability to see where this book could go even when I had not completed that vision. You allowed me to write the book I wanted to write but didn't believe would be acceptable. From our first meeting, I never doubted you were the editor I needed. Tara, I'm eternally grateful to you and your team, especially Alexa Frank.

The Great Ones: And then of course there are those life-giving forces for whom the gratitude is so great it is almost impossible to fathom: the saints and siddhas, the gods and goddesses, the earth, the sun, the moon, the sea, Shakespeare, Tolstoy, Dostoyevsky, Toni Morrison, August Wilson, to name a few.

A NOTE ON THE COVER

Greenland is a remarkable book, unlike anything I've ever read. Is it a love story? A ghost story? Maybe something else entirely? How to give this sweeping, dreamlike novel-within-a-novel—which encompasses so much while effortlessly traversing the reader through time—the cover that it deserves?

I began researching artists whose work might be able to serve as a visual complement to David Santos Donaldson's story. I knew I needed to find a piece that was more evocative than directly representational; something that would serve as an entrance or a bridge the reader wants to cross to enter the many worlds within the book. When I came across the work of Devan Shimoyama, I knew I'd struck gold. His mixed-media paintings depicting Black queer life are surreal, mystifying, and alluring—much like *Greenland* itself. A perfect fit.

–Alicia Tatone